Legacy of the
Kinguard

Legacy of the Kinguard

THE UMBRAGE

Elric Francis

Library of Congress Control Number:		2019911807
ISBN:	Hardcover	978-1-7960-5247-3
	Softcover	978-1-7960-5246-6
	eBook	978-1-7960-5245-9

Print information available on the last page.

Rev. date: 08/13/2019

To order additional copies of this book, contact:
Xlibris
1-888-795-4274
www.Xlibris.com
Orders@Xlibris.com
800530

Contents

To the Word, who continues to leave me speechless.
To the Father, whose hallows hid the shadow waif.
To my brother, whose flame was spent far too soon.

Chapter One

CRESTFALLEN

A tourist couple moved casually down the town's main street, with their arms linked as they chit-chatted happily and gestured back and forth quite animatedly with their free hands, sharing the private thoughts that lovers always have and ever shall. Well-illuminated by the traditional LED post-top acorn lampposts, the two crossed the wide, circular drive. Located here, which encircled the town's oldest tree, was what among the locals commonly called the "wishing tree." As they passed, they glanced at the great and ancient ash, beautiful in its autumn attire, noting the ancient carvings in its heavy bark where, presumably, lovers of long ago had set their marks, swearing their eternal love. They continued on, laughing gaily, as they circumnavigated the great tree which was, as it turned out, quite literally the center of town. They paused momentarily, both eyeing the low, stone wall that encircled the tree and its attendant green area. The stones, like the tree, were also very old, as one could plainly see, and being so ancient, they had a character and a mystique "all their own," not to mention some long faded markings like the word 'Cro' that had almost weathered completely away over time.

Turning away, the two continued across the pavement and stepped up on the curbing on the far side of the town common, directly in front of a local café. There was an illustration on the large picture window of the establishment of what could only be described as a very traditional witch holding a stick and stirring a steaming cup-shaped cauldron.

Directly above the image, in bold, yellow letters trimmed in green, announced the name of the café as The Cup and the Cauldron Café.

The couple entered the door that had an old-fashioned, spring-suspended bell, which danced and jangled loudly, announcing their arrival. A young, fiery, redheaded woman approached them, her outfit a cross of a waitress and a witch's wardrobe. She had a long black dress that covered her from the neck to below the knees in front and hung to just above the girl's footwear in back. The outfit was, however, made of a rather thin material, so both the clothing and the waitress herself could breathe. A closer look revealed a pair of black sneakers with dark leg warmers going up to the girl's knees so that they gave the impression of black boots. Her apron was also black, and as she pulled out a pad and a pen, she waved at them, smiling. "Welcome to The Three Cs! This way, please."

The couple looked around as they passed other patrons smiling and conversing happily among themselves. The café's walls, like most of the other downtown buildings, were made of brick with many framed photographs of witches of various eras in differing ensembles of black and white. Some were actual paintings, artist's renditions one would suppose, and then there were many charcoal illustrations and covers taken from various magazines over the past several decades. The tables and booths were red, as indeed were the cushions of the seats, and they slid into a very picturesque booth by the large picture window they had just been admiring outside. Their table was dimly lit by faux candles both on the table and suspended from the overhead. Menus already lay upon the table even as the couple arrived; the two lifted them to see what was available. They looked up as the red headed waitress asked what they wanted to drink, and the man made their orders, and the waitress was quickly gone, still scribbling on her order pad.

Glancing around, the couple noted that there was an upper floor, actually a mezzanine floor, running around the entire upper area. The walls up there, at least what they could see of them, were lined with tables and additional seating, safely ensconced behind a safety railing overlooking their floor. They smiled, noting what they took to be a few high school girls talking to some oddly dressed girls of the same age group, most probably some classmates at the local high school. They seemed to favor multicolored pigtails and were garbed in some Goth getup. The two couldn't help but love the atmosphere—the place was dimly lit, with just enough illumination to enhance the overall effect of the place without being inconvenient. The only glare of any kind was that created by the large, flat-panel TV screen on the wall, currently displaying the local news. Across the room from them, they could see the counter and a single register where a young Korean American woman was ringing up a group of outbound customers. The register operator waved as the group moved away toward the exit. One of the girls in the departing party could be heard saying her farewell and calling the register person by name.

"Bye, Theresa. Catch you later."

The young woman who had been called Theresa turned to the men to her rear behind the serving window who were preparing the orders. They exchanged words, but the distance was too great to overhear what was being said. Suddenly, the strangely dressed girl leaned over the upstairs railing, calling out.

"Theresa—hey, hi! Are you still going this weekend, you know, to the Winona Dam beach party?"

Theresa glanced up. She looked a bit sad before quickly adopting a small smile.

"I might be late for the beach party. I've been invited to another little get-together."

The pigtailed girl frowned and slapped her hand on the railing, blurting out, "Aw, who?"

Theresa pointed toward the door, and the couple, by now somewhat curious, turned to face the entrance.

The couple smiled broadly as the party entering consisted of three women dressed in white gowns with hoods. They saw the women wore conventional, albeit nonetheless chic boots that were somewhat dirty as indeed were the hems of their robes. The waitress waved at them as they seated themselves in the back of the room at a single table that bore a rather large sign that read, "Reserved," in large, bold letters.

The couple was momentarily distracted as their waitress returned with their drinks. As the waitress placed their drinks before them, the female customer she was serving looked up at her and asked quietly, "Miss, those women, over there in the white robes . . . are they part of the atmosphere, I mean, are they part of the atmosphere of the place, or what?"

The waitress turned and glanced at the three indicated and shook her head.

"Oh, those three, no. They're the real thing, all right. They're actual Wiccans. Some call them White Witches, but they're not any kind of witch—they're Wiccans. Steve, the owner, designed this café with them in mind. He figured that giving them free coffee and a table a bit removed from the general population of the place would make them frequent here and become a draw. It worked like a charm. The décor was designed to make them feel comfortable, and of course, not to offend the public, that's why he used so many movie advertisement posters and magazine cover pages. They come here often, and I'd be with them, but I had to work today."

The couple looked wide eyed at the young waitress, and the woman asked, almost whispering, "Oh, you are a witch too?"

The waitress smiled a small smile, shaking her head.

"We prefer Wiccan, or White Witches even. We are not witches; the connotation of that word is ugly, even fearsome. We are not aligned with any dark power or being. Such a term would associate us with the more unsavory types often heard of in stories."

The woman's eyebrows arched high, while the man's brow furrowed. His companion fleetingly touched her fingertips to her bottom lip.

"I'm so sorry! I meant no offense," she said quickly.

The waitress smiled and waved her hand, palm outward, in front of her.

"No, no—not at all, no offense taken. Um . . . would you be ready to order?"

The couple ordered, and the red-haired waitress left them, walking away and moving in behind the counter. The owner, Steve, caught her eye.

"Amber, you just *had* to mention you are also a Wiccan, didn't you?"

Steve paused as he stood there over the hot stoves, shooting brief glances over the orders hung near him.

Amber gave him a gentle elbow as she walked by, grabbing plates of orders ready to go.

"I am always here, Steve. I don't often get to walk in here to show off. Look at them."

The two looked out to the floor watching the three Wiccans giving their orders to Theresa. The three at the table wave warmly.

"See? They're rubbing it in my face!"

Steve laughed. "Wow, there goes the image of evil women plotting the destruction of our society."

Amber smirked as she left with the orders,

"No, that is what our government is for—oh sorry, Theresa," Amber said, barely avoiding a collision with Theresa as she left the counter.

Theresa, smiling, waved her on and went up to Steve. "Is it okay if I take my last break?"

He glanced at his helper, a young man near at hand, filling a plate, and nodded.

"Sure thing, Tee. Jack and I got it covered."

Taking off her apron, Theresa hurried toward the door, as the younger man looked on longingly.

"I wish I could help her," Jack said under his breath.

"Yeah, we all do," Steve said with a lopsided smile. "But what do you say to someone in such a situation? I can't imagine losing my best friend in a suicide."

Theresa went out the back into the alleyway and was suddenly choking her tears so badly she doubled over. Her sobs echoed loudly.

People passing the mouth of the alleyway would occasionally glance her way. Recognizing her, they shook their heads in sympathy, hurrying on and letting her be. Theresa wiped the worn picnic table (the café's employees utilized for their coffee breaks) off and sat down holding her face in her hands. She screamed into them with no attempt to muffle the sound. She continued to sob for several minutes before regaining control of herself and lifting her head. She glanced down the alley, noting that the entire town was already shrouded in the shadows of the high hills which completely encircled the town. Looking up, she thought, *The sun has yet to set around the rest of the world.*

"It's seems so dark and empty out there. The whole world is," she choked a bit as she tried to speak. "Why am I feeling so sorry for myself?" she asked no one in particular before continuing, "I can't stop thinking that I should have done something, something to help her. Oh, Heather—"

Hearing the sound of the back entry to the café creaking somewhat, Theresa straightened, and taking a deep breath, sighed heavily as the door swung open. Quickly, she dabbed at her eyes and wiped her face even more quickly as Jack poked his head out.

"Theresa, oh . . . um . . . sorry, there's someone here to see you," he said quietly.

Theresa turned and started gathering her things, doing her best to hide her face for a couple of moments longer.

"Okay, Jack, be right there," she said softly.

Theresa stepped in through the door Jack had left open and followed the short hall out to the main floor of the café where she saw that her visitor was her stepbrother, Joshua. She just couldn't help it, and upon seeing him returning from the Army, the tears came again. She caught his eye and tried to smile bravely. He stood there, a sympathetic half-smile upon his features. He was wearing a clean, olive dress coat, shirt, slacks, and tie, all of which were topped off with a beret. The young black man opened his arms as she rushed across the floor and all but fell into his welcoming arms, hugging him tightly.

"I heard what happened. I came as soon as I could," he said, smiling warmly down at her. He held her a second longer, ruffling her long black hair before letting her go.

"The important thing is you are here now, Josh," she murmured, meeting his eyes.

The tourist woman smiled at them and, glancing back at her companion, spoke quietly to him. "They're a cute couple."

Steve and Jack just stared at each other, a knowing smile on their faces, as Amber choked back a small laugh.

"Oh no," Theresa said, glancing at Steve, who nodded, indicating that she could leave early with a warm smile.

"We're brother and sister, can't you tell?" The man in the uniform said with a small smile as he eyed the tourist lady.

The lady tourist glanced at her companion, returning to her dinner more than a little embarrassed.

Theresa and Joshua left the café behind as they moved out onto the sidewalk and started moving away down the main street. Joshua breathed in deeply, glad to be back. Fairmount was a small town, with a population of perhaps a little over three thousand. It lay nestled in the surrounding Suntaug Hills in the state of Massachusetts, Essex County. The downtown business buildings were almost entirely built of brick, as were the roads on the outskirts of town. Neon signs were already aglow in the darkening sky. They passed in silence the now glowing windows of various shops and centers catering to the various populaces, eyeing their equally silent ghostly images reflecting back at them in window after window.

"I can very well guess how you are dealing with this, Tee," Joshua said, looking straight ahead and licking his lips somewhat nervously.

"Why didn't you ever tell her how you felt?" Theresa asked, holding his arm tightly as they walked. She looked up at him briefly before letting go.

"You know my condition, Theresa," Joshua replied. "I couldn't pull her into our family problems."

"Still . . .," Theresa murmured and then fell silent.

Joshua gestured to some benches near the wishing tree, and the two sat briefly, enjoying the privacy afforded to one sitting there, a place where they could see all around.

"I want to know," the soldier said, "but . . . if you're not ready—"

"You need to know," Teresa responded. "The day was just like any other. We came back from school, and we watched some streaming shows we liked before. We painted the glass stones like her therapist suggested. She had just gotten a checkup. Her meds were helping, and she was showing signs of improving. At least, that's what we thought."

She sniffled, and Joshua handed her a handkerchief. She blew her nose loudly before continuing.

"We were in good spirits. When we went to bed, nothing, and I mean nothing, seemed out of place. Her attitude was light and cheerful! We-we talked about going out with Jack and Steve on a double date."

Joshua closed the gap between them and tightened his grip on her shoulders, waiting patiently for her to continue.

"When I woke up and saw she wasn't there, I figured she went to the bathroom and thought nothing of it, until I heard a muffled crash coming from the hall. I called out to her, but there was no response. That's when I started to panic. I rushed out of my room and saw the bathroom light shining out from under the door. I started banging on the door and calling her name, then Marcus and your mother joined me, and Marcus didn't hesitate. He hit that door like a runaway freight train—just one shoulder thrust, and that door went down."

Theresa put her hand over mouth, and her eyes grew wide as she lay tight in Joshua's arms. Slowly, her head sank upon his chest.

"Her blood, Josh, there was so much! She passed out, trying to cut herself for a second time! Marcus scrambled and took her into his arms, trying desperately to stifle the bloodletting. I passed out, and when I came around, He had already called for an ambulance, and as I looked around, Tara was crying. I must have passed out again because that's all I remember until I woke up the next morning. I thought it was a bad dream until Tara sat down on the edge of my bed and told me about it. I couldn't think or function at all that day. I didn't feel like breathing, much less going to school that morning."

"I'm sorry I missed her funeral yesterday. I tried, Tee," he said, shaking his head.

Theresa shook her head. "You're fine, Joshua," she said, all but whispering.

Theresa lowered her head once more onto his shoulder as he held her gently. For a long while, the two sat there silently in the shadows, under the wishing tree at the center of town, as both people and vehicles passed them by, wholly unaware of their pain.

After a time, the two rose slowly to their feet and turned their faces toward the more suburban area of town. The homes seemed to fly away from the center of the town, lining the street with variety of white picket fences and well-groomed lawns. They were always impressed by the homes and how very nice looking the whole street was. The lights were coming on within the residences, and here and there, a streetlight could also be seen to flicker, owing to the long shadows cast by the surrounding hills.

"Do Mom and Dad know you are home for a while?" Theresa asked, finally breaking the silence.

"No. I knew how hard-hit you would be by her death, so I hadn't the time," Joshua said quietly. "She was special to all of us, you know."

Theresa looked down at his hand and saw the ring on his right hand. Following her eyes, Joshua smiled wanly. "It's just a preventive measure, Theresa."

"I'm just so glad you are back safe and sound. How long are you staying this time?" she asked, looking at him. She grasped his arm tightly as they approached their parents' home.

"Three months, heading out right after Christmas," he said, smiling.

"Are you kidding me? This is great!" she said excitedly.

He smiled, looking around and wondering who in the neighborhood might have heard her as they crossed the street. "Okay, okay! Keep it down, sis," he said, patting her hand.

Theresa paused, hugging him as they stood there on the sidewalk, and a single tear freely found its way down her cheek.

"You are the best brother and friend in the world. I need so badly for you to be home," Theresa said, struggling to hold back her tears.

They stood in the center of the sidewalk, between two streetlights, holding each other for several more minutes before continuing toward home. Absentmindedly, Theresa noted that not a single car had passed along the street during the time they had been standing there.

*   *   *   *

"Okay, so how are we on food?" the dark-haired man asked his wife as she glanced back at him, faking a dirty look in their living room.

"Better call the pizza guy," she said with a loud sigh.

"Tara, you are so hopeless," the man said in a charming, disarming way. Smiling, he pulled out his phone.

"It got really busy at work," Tara replied with a twinkle in her eye. "Besides, how could you not have noticed?"

He smiled sheepishly as he started to make the order. As he did so, she drew her hand through her short blonde hair and batted her clear blue eyes at him while smiling.

"You stayed over too, Marcus," she said playfully, slapping his arm. He feigned injury as the two smiled. She left the room and returned to the kitchen as he finished the call.

He stepped into the kitchen to give her a hand with the dishes.

"We are working too hard these days, Marcus," she said as he picked up the drying towel. "We can't keep this up forever. We need a solution before the town falls apart. Everyone's depending on us. What are we going to do?" she asked, the matter preying on her mind and finally taking precedence over her normal bubbly sense of humor.

"I don't know," he said solemnly. "The money we collected and saved over the last twenty years is being sucked dry by the economic downturn. Carla said they might have to move, and the Davis family has already shut down their shop and left. They moved clear out of state, looking to find a more stable life for his family."

"You can't really blame them, Marcus," Tara said, sighing again. "The town is becoming a sinking ship."

"I don't," he said, looking out of the kitchen window into the backyard, memories of better times filling his mind. "The council is going to meet next week to discuss some new ideas."

"We couldn't keep it from them. We are good for a few more years, but after that, who knows."

They both heard the door opening and voices coming from the living room. The two put down their gloves and wash cloths and started heading into the other room. The living room was spacious with various cabin themes about. The walls and ceiling were constructed of natural woods, although the furniture was decidedly modern. Marcus always wanted to own a cabin and brought the feeling home with its design. The lamp on the table was made of fake antlers. Two figures stood by the door, with a stairway immediately to their left. The closet door to their right, however, was open as they were hanging up their coats.

"Theresa, I thought your shift didn't end for another—JOSHUA!" Tara exclaimed excitedly as she ran up to her son and held him close. "Josh—oh my god! You're home! You're really home!"

Theresa stepped over to Marcus with her arms wide as she said with a huge smile, "Surprise!"

Joshua, nigh onto being crushed, waved. "Hey, Marcus—Mom, please."

Marcus waved back as he hugged his foster daughter, smiling as he looked at the mother-and-son reunion.

"Welcome home, Josh," Marcus said through his big smile.

Tara escorted her son to the couch. "Sit here, you. You hungry? Want something to drink? We've just ordered pizza."

Marcus looked at Theresa as she innocently asked, "Marcus, were you two late getting home—again?"

Waving away Theresa's question, Tara asked Joshua over her shoulder, "So how long are you home for this time?" as she left to get drinks for everyone.

"Here until Christmas, Mom," Josh called after her as he smiled brightly.

As Tara reentered the room, she, Theresa, and Josh were grinning from ear to ear.

The night had settled in as the four reminisced, and finally, Joshua rose to his feet and made his way to the front door. Opening the door, he stepped through, waving to his family as he did so. He stepped onto the porch, saying he was calling it a night. The porch was one of those long ones that ran the full length of the front of the house and partially around the corner. The lights on the porch played out upon the walk and the attendant green of the front yard. Slowly, he stepped out, making his way down the porch steps toward the sidewalk, and absentmindedly leaned on the hand railing, deep in thought. He glanced across the yard, looking for anything that might have changed during his four-year absence. Upon hearing the door close, he glanced back, seeing that Marcus had followed him out of the house.

He joined Joshua at the bottom of the porch steps. The two stood there quietly for the moment, taking in the night. Leaning his back up against the hand railing close by Joshua, Marcus continued to peer out into the darkness. After a moment, he spoke quietly. "I remember when I was twenty," he said, his mind adrift upon a sea of yesterdays. "I was fresh from service. Life seemed stretched out before me as if the world was waiting, waiting to form up around me. You know, as if it was all for me and me alone to enjoy."

Joshua smiled briefly, looking down at his feet, with his eyes flicking quickly over to the edging of flowers separating the bottom edge of the porch and the grass of the lawn. Again, he lifted his eyes up and let them play over the well-kept yard.

"Yeah," Joshua said almost absentmindedly. "I've often wondered how others felt, you know, sometimes. If they felt anything like I do even if they don't have the problem of my condition."

Marcus stepped around in to stand beside Joshua, nodding. "I may not be your dad, but I think we both would agree that everyone, regardless what walk of life they might come from, have many of the same feelings when they were your age. Gregory King would be proud."

Joshua pushed off the railing and walked away, heading down the sidewalk. Marcus silently followed him. The two went out through the waist-high iron gate that separated the front yard from the public sidewalk. Both of them turned to look back at the house. It stood there some two stories high, the walls shining somewhat dimly in the slight glare of the streetlamps. The window on the second floor, which gave on the hallway, and the matching windows that gave on his parent's bedroom glowed warmly.

"You know, its home, and yet it's not. Not for me, anyway," Joshua said, his hands in his slack's pockets.

"Then it's a sanctuary for you—to get away from that world you've been living in the last four years," Marcus said, patting his stepson's shoulder.

"The problem follows right along with me no matter where I go, Marcus."

Marcus glanced at Joshua for a moment, and then he returned his attention to the view of the house.

"I take it you're not exactly here on leave, then?" the older man queried.

"I wish I was. If I could be anywhere other than here, Marcus, I would be. I can't stop thinking of her. What could have been, if only . . ."

"You know someone has desecrated Heather's grave."

"Theresa and Mom don't know about it yet, do they?" Joshua queried, eyeing Marcus.

"No, and I don't want to take off too quickly. It might make them suspicious," Marcus said, grasping Joshua's arm and holding him in place.

After a long moment, Marcus turned away, saying, "I'll get the car out. We need to stop by the cemetery so you can look things over."

"Okay," Joshua said. "I need to make a call anyway."

Marcus had moved off several steps when he heard Joshua's voice start to fade in the steadily increasing distance, although he could still make out some of it. He was talking on the phone.

"Yes, Sara, the family is fine. I'll be returning with Marcus."

The Fairmount Cemetery was on the outskirts of town just a bit northeast of Lorelabs and west of Little Elders pond. The air became a bit chilly as they drove through the ornate front gates. Marcus had a bad feeling as they moved toward the east side of the graveyard. The trees near Heather's resting place were illuminated by high-powered lights, but the grave itself was still just out of sight as they made the final turn.

*   *   *   *

Some distance away, a young woman watched as they rounded the final turn to the source of light. She watched them disappear from sight and slowly rose from a kneeling position to her full height. Had anyone been observing her, she would have been taken instantly for a young, Native American. She leaned against the welcome support of a tree. In one hand, she carried what appeared to be a pair of white, high-heeled shoes, which had no doubt been a fashionable accessory for what had been a white dress she wore. Both were, however, in quite a notable disarray, being covered with dirt stains and bits of wood, some of which fell away from her person as she quietly moved away. She paused and glanced back only once, tears creating little runnels down through the dirt encrusting the pale golden brown of her skin. Her dark, rather disheveled hair swirled about wildly, caught by a restive evening breeze as she immediately disappeared into the dark, woody terrain behind her former position.

*   *   *   *

Theresa smiled wanly as she waved at her foster mother. She was going upstairs to the bedroom level, and she paused to look down from the second floor balcony before she waved goodnight one last time to her, with her loving smile once again showing signs of cracking. The girl walked into her room and closed the door without turning on the lights. The room was quite dark, the only illumination being that from the streetlights outside, filtering in through her lightly curtained bedroom windows. The pretty little edgings in lavender and pink pastel, which were the predominate theme of the trimming throughout the room, were lost to the darkness. She could make out the heavier shadow against the wall, which was, in fact, her bed. She could not, however, make out the numerous stuffed animals that took refuge there. As her eyes started to adjust, she found herself able to make out dimly the nightstands and the lamps upon them.

On the far side of the room, directly opposite of her, was a nook with a single window. The window seat it hosted doubled as a storage unit. The drapes were light and fluttered about as the wind made its way in via an open window. A tree just outside the window rustled quietly. Its branches could almost reach her window. In the corner was her vanity, holding the usual beauty accessories, cosmetics, combs, and brushes, and a dish filled with lavender and gold-painted glass stones. The mirror was covered in pictures of her friends. Some of the photos, thanks to the errant breeze swirling in through the open window, were at the moment scattered on the floor. The low-backed stool that was a part of the vanity set rested nearby, and although she could not actually make out the colors, she knew the settee cushioned in white and trimmed in pink, both the seat and back. Directly against the wall on the other side of the room were two short dressers, upon one of which rested her laptop, which she could not at the moment see. She could see, with her mind's eye, the various schoolwork and accompanying books. On the other, she thought, would be her silent media player.

She moved to her left, which brought her close to her closet. She began removing her clothing as she crossed the soft off-white carpet that helped brighten her room even with the lights out. She changed her clothes in the dark, changing into a white night gown. She plopped down on the vanity's settee and flicked on a small overhead light and lifted her head as she brought up a brush. She brushed her hair for a time, enjoying the relaxing feeling of the brush as it kind of scratched her head and pulled out the tiny tangles of the day. Her brushing finished, and she dropped the brush upon the vanity and opened its left-hand drawer.

She laid out the paints and brushes she had taken from the drawer and then took up a single glass stone out of the dish that contained an assortment of glass, gold, and lavender stones. She paused as a sudden sob found its way unbidden to the surface. This, however, was but a momentary breech of her self-control, and then she was once again mistress of herself. Although the sound had ceased, the tears still flowed, but with a shake of her head, she ignored them and began painting the selected glass stone gold. After a few minutes' work, she set it aside, waiting for it to dry. As she waited for the quick-drying paint to dry sufficiently for handling purposes, she glanced at the pile in the small dish and noticed there were a growing number of gold stones compared to the lavender ones. Suddenly, she threw the dish to the floor, scattering the stones out across the carpet, with some rolling under the bed while others made their way under the bureau of drawers. She shook her head as the sobbing commenced yet again, and she laid her head down upon her vanity out of despair.

"Why, Heather?" she choked out. "Why? What made you feel like you had to end your own life? Why wasn't I able to save you from yourself?"

She continued to cry, and anyone passing near her home would have encountered no problem in hearing the sounds of her anguish through her open window.

A large, lone Malamute crossed the street and moved slowly toward her house. The animal obviously took note of the sounds of pain carrying plainly to his ears. He lay down, facing the house, on the sidewalk just outside the picket fence, with his eyes locked on the dark window from where those disturbing sounds came. He whined softly into the cool night air.

Chapter Two

THRESHOLD

The lunchroom of Fairmount High was really quite spacious for such a small school. In years gone by, the school had been bustling with teenagers. However, in recent times, so many families had moved away, taking their teens with them and leaving more than ample room for one's personal little clique to find a place of semi privacy for their private discussions among the wide assortment of available tables not taken by other various cliques.

In one such location near the windows that gave on a nice view of the outside are a group of seniors who were sitting apart and keeping to themselves while obviously enjoying their conversation. Amber, her fiery red hair standing out among the crowd, sat near Theresa who was enjoying her meal with Jack, sitting directly across from her. The clicking of overly large heels caused the three turning to see Karin approaching. She looked very different than she did last night. She had a dour look on her face, which caused a poorly concealed smirk to manifest itself upon Jack's features as he sought almost desperately to keep from laughing outright at her obvious self-consciousness.

She was dressed in tight black jeans, and she wore pink heels that were covered with various Japanese phrases highlighted in glitter. Her top was a short sleeved thing of light blue, which contrasted rather sharply with the black nail polish she wore. Her hair was back to black, which was her normal color, as the red and blue of the previous evening now washed out and hung freely instead of bound into pigtails like how it had been last night.

She stuck her tongue out at him and magically switched moods, turning suddenly cheerful.

"So party?" she asked, glancing back and forth from Theresa to Amber and Jack and then repeatedly saying, "Party! Party! Party!" over and over.

"If I shove this plate of food into your face, would you shut up?" Jack asked as he grabbed at his plate, which caused the girl to flinch as she plopped into a seat on the far side of Theresa and across from Jack next to Amber.

"Well, is it on tonight?" Karin asked again, twirling her hair in one hand while she ate with the other.

"The cabin party out near the dam? I'm there," Amber responded.

"Ditto," Jack replied.

"My brother just came home on leave. Elizabeth canceled hanging out to go to this thing. I might . . . not sure yet, you know, to be truthful." Theresa responded, looking around at her friends sheepishly.

"Aw, c'mon, Tee. Please?" Amber begged. "Most of the school is going to be there."

"I heard Steve will be there," Karin said, throwing Jack a haughty, taunting look. Jack responded by casting a dirty look at the girl, scowling briefly as he did so.

"He will be?" Theresa asked, smiling.

Karin nodded emphatically, grinning from ear to ear.

The conversation continued back and forth around the table until Amber glanced over her shoulder and saw another student approaching them, whereupon she went silent. The group turned to see a young black woman approaching them. She wore a matching green-blouse-and-jeans outfit; the blouse was rather loose fitting, and she wore it well. Around her neck, she wore a medallion portraying the three beings of the Wiccan pantheon—Diana, Pan, and Hermes.

"Still pretending to be one of us, Kala?" Amber asked, watching the new girl holding her tray and walking up to them.

"I hope to be forgiven by the coven someday, Amber. Your spirit is as bright as ever, I notice." Recognizing Jack, the young woman nodded. Turning away slightly, she smiled at Karin. "Beautiful one, ever your spirit slumbers in peace," she said, greeting her.

"I understand why, but I miss you sitting with us every day," Theresa said, smiling.

Kala started to speak but noticed something was somehow off about Theresa. Her mouth fell open in surprise, and her eyes widened. She glanced at Amber and back to Theresa.

"You, you are an illusion!" she said very softly, her voice suddenly tremulous.

She bowed to the group quickly and left them. They watched her walk away, then Theresa spoke softly. "What did she mean by that?"

"She saw something in you, Theresa," Amber said solemnly, almost reverently. "Kala was the most promising among us in the gifts of Diana. She was well on her way to becoming a high priestess of the coven, if not for her attempting to utilize the dark arts as she tried to force Steve to love her."

"Magic! Not buying the whole magical angle," Karin said, shrugging and returning her attention to her meal.

"You and Theresa should join us sometime," Amber said casually as she finished up her meal. "Please, Theresa, if you can make it, call me. I'll provide the ride."

"I will," Theresa said, watching Kala eat her meal alone at the table on the far end.

*   *   *   *

A few hours later, Jack and Theresa stepped off the bus and waved to their classmates as the big, yellow vehicle pulled away and turned to an adjacent street. They watched it disappear from view before starting their homeward walk as they had always done.

"I-I think I'll go," Theresa said quietly as though thinking out loud.

"Oh!" Jack said in a rather deflated voice, very much as if the wind had been let out of his sails.

Theresa glanced his way briefly, her brows furrowing slightly, but she said nothing.

"Hey, look, Theresa. A squirrel," he gestured toward a tree just up ahead of them and moved over to it.

Theresa smiled. "How do you do that?" she asked.

Jack reached out his hand, frightening the creature momentarily, then suddenly, as though curiosity had gotten the better of its fear, it climbed down from the tree and slowly started to move toward his hand, resting just below it on the trunk of the tree. The squirrel ran along his arm and settled on his shoulder.

"I inherited the trick from my father," he said almost to himself. "When I was young, my dad would cheer me up when I was down by having our backyard filled with wild animals. It wasn't like he commanded them—it's like they thought he was a part of them. Sadly, I am not as talented as him, not yet at least." He smiled briefly at Theresa before the squirrel ran off his arm and up into the safety of the shadows of the tree's upper boughs.

"I wish I had such hidden talents," Theresa said wistfully as she watched the squirrel vanish into the high, leafy bowers of the huge tree.

"If you had some sort of talent or power, what would you want?" Jack asked as they crossed the street, drawing closer to her home.

"Well," she said, deep in thought. The two were silent awhile before she said, "Well, I think I should like to be able to see the past."

As if a bit taken aback, Jack stopped and looked down. "Tee, why?"

Theresa frowned. "I never knew my parents. Dad died trying to save Doctor Tyr and my stepmother's first husband Greg. My mother abandoned me while pregnant with my brother or sister, I don't really know which." She shook her head. "I never felt like I, you know, like I quite fit in anywhere. I've been told it's because I'm a foster child, or it's because I'm of Korean descent." Theresa shook her head as they crossed the last street before her house. "I sometimes feel alone, even with friends and family all around me. Considering everything, I should feel lucky, and I know I am lucky, but still, I find that I'm often left feeling alone somehow. Out of place, even."

As the two approached Theresa's place, they could see Amber's convertible in the driveway. Suddenly, Amber stepped out as the car's roof started to lay back and down. She started waving as they came up to the front gate giving on the front yard.

"I need to go, Jack. Amber is eager to get ready for the party. You will come, won't you? Please?"

Jack sighed deeply. "Yeah, sure."

Theresa suddenly hugged him once then, or so it seemed to him. She was passing through the gate, waving back at him. Jack returned the girl's farewell wave and turned down the alley running alongside the house. Taking advantage of the short-cut it afforded, he headed for his own home nearby.

Amber wrapped her arm around Theresa's and proceeded to rush her inside and gently guided her to the stairs. The two were smiling and laughing on the stairs as Joshua passed by and headed toward the front door. He waved to the girls and was just that quickly outside. He stood around, waiting on the porch for a short time before a black SUV pulled up, with a young, blonde woman behind the wheel.

Joshua entered the vehicle. The SUV was suddenly underway, and the two were gone. They left house and street behind as they started for their hotel apartment.

*　*　*　*

"Sara, what are the preliminary results at the site?" Joshua asked. His face contorted slightly as though he was distraught.

"Well, the dirt was pushed up and out from below ground as we thought, not dug up from the outside. The coffin was also strange—there is little doubt that it was forced open from the inside."

"So I am to assume we're dealing with a ghoul or vampire? That's insane."

"I'm not really ready to report this to our superiors—not quite yet. We simply don't have enough information," Sara said, referring to the limited information they had available. They drove on until they came to the parking lot that serviced the town's only hotel. They turned in and parked in an available space near the walk leading to the hotel's front doors. The two made their way up to their room. A few moments later, Sara was sitting on the bed, and Joshua had plopped down into one of the two easy chairs that occupied the room. She retrieved her phone from her pocket and started punching in some numbers, making a call. She removed the initial findings from folders nearby as she waited for a response. He started skimming the reports.

Soon after, the young woman laid her cell phone on the dresser and started to undress.

"So find anything out of place?" she queried, pulling her blouse over her head.

Joshua stared at the reports, going back and forth through the pages, as he heard the sudden sounds of the shower through the bathroom door. Sara had left the door ever-so-slightly ajar so that the two might continue to discuss things as she availed herself of a much-wanted, relaxing shower.

Joshua nodded to himself as he responded, "Yeah, it's only hinted at, but she's no zombie or ghoul." He fell silent for a moment as he stared at the photos of the burial surface and its surroundings. Then he continued, "This was no mindless creature that came up out of there, wearing high heels, which it then took off, and walked away barefoot into the woods. And no, they've found nothing else so far, but a thorough search is currently underway."

He stood up and walked to the room's window that faced the parking lot. He stared silently out as he raised his arm to the window frame and leaned his head against that arm. The sky darkened as the sun settled behind the surrounding hills. He glanced back at the bathroom door before opening his phone and making a quick text.

She walks, DeSantos. Trying to avoid General's suspicion.

With the text sent, he closed his phone and put it away inside his jacket and returned to staring out the window. He saw a car packed with what he recognized was some of his sister's classmates passing by the hotel.

Find her. Keep her safe, he thought, watching the car disappear into the gathering darkness.

*   *   *   *

They were loud, boisterous, and cheering happily. They were seniors and some juniors from Fairmount High, speeding out of town in a flashy, bright-red convertible, outward bound for a night of fun.

"You ready for the night of your young life, Ms. Roh?" Amber asked, checking on Theresa who was slumped down in her seat, bare feet dangling out over the side of the car, and her shoes resting semi forgotten on the convertible's floor.

"Well, my brother coming home so unexpectedly really has me feeling really good, so I'm going to try to enjoy myself tonight," she said, smiling fully for the first time in weeks.

"He's certainly a miracle worker. We couldn't get you to leave your room for. . ." Jack fell silent, his comment stopped as a finger was gently pressed against his lips.

"Don't ruin the mood, stupid," Karin said softly, giving him a "duh" look. Jack nodded as he lost himself momentarily in the effect of Karin's ensemble. She was dressed in in a frilly black miniskirt with purple hemming. Her slim waist hosted two studded belts, loosely crossed so as to hang most fetchingly down on each side of her slender hips. He took in the black and white stockings that ended at her black, military boots, which were covered in black, tattered, bits of cloth. He liked the blood red blouse she wore, covered by her shredded black, jean jacket with its bright red lining. She wore a dark choker of some kind, and her makeup was also dark and served to bring out her eyes. Her hair was teased again and ended in pigtails of red and black stripes. Her arms were covered in striped, filmy satin sleeves, and the laced fingerless gloves put a finishing touch to her wardrobe.

Amber wore a matching blue, lacy-sleeved top, which barely covered her midriff, and a blue, rather full skirt that she was required to sit upon to keep it from blowing up over her head. She wore matching blue heels and natural, blue, silk anklets, turned down smartly to form a nice cuff. Theresa glanced back at Jack and smiled a silent "Thank you" at him. She herself was wearing a light white, tunic like dress drawn snug around her waist with a barely-there black belt. Her right wrist was adorned with black and white bracelets and those she matched with matching black and white star fish earrings, and necklace. Her shoes were a pair of simple black slip-ons with a small, silver buckle. Jack felt a bit underdressed as he reflected on his own simple apparel, which consisted of blue jeans and branded T-shirt. His rather plain, red, high-top tennis shoes were really the only highlight of his plain garb.

*   *   *   *

The convertible, which was Amber's, moved slowly along a wooded lane that brought them to an opening in the trees bordering the lane. The car moved into the opening, which found them all on yet another lane, smaller than the previous one and somewhat less than a half-mile long. The lane emptied into a makeshift parking lot just a bit more than a quarter of a mile in. Cars were parked here and there, with some people starting the party before even setting out for the cabin itself.

"We're here. From here on, we walk," Amber said as the car came to rest amid several other vehicles already seemingly abandoned. They could see couples going into a light scattering of trees and moving along the path to the cabin, engaged in highly animated conversations among themselves. The group quit the red convertible and made their way across the lot and into the tree-sheltered pathway.

"Who owns this place?" Theresa asked as the woods blocked out the stars that were beginning to appear somewhat dimly while the sun surrendered the land to the night.

"Well, Steve, but . . .," Amber quickly added as the others turned to her with expectant looks.

Theresa and Jack looked at each other, and both of them started waving at Amber as they ran ahead.

"Remember, you guys, if we get busted, he'll be the one who gets into trouble."

Amber smiled, giving Karin a knowing look.

"Apparently, this is his present to the seniors. Besides, he and Elizabeth are there to keep things from getting out of hand."

"The coven's high priestess will be here," Theresa said a bit too loudly.

"The entire coven is here. Hey, Wiccans need to relax once in a while too," Amber said as she ran gleefully into the crowd, laughing.

They could hear the party long before they could actually see the cabin itself. The thinly wooded clearing ahead was just becoming visible as the previously unseen path lights blinked on, shining out from their hiding places amid the brush and shrubbery running thickly along both sides of the pathway. The new, low illumination threw weird shadows all up and down the path as the shadows under the trees became heavy enough to trigger them. Even before the group rounded the last bend in the pathway, the bass was prominent enough that they could actually feel the music on their bodies. They all smiled, coming out into the clearing occupied by the cabin. There were people milling around outside and within the two-story cabin. The large pool off to the side in the back of the cabin was already packed with people splashing about, their laughter and shouts nearly as loud as the music itself, which all but deafened one to any of the other surrounding distractions.

"All righty, then," Theresa said, suddenly running ahead of Jack. "I'm going to look for Steve."

"I am going to find the other priestesses and see if they've seen any cute guys I can sink my claws into," Amber said, turning around and making a clawing gesture of farewell to Karin as she bolted after Theresa, and the two were suddenly lost in the crowd.

"Less than a hundred and fifty graduating seniors," Jack said, looking around. "And I think about every one of them is here!" Karin sidled up close to Jack and gave him a slight nudge with her arm.

"Want to get us some drinks?" she asked mischievously.

"Yeah, sure," Jack said, moving away toward the long porch in the front of the cabin.

Karin followed Jack at a considerably slower pace, off toward the coolers on the long front porch that could only be seen sort of periodically as people parted and merged, blocking and unblocking one's view. Jack barely heard anything as he made his way to the coolers, his eyes constantly scanning the crowd, trying for a glimpse of Theresa or Steve, or worse, the two of them together.

Karin walked up onto the porch and waved at everyone, all who moved quickly away, giving her a wide berth. Sheepishly, she accepted the paper cup Jack absentmindedly handed her. As she started to take a sip, a young boy swaggered up to her, "Hey, uh ... uh ... Chrissy?"

"It's Karin." Karin said somewhat testily.

"Yeah, right. Anyway, I was wondering, you here alone?" the younger guy asked.

"I'm with Jack," she lied.

"Jack? The same Jack who's had a crush on Theresa since third grade?" the younger guy asked a bit sarcastically as he shook his head and started to move away with a very pronounced smirk. Karen could smell the alcohol on him and suspiciously sniffed the drink she just received.

A younger guy, noting her sniffing her drink, spoke quietly. "Steve wouldn't allow us to bring it on his property. We snuck these in, and more is back at the parking lot where you just came from. If you want, I can get you some. Just don't tell him, or you'll ruin the fun some of us are having."

Karin wedged herself between the refreshments table and the drunk boy. "Uh, yeah, whatever. Excuse me."

"He doesn't want you, Karin. Why not date a guy who will settle for you?"

She looked at him with a mixture of hurt and anger. She looked back and forth between Jack and the boy a few times. As she started to walk off from the boy in disgust, she clearly heard him murmur the word, "Slut." She paused briefly and started to turn back to face him but instead took a deep breath and moved back to join Jack who was still scanning the mobs of party-goers.

"Here," she said dryly, thrusting her drink roughly into Jack's hand. Slightly irritated by her attitude, Jack gave her a "what the hell" look and went back to searching the crowd as he was still focused on finding Theresa. Karin glared at him for a moment more before settling beside him. She mumbled into the new drink he'd handed her in exchange for her first one, and the two walked around to the pool's edge as he continued to scan the crowd, adding to Karin's irritation.

"CANNONBALL!" someone yelled loudly.

The crowd cheered as the class clown jumped into the pool, his arms clutched tightly around his knees. He had a bra on his head and was wearing a pair of bunny slippers, both of which were torn from him as he impacted the water. Steve, standing at the edge of the pool, reached down and snatched up the bra as it washed up against the side of the pool. He glanced at the piece of intimate apparel for a moment before lifting the lacy item over his head.

"Okay, who does this belong to?" he asked, glancing around.

"Mine. Can't you tell?" the jokester said, emerging from the water, grabbing his pectoral muscles, and doing his best to shake them.

"You're obviously drunk," Steve said dourly. "Go home, Franklin, before Liz lays a curse on you."

The young man looked beyond Steve to see a slightly older woman in her mid-twenties, her long tresses of gold falling casually and draping down about her shoulders. He could not help but admire how good she looked in the long, pink evening gown she wore, until his eyes found her hand, which held the necklace of a Wiccan medallion intertwined through her fingers. The medallion itself was thus allowed to swing all too innocently just below that hand. The would-be comedian promptly scrambled out of the pool and stumbled away. His eyes, constantly flicking around to look back at her, occasioned several instances of his running into more than a few of his fellow seniors, who laughed uproariously as he executed his hasty exit of the area.

"You are very forgiving," Elizabeth said, extending her wine glass in salute, "considering these guys sneaking alcohol into the party could land you in a lot of trouble." Steve followed suit, extending his own glass out to meet the one in Elizabeth's hand.

"Better we make sure they don't hurt themselves," Steve said quietly with a small smile, "or others, for that matter, as they most surely would do if they wander off somewhere by themselves to do whatever on their own."

"Well, really, I'm a bit surprised," she responded in a low murmur. "These boys are mostly behaving themselves pretty well."

"Really, they do seem to, huh? I'm glad," Steve said, nodding. "I threw the party believing that I was well enough respected that they would go by my rules, and for the most part, our younger friends and old underclassmen do seem to be doing so."

Smiling, she took his hand and led him inside the cabin. The party was going strong within, the furniture was all covered with blankets, and the large media rig in the living room was blasting tunes with enough bass to make the windows shake. He glanced around quickly to ensure that people were, in fact, behaving themselves.

"No worries," she said softly. "I directed the coven to keep an eye on everything," she said, smiling as she extended her glass and waved it back and forth across the room in general. Hands popped up, drinks in hand, in response to show Steve that her coven was indeed watching.

"I can see where it would be a good thing to be high priestess," he said as they made their way up the stairs, glancing back down on the noisy merry-makers one more time before she pushed open his bedroom door, and they moved inside, closing it quietly behind them.

*   *   *   *

"Where is he?" Theresa whispered to herself as she made her way to the back where the pool was located, albeit a bit too late to see Steve. She walked around the edge of the pool looking for him. Jack and Karin found her paused at the pool's edge. Karin stared back and forth from Theresa's form to that of Jack, in growing frustration, as Jack watched Theresa so very intently. Karin crossed her arms, looking around, willing to look at anything other than Jack's seemingly mindless infatuation with another girl. As she glanced about, she saw a couple of rather intoxicated guys laughing as they were being escorted from the party by one of the Wiccan priestesses who graduated the year before. Karin turned back to Jack, gave a rather disgusted sigh, and pushed him off the edge and into the water. Shaking her head, she turned to leave.

Jack fell with an ungainly splash, which attracted Theresa's attention as he surfaced and stared over at her, feeling somewhat stupid. Theresa laughed as she moved around the pool and knelt to assist Karin's victim.

"So," she said laughingly. "Come here often, stranger?"

He pulled himself up onto the pool's edge and out of the water, with Theresa doing all she could to assist him.

"Actually, my first time. You?"

Jack sat there on the pool's edge, his feet dangling in the water as Theresa retrieved a nearby towel.

"The same for me. Here. Having fun yet?" she asked, smiling broadly.

Jack started wiping his face and hair and looked up into those eyes he so adored.

"I am now," he whispered.

*   *   *   *

Karin stormed away to the front porch, down the stairs, out, and away from the cabin. She noted that she was catching up with the two guys being escorted out. They were, rather unwisely, arguing with the priestess who was dressed in normal evening clothes.

"Come on, baby," the blond one said somewhat disjointedly. "We were just—" The young man fell silent as the Wiccan put a hand up front of his face, which, even in his drunken state, made him take a step backward before stumbling. He would have fallen, but his dark-haired companion managed to hold him up.

"You refused to go along with the rules," she said flatly. "You need to go."

"Come on, Craig," said the dark-haired boy holding him up and sneering at the girl ordering them out. The two turned away from the debate with the Wiccan and stumbled away along the path to the

parking lot. Karin brushed past the priestess and hastened to catch
up with the two guys.

"Hey, guys, I need a drink. You got any left?" she asked, taking
Craig's other arm and helping him.

"You bet your ass we do," the dark-haired guy responded.

*   *   *   *

Theresa and Jack were cutting-up, laughing, and carrying on,
but as time passed, he took notice of her glancing around a bit too
much. His frustration mounting, he sighed heavily, saying, "He's
with Elizabeth, Tee," and his irritation finally getting the best of
him. Theresa turned to face him directly, just staring at him and
bordering on shock.

She got to her feet and stood, glaring down at him.

"Just how long have you known?" she asked softly.

He averted his eyes briefly, realizing all he was doing was causing
her pain.

"Over a month now, at least," he said reluctantly.

She spun on her heel and walked away and started to push her
way through the crowd on the pool deck, heading indoors.

"Theresa, wait," he called out, jumping up and running after her.

*   *   *   *

Karin and the boys made their way along the path, heading
for the area where everyone had parked their cars. One of the boys
leered over at her.

"Karin, I had no idea you could be so much fun." It was the
dark-haired guy.

"Wait until we get back to that keg sitting in the trunk," the other
boy said as he moved his hand around her neck so that it lay upon her
breast. As she moved to remove it, a deer suddenly ran across the path
in front of them, causing the two guys to lurch abruptly and stumble.
Going down, they nearly took Karin with them, but she was able to
break free, causing them both to fall without her.

She glanced up, sure she saw a deer, just as something ran across the path, chasing the deer. *A dusky-skinned young woman in a white dress,* she thought whoever it was dropped a single open-toed white shoe. Picking up the shoe, she slowly lifted it where she could see it better, and she was beset with unbelievable feelings of mixed terror and fascination. She felt like her heart was about to explode.

"No way!" she said explosively.

*   *   *   *

Theresa moved into the cabin and started asking around as to where she might find Steve. After looking about in the main building, she moved to the stairway and made her way upstairs. As she moved along the hall, she saw a couple of guys who were classmates she recognized, and they were arguing. A woman, trying to break up the argument, was pushed backward and fell into the arms of the star quarterback of the football team. He moved in-between the guys who were arguing and the woman who had been shoved aside, and he and a couple of his teammates who were with him quietly handled the situation, breaking up the argument, which the young woman appreciated very much and for which she gave a great deal of thanks. Theresa shook her head and passed them by as she continued her search for Steve.

"Now, you guys are going to play nice and have some nice, nonalcoholic beverages, and we'll be cool," the quarterback said, smiling.

The boys looked warily at him for a moment, and then shaking their heads and nodding their agreement, they turned away and made their way down to the main floor.

Theresa took the opportunity to tap the quarterback on the shoulder, addressing him by his name.

"Have you seen Steve, Cody?" she asked as casually as possible.

*   *   *   *

Karin continued into the woods, pursuing the woman as best she could. Her clothing was torn and caught up on the branches and brush. Ignoring the stinging pain of the scratches and bruising impact with tree limbs and such, she broke into a small opening and gazed upon a horrifying scene. A young woman stood there in the middle of the clearing in a tattered and dirt-encrusted once-white dress. She stood over something that looked like it was or had been burning. Absentmindedly, she noted a white, tail-like appendage seemingly turning dark as it disappeared back under her dress. The strange young woman turned to look directly at her.

The woman's mouth gaped slightly open, exposing very distinct fangs in her mouth. She stood stock-still, obviously in something of a state of shock at being seen. Still terrified by the shocking sight of the woman with the fangs, Karin's attention was attracted to something at the girl's feet. She saw what looked to be the ashen head of a deer broken away from the rest of its body, and as it toppled over, it crumbled into a very fine ash, leaving literally nothing. Karin's eyes flicked back to the young woman's face and, surprisingly, found her to be in tears.

As full recognition became suddenly manifested in her mind, Karin murmured a single word almost dumbly.

"Heather?" she whispered simply.

Heather slowly reached out to her, "I-I just wanted to see everyone again. I-Karin—" she explained but got no further as Karin interrupted her, who was screaming out loud and turning to flee the scene.

Heather took a step toward Karin's retreating figure, but as if she couldn't summon the strength, she fell to her knees, sobbing.

"I never asked . . . I never wanted . . . I . . . I miss you all so much."

* * * *

After walking completely down the hall, Theresa came back to where Cody had been required to end the argument a few minutes, only to find that Jack had followed her and was standing with Cody and his two teammates, and the woman who had tried to stop the altercation had already gone. A puzzled look clouded Theresa's features for a moment. She nodded to herself and turned and started for the first bedroom door a few feet away. Quickly stepping forward, Jack grasped her arm, momentarily preventing her from accessing the door.

"Theresa," he said quietly.

"Let me go, Jack," she said quietly, struggling to control her voice. "I have to know, I need . . . I need to know." She bit her lower lip in an effort to keep her from saying something she would later regret.

"Jack, I—"

Both Jack and Theresa suddenly looked out at the big picture window that overlooked the front area of the cabin property and out toward the path leading to the parking area. Suddenly, Jack was distracted as Theresa suddenly collapsed, grabbing the small of her back as if in severe pain. No one seemed to notice as the football players had moved off along the hall toward a second set of stairs at the far end of the hall. The music from below was still blaring. Jack knelt, moving to support Theresa as she was doubled over in obviously severe pain.

"Theresa!"

*   *   *   *

Karin broke back onto the path and ran for the cabin, calling for help. Just as she was about to break out into the clearing, she was suddenly grabbed from behind by her coat and thrown against a tree. She could feel her ribs snap upon impact with the tree, and her right arm suddenly went limp. She slid slowly down to the ground as she began coughing up blood; she was finding it hard to breathe. Looking up, she saw the silhouette of a female figure standing over her, and as she looked on, she saw huge, bat like wings unfold, blocking out the lights of the cabin across the field, and again, she saw a tail of some kind flipping around as if in agitation. Karen lifted her one good arm as if to ward off her assailant, but the figure simply grabbed her hair and started to drag her into the dark woods while Karin screamed for help.

*   *   *   *

"Theresa, what's wrong?" Jack asked when she glanced up; limbal of her eyes flickering gold.

Jack's feelings were not those of sadness nor even pity but anger and fear and a sudden bloodlust. Jack, lost momentarily in the bloodlust, turned first this way and then that, and he felt a need to flee, but he could not. He glanced back, only to find that Theresa was gone. He ran to the stairs and paused partially down, looking out over the railing and scanning the floor below. A sudden gust of wind blew inside through the wide open doors to the pool area, and he saw her running out across the deck. Jack was down the remainder of the stairs and bolted through the patio doors so very fast as he tried to reach her, but she moved faster than he thought possible for anyone. In shock, he saw her run to the pool and cross its surface before leaping over the railing surrounding the patio! Jack skirted the pool around to where she had gone over the railing and looking out across the back clearing just in time to see her running into the woods. He launched himself over the railing and gave pursuit.

*   *   *   *

Heather ran further into the woods for a long time before calling a halt to her awesome pace. As she glanced around, she found that she had stopped near one of the lavish homes the area was famous for and was, in fact, just across the fence from its backyard. She leaned against the fence, breathing heavily and trying to calm down. She slowly slid down the fence into a sitting position and covered her mouth as she suddenly started to cough. She felt like crying but knew it would be quite unwise to make any noise, so she did her best to control her inclination to sob out her woes. She looked up into the night sky as if making a wish and closed her eyes. She sat there for some time, pulling her legs up to her chest, and she hugged her knees with her arms, resting her head on the two.

A large Malamute came up to her quietly from the woods a few feet away, but Heather, absentmindedly aware of the creature's approach, remained seemingly oblivious to the animal. The dog padded quietly up to her side and nudged her with its nose. The nudging of the dog's nose effectively broke her out of the trancelike state she was in. In an impossible fast speed, she bolted to her feet and backed away from the dog. The dog just sat there, looking at her for a long moment with slightly illuminous, silvery limbal eyes, and then padded casually up to her again. She reached out her hand and started to pet the animal, speaking to it through clenched, fanged teeth.

"Well, at least, you don't seem to be afraid of me. Are you?"

The dog just looked at her with big, fearless eyes. She leaned forward and took the big animal into her arms, hugging it tightly, and though she continued holding the great creature like that, in a hug that she was certain would have driven the life's breath from anyone, the animal moved not an inch but simply stood quietly, accepting her. After several minutes, she released the big fellow and smiled down at him.

"Karin is scared of me. I knew when I dug myself out," she said haltingly. "I was some kind of vampire or something such. But like the deer, you don't fear me. It didn't even fear me when I drained it of its blood. You might want to run away before this monster gobbles you up too."

She stood there and suddenly realized she lost both her shoes, the incongruity of which almost made her laugh out loud. She quickly clamped a hand over her mouth.

"Oh hell," she murmured instead. "Probably not a good idea to wake the neighbors. I wonder where I am?" she asked as she walked stealthily around the house, looking for the nearest street sign.

"Safford Road, eh?" she said, noting the sign at the end of the lane like drive that served the big house. "I must be in Lynnfield."

The dog simply yipped playfully yet quietly, and again, she knelt facing him. Gently petting his head and ruffling his ears, she stood again and started for the woods at the back of the property.

"Still wanting to follow me, huh?" she asked softly.

The animal looked up at her, cocking his head over to one side.

"I wonder what your name is," she said, kneeling at the edge of the woods, looking for a collar that might supply some information.

"*Johnathan*," the dog responded—in her mind.

*   *   *   *

Jack arrived at the edge of the woods and stared in awe. A path had been created by Theresa's passage. Flames flickered up and down the trunks of the trees that had not yet been incinerated; the solid wood, not burning, beneath the bark exposed to the eye a whitish-yellow color. Smoldering red embers could still be seen, flaring with every little gust of wind that passed across them. He walked across the scorched earth. He glanced back over his shoulder, noting that most were far too busy to have been aware of Theresa's run across the water of the pool, and those who had thought they had noticed something unusual lost interest when he took off after her, putting it all down to too much booze and partying. For once, he was grateful that none of his classmates had decided to play the hero, being too busy having fun.

Theresa was a bit further into the woods. She lay curled up in a fetal position; the ground about her lay untouched. She was having some kind of spasms as Jack rushed over and knelt, lifting her into his arms. As he picked her up, the back of her shirt snagged upon his arm and pulled up, and he shifted her about to better carry her. He saw scars on the small of her back—scars that were moving. He looked on, watching as they danced about upon the small of her back.

"They are unraveling further; healing," he said to no one in particular. Feeling for his phone, he made a quick call.

"Marcus? Yeah, we both sensed something. Yeah, both of us. Her scars, they are writhing about. Yeah, I'm going to take her to Lorelabs, to Tyr. See you there. Bye."

Chapter Three

TYR

Looking back toward the party still going on at the cabin, Jack shook his head. People had definitely noticed the flames, even if they had not observed Theresa creating them. He could see people standing at both the upper and lower railings, trying to see what had happened. One could easily expect some of the more inquisitive among them to come to check things out.

"Oh well, great," he said, lifting Theresa, who completely passed out because of the pain. He shook his head, looking down at the girl in his arms.

"Couldn't wait until we were well away from the others, could you? What the hell did we sense?"

Jack headed deeper into the woods in hopes of losing any overly inquisitive investigators. It was but a short time before the two broke out into the open on the eastern edge of the woodland where they came upon a well-kept lawn with gravestones scattered across the field.

"Too open here. I need to get you to Lorelabs, Tee."

*   *   *   *

Heather scrambled back a good six feet and simply stood staring at the huge Malamute. Her skin paled, suddenly turning white, and wings seemed to just as quickly materialize at her back, spreading wide and out to either side of her, testing the air tentatively. Were one observant enough, what seemed to be a tail could be seen protruding out from beneath her tattered, white dress, flicking anxiously back and forth. Her nails became black and claw like, and her visible veins took on a blackish look, in sharp contrast to her suddenly pallid appearance as her skin continued to become pale and then dead-white. As she opened her mouth to speak, one did not need to be observant at all to see her canines growing into actual fangs.

"Did you . . . did you just speak with your mind?" she asked the huge animal warily.

The Malamute shook his powerful body and then shook his head, as might any denying something.

"*Nope, it's all in your head.*" She felt a feeling of serenity from him speaking.

"How can I tell how you are feeling? How can I hear your voice when your mouth isn't moving?" she asked as she glanced about herself, not quite sure she was buying the idea that this dog was somehow able to make himself heard in her mind.

"*I don't particularly like the word 'telepath.' It sounds somehow, you know, cold. Especially when one can share their feelings to the one he is 'speaking' to. 'Rynspeak' is what my mentor settled on calling it, since telepathy, if it's even possible, is associated with humans, not our kind. Whenever I speak, you cannot only hear my words, you can also sense my feelings or mood.*" The voice sounded in her mind yet again as the animal started to slowly move toward her.

"Whoa. I might be new to whatever happened to me, but I know how to use my power," Heather said, pointing out her hand toward the animal.

"Indeed." The voice came again. *"However, before you do, perhaps you would like to know who you are, what you are, or what you're going to want to do now. Or even, where you go from here. I offer possible answers for your situation. This very town came into being because of our existence. I suspect you are one of the other species I've heard was possible, but I haven't seen any. You're the first Savryn I've met."*

Heather relaxed, albeit ever-so-slightly, and stood quietly eyeing the animal as he ceased his advance and sat back on his haunches in the grass, seemingly waiting for her response. She was obviously listening quite intently to what he was saying. Her expression clearly showed she was absorbing and assimilating everything he said.

"Are you like me? You look like a big dog!" she said softly.

"I was born like this—in this form for a long time. I age seemingly like a human. I can also change, but I look quite different, and I've been told to never show my true form." That silent voice came again with a feeling of compassion and kindness.

Heather walked up and knelt in front of him. She carefully reached out her hand, which returned to her natural almost maple colored skin tone before coming in contact with him. Carefully, she proceeded to scratch him behind the ears.

"Why is that? Who told you never to take your true form? It sounds cruel not to be allowed to be yourself."

"I am actually an Ulryn, from what my mentor told me. He said I have a power called the Umbrage. He said that if I use that power, I could bring ruin to everyone I care about. But I can, however, use it safely on myself."

"How can that be, if it brings ruin to others?" Heather asked, regaining her feet and glancing around. "Huh, maybe best we continue this elsewhere?"

John rose on all fours and quietly followed her as she turned toward the woods and started off in that direction. A crackling sound, not at all unlike that of a fire, suddenly caught her attention, and she turned quickly to see the dog enlarging, his back now coming up to her bosom, and the black markings on his fur erupted in flame—flames that were black. Heather backed off, noting that this fire gave off no light but seemingly absorbed all light around it. The Malamute's face caught fire as the black flames completely enveloped his body. He was suddenly reshaping, and in bare moments, he had become a huge white wolf! She could only stare in awe.

"You are so beautiful!" she murmured.

"As far as I know or have ever seen, the Umbrage can destroy anything except me. For me, it heals and helps me change form." His voice touched her mind again.

Heather cautiously walked up to his majestic form and gently ran her fingers through the silky coat covering his back and up behind his head. She scratched his ears, which he seemed to appreciate.

"Humph, you seem to be a bit of a pushover. So is it you, or do you just know someone who can help me answer those questions you posed earlier?" she asked, falling into place at the large animal's side as they moved deeper into the woods.

"That would also be my Mentor. He resides within the confines of Lorelabs."

* * * *

Theresa could feel herself being carried along quickly by someone or something. The rapid movement caused her long tresses to blow and whip about. Slowly, she opened her eyes to see a gray-skinned man with red hair. The guy carrying her, for he did look to be a young man, glanced down at her, and she could see that he had horns protruding out through his hair just above his forehead. As one might imagine, she was suddenly kicking and screaming loudly.

"Okay, okay, here you go. You're down. Geez, Tee," the creature said as he quickly placed her on the turf in the small clearing they had come to a halt in. Theresa was up on her feet immediately and was three very quick leaps away before it dawned upon her that she recognized the horned thing's voice. Staying in her flight, she exclaimed, "Jack!" as her turn brought him fully into view.

Jack was all but unrecognizable. His skin that was a strange grayish color and combined with the red hair and the Illuminous silvery rings around his eyes were a far stretch from the formerly peach-colored skin tones, blond hair, and blue eyes that comprised Jack's normal features.

"Your eyes—what happened to them? It is you, isn't it, Jack?" she asked warily.

He stood there, looking at her, a big smile creasing his features, and his silver-rimmed eyes seemed to stare into her very soul. She felt strangely vulnerable and self-conscious. His fanged teeth did not add to any sense of security!

He lifted his hands and linked them behind his head and stomped his *hooves*.

"You've got hooves!" she exclaimed, seemingly to herself.

"Well, from what little I know, that is a common trait of a Cinryn. I also used contacts to hide the silver portions of my eyes. Dad's idea originally," Jack replied.

Theresa shook her head, continuing to stare at him. His body was far more chiseled than she remembered it being.

"Sin-rin?" she repeated the word, albeit not correctly.

Smiling, he walked over to a nearby tree and walked into and on through it! He stepped out the other side, looking like the Jack she knew. The tree suddenly began to wither.

"What-what did you do to the tree?" Theresa asked, her eyes flicking from the Jack she knew to the dying tree.

"From what I was told, this is normal. Think about it, all those trees you see dead in the woods. Did they die of natural causes, or do you have a Cinryn nearby? Hmm, I wonder."

Slowly, she walked up to him and gently touched his face. He stared at her fingertips as if they were holy, but the moment she touched his cheek, he closed his eyes as if to soak it all in.

"You look, looked like a, a Satyr, you know, like we see in novels and movies."

"Yeah, apparently, it's what our own kind call each other around humans. Not that I know but one other like me."

"Who's that?" she queried in surprise.

"I'm not really supposed to say. Think, 'secret identity.' He prefers to remain behind the scenes, so to speak. So, umm, any other questions?"

"Where are you taking me?" she said, looking more comfortable now that he'd returned to being regular old Jack.

"To your father's company, I guess," Jack said thoughtfully. "Knowing Tyr, for a history lesson about this town few knows about."

"But why would you take me to him? Why now?"

Jack glances thoughtfully back where they had just come away from then returned his gaze to her.

"How about because you ran across the water in the pool? Not to mention leaving a small section of the woods in a state of cinders and ash," Jack responded. "I was told to watch you. I'd heard you were similar to me, but honestly, we couldn't use our abilities in our human forms. You certainly are special, just like Tyr said."

"Wait, Tyr? Doctor Tyr?" she asked.

"Yup. He was a victim of Lorelabs that was saved long ago from the former owners, or so I heard. But it's not really my place to tell you."

Theresa looked down at her hands and started to go into shock. Jack walked up to her and took her by the shoulder and could see she was visibly shaken, "Tee?"

"Who, Jack? I mean, what am . . . uhh . . . am I?"

*   *   *   *

"We have a while before we get to Lorelabs, considering it's clear on the other side of the township," Heather said as she stopped at the edge of the woods, looking out at the still ongoing party. Being careful to stay just inside the tree line, they circled around the edge of the clearing housing the cabin and the party itself.

"Be wary, Heather. You would shock them if they were to see you now."

"Too late," Heather replied. "I got hungry and chased a deer across the open path to the cabin. Karin saw me and followed. I freaked her out," Heather said, pausing and clutching her chest for a moment.

"Karin?" The white wolf queried as he paused, looking back at her.

"She called me out. It hurt so much seeing her stare at me like I was some monster. I guess in the comics, movies, and TV, you aren't scared because the monsters usually looked human when you first see them."

"The reality is, when confronted with impossibility, humans fear first. It's a survival instinct, fight or flee—the two dominate their subconscious, even in this 'civilized' society they've created for themselves."

"Huh, yeah, you're right. Now, that was really insightful. You sound like there's a lot going on behind those big eyes of yours, John."

"Ugh, Am I starting to sound like my father? Oh now, there's a lovely thought."

"Who's your dad?" she asked out of curiosity.

"That would be a need-to-know kind of thing. He says it's important to hide our identities and maintain the status quo."

The two continue on, moving again ever deeper into the woods, and leaving the party and cabin behind when a thought occurred, "We could have gone faster if I changed. I could just fly us to Lorelabs. I know how to get there," she said thoughtfully.

"As convenient and awesome as that would likely be, it also presents the possibility of being seen. Right now we need to keep to the woods and remain hidden."

"It's night, though, who would see?"

"Let's think about this. A bone-white, bat-winged, young girl with a tail, flying through the night sky? Oh yeah, right. Surely, no one would ever look up and notice something like that, not on a Friday night. Tell you what, let's not chance it, regardless, all right?"

"Oh well, yeah. Makes sense, I guess," Heather said, feeling rather silly by even suggesting the idea. "What do I do about Karin?" she asked, wanting to change the subject.

"I know a bit about her and her reputation for anything animalistic and or fantastic. No one would be likely to believe her. Social stigma, you got to love it."

*   *   *   *

"Here, take my hand, Tee," Jack said, holding his hand out to Theresa who was on a steep slope beneath him. Theresa grasped the proffered hand and clambered up to stand beside her companion, and in so doing, she saw the tall fence that designated the outer boundary of the Lorelabs' property. Well beyond the fence, one could just make out a building, which, if truth be known, looked rather dilapidated on the outside but played host to very modern cameras positioned on every corner. The grounds were well-kept, but the parking lot along one side was mostly empty, save for some nine or ten vehicles resting on the cracked and broken pavement currently somewhat overgrown by the returning vegetation. The windows look cracked and unkempt. The two followed the fence around to the high, heavy gate that was the entrance to the place, and the gate, surprisingly, opened automatically.

"Oh, they saw us on the cameras, and they're letting us in." Theresa observed as they started walking down the paved drive toward the parking lot and the front entrance. The doors, when they arrived at them, were old but quite functional. They merely walked up to the double doors when a beep sounded, and the doors swung open.

"I haven't been here for a long time. Why is it so rundown?" she asked, looking around with furrowed brows.

"It was in part on purpose. The facility was famous, at one time being the greatest pharmaceutical company in the world. It made few medications, but the products sold for millions a pop. At least, that's what I heard before the takeover. Now, it's just a headquarters for factories making lesser quality medications elsewhere," Jack was saying when he heard a beep on the wall phone close at hand. He moved to answer it.

She noticed the big smile creasing his features as he turned back to face her.

"Good news?" she asked.

He nodded, starting to walk down the hall, leading her on toward a set of elevators.

"We are to hit the down button when the elevator arrives," he said quietly.

"We're going down then?"

"Yes. We are to wait for them at the cubicles below," came the response.

Theresa turned around to see Marcus walking in the double doors behind them as they awaited the arrival of the elevator, his lab coat waving about as he entered.

"Marcus!" she said, recoiling and throwing a terrified look at Jack.

Jack took her in his arms, smiling broadly. "It's all right, Tee. He knows. He's always known, well, sort of. It's kind of hard to explain. Hey, Marcus."

Theresa saw her adopted father walking up to them with his usual solemn look on his face. It always seemed like he carried the world on his shoulders. Theresa sheepishly tried to back up and get in behind Jack. Noting her action, Marcus smiled.

"Theresa, it's okay. You're no different now than you were yesterday. I love you—remember that as you talk to Tyr."

The doors opened and the three of them stepped inside. Jack caught a look from Marcus and took a step away from Theresa. Theresa noted how he was still trying to protect her. She moved into her foster father's arms and hugged him tightly. Marcus held her the entire time they were descending.

*   *   *   *

There came a dinging sound, and the doors opened. Unlike the floor above, the floor below was far more modern and clean. It was a simple room, really. The center was filled with cubicles, and across from them was Marcus and Tara's office. The others in the middle were for various specialists with their tools for their testing and experiments. The other rooms were always locked away from her as they came to Marcus's office and entered it. It was like taking a step back in time to her childhood. Nothing had changed. From the various baseball trophies her dad won when he was in high school to the various pictures of her and Joshua with more added as they grew up. Among them were also pictures of a large white wolf.

Theresa walked over to the pictures and picked one of them up and looked into the eyes of the animal. Intelligence lurked deep within those eyes—those were not the eyes of an animal. It was almost as if the animal's body concealed a human intellect. She was lost in looking at the picture when she heard the door to the office open.

A large, nearly naked man walked about inside the office, blocking her view. He was wearing little more than a medical gown to cover his muscular frame. His hair was gray, and he had a rather ragged beard. Old, jagged scars covered all of his visible body, although somewhat hidden by thick body hair. As she studied him, she noted that his limbals had a ring of gold, and she could have sworn, even in the normal bright light of the office, that they were glowing. He hobbled inside and smiled upon seeing the group.

"Tyr," Marcus said in greeting, indicating a seat. Jack gave the man plenty of space as he slowly lowered himself into the seat, wincing.

"That's Doctor Tyr, Jack? I remember him but somehow different," Theresa whispered.

"Most who meet me do, young lady," Tyr spoke. His voice was deep and grainy.

"Tyr, do you know what the matter with me is?" Theresa blurted out.

Tyr glanced at Marcus briefly then back at Theresa before continuing, "We're waiting for the others to show up."

Almost as if on cue, the sound of something falling to the stone floor outside grabbed the group's attention.

"They've arrived," the gray-haired man said quietly.

Jack and Theresa looked out through the one-way glass in the closed office door then back at Marcus and the seated older man. Shocked by what they saw, they nodded at each other, and Theresa rushed for the door, while Jack hung back his mouth agape.

Marcus looked at Tyr, and the two smiled as he pushed himself off his desk and walked up to Jack.

"It's impossible," Jack muttered about what he was seeing. Marcus looked down at him briefly before looking back as two friends were reunited.

"Why is John here?" Jack asked as Marcus raised a hand, indicating that he should hold his questions.

"Heather!" Theresa cried out as she rushed through the throng of cubicles to Heather who hurried forward to meet her. They all but crashed into each other as they hugged tightly. The two of them started crying, laughing, and talking all at the same time. Then something in Heather remembered what she was, and she backed away from Theresa. Theresa was having none of that, however, and immediately closed the gap.

"Stay back," Heather said, her hand outstretched as if to ward her best friend away.

Theresa, still in tears, was overjoyed, and her face contorted in pain at her friend's words.

"Why? Why should I keep back?" Theresa almost sobbed. "I am so happy you are alive, Heather, why are you pushing me away?"

"Tee, I . . .," Heather started to say something but seemed lost for words.

"She is assuming she's an evil vampire, and she will gobble you up."

Theresa felt the words flow into her mind. She didn't hear but actually felt them. The pain in her back returned, but it wasn't as painful as before.

The words felt comforting and seemed to think aloud so as to not hurt my back, she thought. *My back!* Theresa stopped in mid thought.

"Why am I feeling this? What happened to me?" she asked as she took Heather's hand, even though her friend reluctantly tried to pull away.

"No!" Theresa said loudly. "I'm not letting you go again, whatever you think you are and no matter what is happening to me. We are going to get through this . . . together."

The two teared up and again fell to hugging each other.

Tyr watched for a few moments before he broke it up.

"This is rather emotional. I'll be in the office when they get over themselves."

Marcus turned and entered the office behind Tyr. Jack looked at Marcus through the open office door and then back at the girls before returning his gaze to the older man.

"Tyr's like that," Marcus said with a trace of amusement. "Not big on feelings, but then, feelings are not all he has to offer one. Bring the girls inside, Jack, when they've calmed down."

Marcus went inside, and as Jack walked around the large white wolf, he stared at the wolf in passing, catching its huge sliver ringed eyes. It turned its head toward him, and suddenly, Jack heard a voice in his mind!

"Hi, Jack."

"Why expose yourself now?" Jack asked in amazement.

*   *   *   *

The girls entered the office, and Marcus gestured for Jack to close the door. The two young women continued to talk excitedly to one another until Marcus coughed loudly, causing them to go silent but still exchanging knowing looks with each other. The two turned toward Marcus, who gestured toward the tall burley man known only as Tyr.

"Done acting like children? Good. Cause you're not children, and at least one of you isn't even human." Heather frowned and averted her eyes from those of her friend, casting them down to the floor. Theresa tried to speak to her, but Heather wouldn't respond.

"Okay, I don't know what happened to her, but to go on treating her like a monster is a bit much, don't you think?" Theresa asked a bit caustically.

"Dear lady, I wasn't talking about her. She is a given," Tyr said simply.

Theresa looked toward Marcus as if expecting him to come to her defense, but he said nothing. She then looked at Jack, but he only shrugged.

"I'm not human either. I die—wait, what?" Heather looked far more confused than ever before, her head rising upon hearing this new bit of information.

Theresa looked aghast and stared at him then back to Marcus before finally bringing her eyes back to Tyr. For the moment, she was completely speechless. The moment, however, passed quickly for Heather.

"Wait, okay, I dug myself out of the grave, and I've been feeding on living creatures until they turn to ash, and *she's* not human?" Heather finally said.

"Girls, I don't know how to address this, but I will explain if you'll be patient. A long time ago, before you were even born, Theresa, there was the other owners of Lorelabs. These men and women did horrible experiments with animals involving genetic manipulation. They were trying to recreate an Ulryn using a wolf named Tyr."

"The hell!" Heather said, looking at John then back at Tyr. Theresa' mouth slightly parted as if she wanted to say something, but she chose to remain silent.

"Theresa, you and your biological father were captured. Joon and the others were experimented on. It was hoped it would advance what they had done to me by using two living samples of the children of Ryn."

Heather and Theresa said in unison, "Children of Ryn?"

"I have no idea what Ryn even means. But they did call one a Cinryn, and your father Joon a Vulryn, but they were both Ryn. An opportunity eventually arose where we could escape. Most of us escaped alive, save two. Sadly, it cost the lives of those who did the most to save the rest of us. Gregory King, Joshua's father, died in an explosion, and Joon Bok died going back for him when the explosion occurred."

Theresa's mouth dropped, and Heather covered hers, her eyes large as saucers as she had always asked about Josh's dad and why he avoided talking about him.

"He said he was a hero," she murmured.

"Greg and Joon saved us. Marcus and Tara, Greg's widow, were among those who were saved. Marcus and Tara were also among those who supported the coupe and decided to stay and clean up the place, making it a legitimate pharmaceutical company. Without the drug that also helped create me, the company has had huge losses and is but a fraction of what it once was.

"I learned some things from them as they were not fully aware how sentient I was. For instance, the name Vulryn, Cinryn, and Ulryn. There were two other races among the Ryn. One was called the Lucryn. I know nothing about that branch of the race of Ryn. Well, except they are also called the Immortals. The last is what you may very well be, Heather. However, I know almost nothing about your race, if you are, in fact, an Immortal."

Heather walked up to Tyr. "What do you think I am?"

Tyr looked down and away before responding, "You are of those called the traitors of the Ryn—you are a Savryn."

Theresa came up for air. "She is no traitor to us or anyone!"

John padded up to Theresa and rubbed his head alongside her hips.

"It's all right, Theresa. He is implying what the race as a whole was known as. He isn't speaking of individuals present."

"So you are a talking wolf, John; one I assume has a human form. The old owners were trying to recreate this Ulryn thing. Theresa and Josh's dads were heroes, I am a child of Ryn, one of a long line of traitors called Savryn, and Theresa is a Vulryn," Heather murmured softly, still very close to the gray-haired man.

Tyr stood and towered over her. "Yes, young lady, you sum it up well."

"Well, hell," Heather mumbled, backing off and walking back to Theresa. The two stood there close to each other, holding hands, each a comfort to the other.

"So we're both not human. What do we do now?"

"For Theresa, she will soon undo the bindings her father placed on her so she could live a normal human life. Funny thing is, he said that it should have lasted her entire lifespan and more. What is her power that could undo something so potent, so early in her life?"

It was Theresa who broke away and let go of Heather's hand as she stood before the imposing Tyr, but unlike Heather, she was unflinching.

"What is this binding you speak of, Tyr?" she said curtly.

"It was a small stone made of solidified sulfur. It has many names. In China, it's named *zhūlóng*. In Japan, *magatama*, and in Korea, a *gogok*. It's completely harmless to humans, Joon had said. It would only affect himself. He said there are many powerful artifacts humans have obtained that are completely inert in their hands but not in the hands of the Ryn or their children, or in your case, under your skin. A powerful rune totem can do various things, but for you, it binds your power. However, it's very apparent that its power is weakening.

"Girls, this kind of knowledge endangers us all. If anyone learns of this and informs your government, I would fear for all of our well-beings," Tyr said, standing and walking toward the window, staring out intently into the empty cubicles.

"So I assume Theresa cannot change yet," Heather said, standing up and distancing herself slightly from Theresa.

Everyone heard Heather's words and turned toward her, and the others backed off as they saw before them a creature few would call a vampire. Her skin was bone white; her black veins could be seen just under her skin. The contrast made them more apparent than on humans and their veins. Her nails turned sharp and as black as the deepest night. She unfurled her wings from behind, and the flesh of her wings was covered by the same black veins but was much more transparent. They saw a tail protrude from underneath the remnants of her soiled white dress, which swung lazily back and forth. Her lips parted, and they could clearly see her fangs.

"So am I a Savryn?"

*   *   *   *

The hotel outside Fairmount was quiet with the sounds of a gentle rain. The wind gently blew through the trees, and the pattering of rain on the hotel's windows was the loudest noise of the hour. Inside, all but the night staff slept soundly in their beds. It was another night like any other in this small town—seemingly.

Sara woke first, hearing a noise, owing to her being a naturally light sleeper. Joshua was sound asleep as Sara silently crawled out of her bed that lay next to his. She slept in purple satin shorts and a lavender tank top. Her bare feet landing on the soft carpet, she listened intently to the door and heard the clicking of the doorknob. She reached for the holstered forty-five-caliber lying in the open bottom storage area of her nightstand and slowly moved to approach the room's door, unsheathing the weapon. She looked back at Joshua briefly and thought, *If I wake him, the perp might hear and flee. Better to catch the person or persons in the act.* She crossed the room, passing the room's private bath on her left, and she closed in on the door quietly.

Her hand reached out for the knob and quickly jerked the door open, only to find an empty hallway. She looked down the left and saw the other closed doors and the elevator at the end of the hall. To her right was only one door before the window at the end of the hallway with a small table and flowers in a vase. It was then she heard the slightest creak in the floor and the shimmer as she took aim. "What the hell is up with this sci-fi shi—"

Sara's gun flew from her hand, and she found herself floating in the air with the life being choked out of her.

"*Where is Heather?*" a disembodied voice queried. Sara felt its feelings—the thing was filled with murderous intent. She was starting to float back into the room, and as she did so, the door closed seemingly of its own volition. Suddenly, out of nowhere, Joshua tackled something, and Sara fell to the ground, choking. Everything spun before her eyes as Joshua was flung to the bed, his arms pinned.

"*Oh, how I will enjoy torturing you,*" the voice growled in his mind. The sensation he felt from the voice in his head was malevolent and vicious. He could feel a hand over his mouth, and he grabbed onto something and tried to push it away, but it was far stronger than him, and suddenly, his left arm was torn from his body. Sara screamed herself, hearing Joshua's muffled screams of pain.

"You son of a bitch!" Sara yelled and just as quickly went silent as something covered her mouth, and she fought to breathe once more.

"*Now, where was I?*" the disembodied voice whispered to him. And then Joshua's own disembodied voice responded oh-so-terribly coldly.

"*Thank you.*"

The intruder could hear his Rynspeak, and furthermore, it could feel its relief and joyful anticipation. Joshua was suddenly smiling as a shadowy mist began to envelope him, and then he was free, and Sara was dropped.

The entire hotel awoke as something inside their heads screamed in horror. A terrible fear had encompassed something—a fear they could not only hear but one they could also feel, and they too were terrified unto their very souls. The terrified thing, knowing a fear such as no current human had ever known, was screaming in absolute and utter terror. Whatever it was, it kept screaming in their minds,

"ULFYR!" There came a great crash as something smashed out of Joshua's hotel window, and a shimmering, nearly invisible creature fell from the second-story window, falling onto a parked vehicle, which roof caved in as the creature landed hard and then collapsed, entirely caving in. The creature rolled off the crushed vehicle and into the side of another vehicle, severely damaging its side door. As the rain made the creature partially visible, it looked up as it saw in the broken window a tall, shadowy form. Tall and imposing, the figure had unusually tall ears and distinctive, even slightly illuminous, silver limbal rings that marked its eyes even in the dark as it looked down on the creature as the mist took form.

"I hunger," the dark beast's Rynspeak whispered in the semi-invisible creature's mind, and there was about it a terribly mocking sense.

The injured intruder continued to stand, looking up but for a mere moment longer in the rain as if in thought. However, in the end, it apparently thought best to avoid the shadowy beast, and it took flight, flying in the general direction of the town and the heavy woods beyond.

Sara was surrounded by the mist, and it had acted as if it were a living thing, alive and deadly. She was well aware of its deadliness but knew it would not come near her and that it would purposely avoid her whenever she approached. She ran to the bathroom, and in it was stored a large cooler. She flipped it open, and it was packed with frozen meats of various kinds.

She ran back to the door where she could see the dark creature's silhouette still staring out of the window.

"Josh, the food is waiting, if you want to pursue her," she called to him.

She shook her head, still amazed, even after all these years, to see the tall, black, short-haired, jackal-headed form she both admired and feared when she saw him like this.

The transformed Joshua shook his large head and started turning gray. Suddenly, the mist withdrew, seemingly into the jackal-headed being's form, and the shadowy outline of Joshua's human form seemingly materialized out from within the ashen form of the beast, and Joshua stood there where the fearsome thing had been. He seemed to be slightly groggy.

Sara approached him and helped him sit on her bed as she walked up to the broken window and the pile of ashes on the ground. He stood there, flexing and checking out his fully restored left arm. Sara gave him one more glance before walking over to where the arm he had lost was. It wasn't much of an arm, though—it was now ashes. She retrieved the ring from among those ashes and placed it in his hand. Joshua took it gingerly from her and replaced it in the middle finger of his new left hand.

"I'm going to pull something from the ice chest and fix you something to eat. You need food after that ordeal."

Joshua nodded as he stood, and they both could hear the raised voices outside as he approached the window. He could see people running around, yelling about their damaged cars. They looked up and saw his broken window and Joshua standing there looking down at them. The people, many still in their pajamas, started to yell at him.

"Go downstairs and explain a burglar attacked us while we slept. At least, it's not a lie this time," Sara suggested. As he started to leave, his phone started to ring.

"Who the hell would call in the middle of the night?" Sara exclaimed from the mini kitchen.

Sara became concerned when she saw Joshua's mouth drop open. Slowly, he turned to face her as he finished the call.

"Heather—they've found her," he said, a small smile touching his features. "She's safe at Lorelabs, Sara. Tyr suspects she's a Savryn."

"That thing may have been looking for her or trying to stop us from finding her," Sara said, walking over to Josh and replaying the events of the last several minutes in her head.

"Are they still going to go ahead and use that stupid idea and try to readmit her, saying she is Heather's long lost twin?" she continued the thought, glancing back at him as she turned to go back into the kitchen.

"If that thing is looking for her, its best she stays in the public eye, at least for now," Joshua responded so quietly as to be almost speaking to himself.

"She'll have to stay at Lorelabs, though. It is the only secure place that is meant to handle your kind," Sara said musingly.

Joshua replaced the phone as he started for the door. "Perhaps, perhaps not. I think I've got a better idea."

Chapter Four

GOLDEN EYES

It was a brisk October night. The streetlights reflected off the damp, brick-layered streets that were one of many major advertising points for the tourist trade, which, of course, brought in a goodly portion of the town's funding every year. The more dimly luminous, antique styled streetlights that were utilized in and around Center Street, which encircled the town's "Kissing Tree Common" and reflected more softly off the old stone and brick walls, were the recognized trademark of the town.

"Welcome to The Three Cs," Amber said graciously to the returning couple she recognized as two who were on vacation and had visited the café many times recently.

The two nodded as they were shown their seats and received menus from her. The two had seemingly grown to quickly love the place, and it was quite obvious it pleased them as they glanced around, being as unobtrusive as possible. They admired the atmosphere of the place, where young and old seemed to mingle and interact without friction. It was a café that was in reality more of a gathering place where people of all ages could gather and feel comfortable.

Everyone chose their favorite patrons encountered during previous visits and sat around talking among themselves, settling in for an evening of light-hearted banter. Just as the waitress turned away with the couple's orders, there came the sound of the bell above the entry door, announcing another arrival as someone entered the café. The young redhead paused as she was walking away, touching up a note or two to the order she'd received. Glancing back at the door, she gasped quietly. The couple turned, curious as to what might have caused such a reaction.

A young Native American woman wearing a pair of old jeans, a colorful blouse, and cowboy boots stepped through the door. The sleeves of her loose blouse were confined by armbands, which tinkled lightly as she shut the door. The waitress simply stared agape, and the entire room fell silent as everyone turned to look. The couple looked at each other and then glanced around, wondering what had happened to the once gay atmosphere.

The young woman stared at the waitress and nodded somewhat sheepishly.

"Hello, I'm Chrissy Blackfeather. I'm looking for my twin sister, Heather."

The whole room remained strangely silent as Theresa slowly moved closer to the young woman. She stared silently for a moment and then softly spoke. "You, you can't be her . . . you, she . . . I can't believe it . . . she has a twin!" she added, barely speaking above a whisper.

"Afraid so, although I'm not at all sure that she was aware of it. We were separated at birth," the newcomer replied, eyeing everyone and in the process noting Karin's perplexed stare.

Karin stood there quietly, dressed rather unusually normal (for her) in tight jeans, black boots, and a comfortable red top. Taking notice of Chrissy's rather bold and somewhat challenging stare, Karin moved silently past her to the door and went to leave the café.

"I know it's you!" Karin whispered as she passed close by the girl.

The girl called Chrissy eyed Karin all the way out the door and then turned back to face Theresa, who seemed to be on the verge of tears. The sad-eyed girl murmured softly to the new arrival.

"Your, your sister, she's . . ."

Amber stepped beside Theresa and placed a hand gently on her shoulder, eyeing the newcomer intently.

"Chrissy, right? You'd best be sitting down for this," she said, waving her hand out in the direction of an empty table.

The girl named Chrissy could not help but take note of the serious tone of Amber's voice and Theresa's pained look, not to mention the way Theresa was sinking her teeth into her bottom lip.

Nodding absentmindedly, she slid slowly into a seat at the indicated available table.

"Okay."

*   *   *   *

"So was I any good? I really thought I should have gone into the acting trade after graduation and maybe become an actress," Theresa said proudly as she walked with her friend a short time after work just outside her home.

"Don't quit your day job, trust me," Heather, now "Chrissy," responded, smirking mischievously, indicating the porch that ran across the front of Theresa's home.

The two settled down on the porch swing with drinks they had picked up on the way home and sat swinging quietly for a time, simply enjoying each other's company.

"So the next step in our master plan?" Theresa said thoughtfully.

"Tee," Heather said as she turned to face her friend, "I don't have a clue what to do with the rest of my life. I see where we are right now, and I wish it could all just stop and allow me to breathe, you know, to focus, and to think. I killed myself, I awoke in a coffin, and then, half-crazed, I clawed my way out, all the time thinking I was some kind of monster. I couldn't think straight, I just wondered around aimlessly, really, until I saw everyone going to that party. I watched all of you from the woods."

Heather rose to her feet and moved away from her friend, over to the porch railing, where she turned, placing the small of her back up against the firm support of the railing, and continued the conversation distressed and more than a little dismayed over it all.

"Theresa, what do I do now?" she asked, not really expecting an answer. "I was adopted by my parents four years ago who, as fate would have it, lived just down the street, as you well know. I mean, they were good to me and never treated me like I was adopted. I lived there for some time. I died, and now I've come back to treat them, more or less, like strangers! My 'twin's' return hurt them so much they quit their jobs at Lorelabs and will be leaving town soon, simply because I remind them of their dead, dearly departed daughter entirely too much."

"Do you want to tell them the truth?" Theresa asked, or more accurately, suggested, as she too gained her feet and made her way past Heather to the front steps, descended to the walk, and moved on down the sidewalk toward the gate at the far end of the concrete pathway.

Heather pushed herself away from the railing and followed her friend, matching her pace as she caught up so that they were walking together.

"No. I've put them through enough. I've been selfishly thinking of my own pain only, not considering how my 'death' would have been affecting them and others!"

The two were silent for a while as they crossed the street heading in the general direction of the high school.

"Heather?" Theresa started somberly.

"Huh?"

"Do-do you hear the voices anymore?"

"Funny thing, Tee, no. I mean, it was just one voice . . ." She paused, falling silent, a sudden realization manifesting in her mind.

Dread grabbed her heart, momentarily staying her breath, and her knees felt like they were going to give out. She knelt down to the ground, grasping the center of her chest.

"Heather! Are you okay?"

Heather turned to her, and Theresa recoiled involuntarily, seeing the alarm in her eyes.

"Tee, it was one voice. It was a single, vile voice that made me feel so hated, a voice that told me how much it wanted to kill me. A-a sort of disembodied voice—it called me all kinds of names . . . like it was Rynspeak!"

"Shhh," Theresa murmured as she knelt beside her friend, holding her arms and rubbing them.

"It'll be all right."

A single tear escaped Heather's terror-stricken eyes. "It said it wanted to kill me because-because I was a-a worthless Savryn!"

*   *   *   *

Joshua walked down the brightly lit hallway of the hotel, back to the same room where he was the night before. He walked through the door, its electronic lock temporarily disabled to allow the repairmen access to perform their work. He passed the two beds and moved to the, as yet, still broken window, which at the moment was still covered with heavy, plastic sheeting. The wall was already repaired, at least, for the most part. The workmen were doing quick (and relatively inexpensive) work, trying to get the room ready for occupancy again as quickly as possible. He pulled the plastic cover over to one side and stared again out the window.

Sara, clad in light blue pajamas, stepped into the room and moved slowly to his side.

"Can't sleep?" she asked softly as she placed a hand on his shoulder.

"She's in danger," he said aloud without meaning to. His fear for Heather's safety made Sara wince.

"She's safe with Theresa and her parents. John is also there. It was a good idea."

He turned away from her and let the plastic sheeting drop down over the window as he did so. Continuing on, he left the room, and Sara turned quickly to follow him.

"What is my half-brother supposed to do against a Savryn? Ask it not to kill the entire family? It's not just Theresa, Sara. My mother is there too!"

"Your mother isn't as capable as you, but she can take care of her family."

"She's barely able to restrain herself without her jewelry. No, I need to move back home, at least for the time being."

"You know you can't now. We are here because of Heather's unusual circumstances. Our vacation was voided the moment we discovered her death was under special circumstances."

"You going to stop me if I go?" Joshua asked, pausing, his back still to Sara.

"I—" Sara started to reply, but he resumed before she could continue.

"I know I selected you to be my tether. I also noticed the last time I changed on our last mission, I had terrified you. I've noted the silver-laced tranquilizers you try to keep hidden from me."

Sara's face grew red. "Josh, does it matter that I love you? Do my feelings mean anything?"

"I will always love you, Sara—"

"As a friend," she said softly, finishing the statement for him.

"I will go to protect them all. You are welcome to move in so my tether isn't stretched too thin."

"I've never thought of it like that. I just wanted to—"

"Protect yourself and others from me. I hate myself for making you feel the need to."

Turning away again, he walked to the elevator and, punching a button, quickly entered.

Sara watched him as he entered the elevator and stood looking at her. Her heart lurched within her breast, and then forcefully composing herself, she forced all emotion out of her features and made her face stern and stony as the doors closed.

She turned around and shuddered, her lips pursed, and she was trembling as she shook herself. Taking a deep breath, she slowly returned to their room.

Josh left the elevator and had just started for the entrance when Theresa and Heather came bustling in through the door.

Joshua's face was a study in shock, seeing Heather standing there before him.

"Heather, it . . . it's late!" he said.

"You're going to want to hear this in a more secure setting, like maybe back at home." Theresa said, holding her friend's hand tightly.

*   *   *   *

They made their way to Theresa's house. Slipping out in front of the girls, Josh opened the door, pausing a moment to allow the two to enter first. As they passed close by, he queried upon entering the living room.

"Is this about what happened to Sara and me?" Joshua asked, closely watching Heather's reaction.

"I know. We've barely had any time to sleep since late last night," Theresa said, obviously thinking back on meeting Heather late the night before.

"Early morning, actually. It was after one-thirty in the morning," Joshua said pointedly.

Both Theresa and Heather threw him dour looks, and the young man grew silent, gesturing for the girls to continue.

"I don't think my suicide was anything like just my doing. I was being driven to it by someone who not only used Rynspeak but also knew I was a Savryn."

For a moment, Joshua stared thoughtfully at Heather and then nodded.

"I wish nobody was using Rynspeak," Theresa said somewhat caustically, "especially since I can't use it. I can only receive it when allowed."

"It's only because you've been restrained, Tee," Josh said, nodding, his eyes still far away. "Owing no doubt to the binding stone your father placed in you to hold your abilities in abeyance. Heather, on the other hand, has no such restrictions."

Both Josh and Theresa eyed Heather, whose expression was one of sudden surprise.

"Wait," she replied, a puzzled look upon her face. "So anyone could receive Rynspeak, even normal human beings, when allowed?"

Joshua's features momentarily clouded, his eyes remaining locked on Heather. The look on his face was one of slight confusion, as though he had been caught off guard by something. Heather glanced away, a tremulous smile gently touching her features.

"Will you two stop leaving me out?" she murmured. "My powers will be unlocked one day. It's kind of like you're rubbing it in!"

Josh nodded. "I think anyone who is of the Ryn can Rynspeak. I think that such a rationale also supports the theory that no matter what name a clan goes by, all the various types are, in fact, descended from this Ryn race.

"That cinches it—I'm moving back in. Tee, you think there'd be enough room for all of us if I did? It's been a while since I've actually stayed here last."

Theresa nodded, and the two girls looked at each other. "No problem. You've spent the night at our place plenty of times, you know that."

"So is Sara moving in too?" Heather asked, sighing.

"She can if she wants to sleep on the couch," Joshua replied, shaking his head and turning back to the front door. He passed through and, crossing the porch, started for the street.

Heather stood in the frame of the doorway watching him go, and then not being able to restrain herself any longer, she started to give voice to the question bouncing around in her mind.

"Why wouldn't—"

"You and I are in a relationship, Heather," was Joshua's answer, flung back over his shoulder and cutting off the question. He said it aloud so that Theresa could hear his response.

"Oh!" Heather replied aloud, a self-conscious smile spreading across her features.

"I've told you that before." Theresa nodded, smiling.

"May I ask you a few more questions?" Joshua asked.

"*Sure,*" she responded to the Rynspeak's touch. Again, she felt his feelings clearly and without question. It was a feeling very much akin to the warmth felt being in your lover's arms.

"*The voice that haunted you—male or female?*" he continued in Rynspeak.

Heather glanced away momentarily, shuddering involuntarily but responding nonetheless. "*Definitely male. It was terrifying. Whoever or whatever it was, it was all hate and anger, and it—he—feels such despair. He hates me. He wanted my death.*"

"*You have some—er—female looking for you. She's another Savryn, like you. Then there's the other, whoever he is, a male that drove you to suicide, using Rynspeak. What I want to know is just how crucial a cog in their wheels are you?*"

"*I have no idea. That voice, I haven't heard it since, well, you know. The female, she concerns me somewhat.*"

"*I will find her,*" Joshua said vehemently as he returned to the porch. "*And, I will end her!*"

"*What,*" Heather responded again in Rynspeak, but no answer was forthcoming.

A car drove up and parked across the street from the house. "*I see you, guys,*" Sara said in Rynspeak for Joshua alone. "*Can you hear me?*"

"*Yes, unless we are out of range or I break the link, I always will,*" Joshua replied irritably, not at all pleased with her timing.

Sara found herself sighing in relief as she watched the house and saw Joshua had returned to the porch and was ushering the two girls back inside while he remained outside to talk to her.

"*Joshua,*" Heather said in open Rynspeak, purposely to include Sara.

Josh froze in place and looked straight at Sara who just looked away and purposely closed their connection to each other. As she did so, Heather joined Joshua on the porch again.

He sighed heavily. "Heather you should stay inside. It's harder to protect you out in the open."

Heather moved up next to him and sat down on the railing, holding onto one of the porches upright.

"I've got something I want to get off my chest," she said firmly.

"You've know," Joshua said quietly. "You heard what I am. You know why I've avoided you until now."

"Well," Heather murmured back, "I'm like you now, so there's no need for concern."

Joshua took her hand and led her back into the house as Sara eyed the door again and continued to watch dutifully. Giving them privacy, Theresa went up to her room.

Joshua walked past the stairs and the living room to the back of the house to the kitchen.

Heather followed, cherishing the moment and holding his hand for the first time. The two stepped inside the kitchen, and Joshua pulled out the trash and went outside to the garage, only to come back in a moment later tossing some black trash bags on the ground. A faint, foul smell escaped from them.

"Josh? What are these for?" she asked, looking perplexed.

"I need sustenance," he said as the light in the kitchen started to dim, and the entire kitchen started to go dark. Then suddenly, she caught her breath as she saw a dark mist issuing from him as if devouring the light and everything in sight. Glancing behind her, she saw the few night lights in the living room still illuminating their surroundings, but the light stopped at the kitchen. She turned toward the gathering darkness where two silver limbal rings stared back.

"How are you possibly like me?" he asked almost coldly in Rynspeak.

She cringed at first from the surrounding darkness, but the compassion and the love she felt was like a blinding light that tore away the darkness, and she suddenly stepped forward. His eyes went wide with shock, and just as he was about to warn her, the darkness parted. It seemed to cower as though not daring to harm her.

"You are the darkness," she said. "Because it is an extension of you, and you'd never purposely hurt me."

The darkness parted, and his true form stood revealed among the retreating shadows. In all regards, his body was that of a giant wolf man, with fine black hair covering his entire body like that of maybe a Doberman. However, his head was like that of a jackal, with elongated, pointed ears standing straight up.

She reached out to him, and the black mist of the Umbrage withdrew at her approach even more. His lower half was jointed like a wolf's, and his hands were large and seemed to have swallowed her hand as he took it into his.

"You are a cursed Ulryn, I am a Savryn," Heather said softly. "Regardless, I love you, darkness and all. Let me be your light."

Her skin paled to bone white, and her body and hands grew slightly. She smiled, showing her fangs, and her head rested on his chest as her wings grew and covered the two of them. Her tail wrapped around his leg as his tail wagged back and forth in contentment.

Sara could see the kitchen growing dark, and she upholstered her gun, leaping out of the SUV. She quickly approached the house and then suddenly stopped as a scowl crossed her features. She tilted her head slightly as though listening to or for something. Slowly, she holstered her weapon and returned to her vehicle while constantly watching the kitchen windows.

"*Okay, whatever you say, John,*" she said in Rynspeak.

*   *   *   *

Theresa and Heather had been taking a short break outside the gym, and they both exhaled loudly as their break was over and headed back inside. They were helping with the decorations for the Halloween dance, and because Heather's "twin" was new to the school, it was Theresa's job to show her around while they continue to work on the decorations.

"Okay, details," Theresa said suddenly. "I woke up, and your side of the bed hadn't been slept in, and after creeping to the head of the stairs, I see you and Josh being scolded by Marcus and Tara. What was that all about?"

Heather lifted the poster they just finished in a doomed attempt to change the subject.

"Look at that," she said with affected gaiety. "Now that's what I call a great poster for the Halloween dance! You are going this weekend?"

"Oh hell, no—we are *not* avoiding this subject, *Chrissy.*" Theresa said caustically.

Heather couldn't help but smile. "Well, it was all kind of sudden. He had me pinned on the couch and was starting to remove my blouse—"

"Oh gawd, getting sick, I don't need to know what he did to—" Theresa said, going through the motions of faking vomiting. Heather couldn't help it. She laughed out loud.

"Truce?" Heather asked, as though prepared to continue her verbal torture.

"Truce, oh yeah, by all means," Theresa said in-between her ripples of laughter.

"So, Theresa, what was Heather like?" Heather asked, definitely tongue-in-cheek.

"She was, and is, a total ass. You'd really hate your *twin*."

Heather grinned broadly as they passed the gym and made their way to the lunchroom. Even knowing how much enrollment had dropped, the two could not help but note how empty it was in there, at least as compared to when they were freshmen. Both girls' minds couldn't help but fret in silence over what the future might hold for the small town. Small groups were busy here and there, mostly the freshmen helping with the decorations of the cafeteria, which also happened to serve as a theater and dance floor for the upper classmen. In years gone by, they would have all been helping out, all five grades.

"Marcus has a meeting with the town board. They're going to be discussing the town's economy and how to keep the town in the black."

"Is it really that bad?"

"Yeah, definitely, at least, so I hear from Amber." Theresa cheerfully dropped the subject as she waved at Amber sitting across from Jack and the oddly normal-looking Karin. As always, she could see Kala sitting away from the others with another group but still obviously very conscious of the group around Amber.

"Please tell me you are here to help out with the decorations? We simply do not have enough volunteers," Amber said, eyeing the two as they approached the table.

"It's my senior year, Amber—" Theresa started to reply as Heather interrupted by raising her hand.

"I'm new here, but I'll help. Oh, and I probably have a plus one to also help out."

"You didn't," Theresa half-groaned.

"I'm sure he'll come," Heather replied brightly.

The two girls went into a flurry of questions and answers. Amber and Jack flashed annoyed looks as the details started to emerge. Choosing to limit just how many details were actually made public, the two girls moved to the far end of the table. A few minutes later, the question-and-answer session having been dispensed with, "Chrissy" had moved over and pulled Amber aside to talk about helping with the decorations. Theresa shook her head.

"I am never going to hear the end of it," she said, smiling as she watched Heather talking with Amber. She couldn't completely control the smile that seemed bound and determined to break up her features.

"That's been a while. Them talking, I mean," Jack stated, watching the two.

"Too long," Theresa replied, mostly as if to talking to herself.

"So are you going stag to the dance, or are you going with your 'plus one'?" Jack queried.

Theresa laughed and leaned over the table.

"No, not really. He's just my best guy friend. I know he would want to remember his last Fairmount High Halloween dance in a special way with me."

"So not an official date," Jack said, his enthusiasm for the conversation falling away.

"You know I plan on asking Steve, since he certainly won't ask me to the prom," Theresa replied with a sigh.

"But you know—"

"Yes, but hey, thanks for the reminder," Theresa said dryly. "Still going to ask. Worse thing he can say is no, right? My only chance is at the dance, so I have to ask then."

Heather and Amber continued their conversation, while Karin simply continued to focus on the decorations, all the while throwing glances at Heather, who seemed to make Karin, in some way, more and more uncomfortable.

*   *   *   *

With the dance preparations finally finished, the girls moved outside where Joshua was waiting for them with his car. In the back seat of the vehicle, a large, white and black Malamute with light blue eyes eyed them quietly. Heather smiled, seeing Joshua leaning against the car, a big grin creasing his face as he waved.

"Okay, it's not a Porsche, but that's my 'Jake' leaning on it," Heather said, smiling as she ran up and kissed Joshua, while Theresa covered her eyes to avoid seeing it.

As Heather turned back to face her, Theresa murmured, "Jake . . . who's Jake?"

"Oh, you know, the hunk that was waiting for that character when she came out of the church in that one eighties movie."

Catching sight of the large dog in the back for the first time, Heather waved and murmured, "Ah, there you are."

"It's Johnathan," Joshua said flatly.

Heather moved away from Joshua to open the back door to let the dog out.

"Okay, you two are walking so Josh and I can have some time together."

Joshua looked concerned, but Heather started shoving him playfully to the driver's side and opening the door, almost literally pushing him in. Sporting a huge smile, she waved at the two on the sidewalk. Theresa, being somewhat taken aback, simply stared openmouthed.

Joshua maneuvered the car out into the street, repeatedly checking the rearview mirror, as the two on the walk shrank out of sight.

"Why did you do that?" he asked, looking perplexed.

"So we can be alone, dummy," she said as she snuggled in closer to him.

"You caught it too?" he said flatly, eyeing her briefly before his eyes flicked back to watching the road.

"She's so full of Steve that even if she can sense John's feelings, she won't actually see them, you know, be aware of them."

The car followed a route that would take it to The Cup and the Cauldron Café. They took a left, and then hung a right toward the center of town. It wasn't really all that far.

"John's only going to get hurt, you know. She wants Steve," Joshua said reflectively.

"How long have we stood by and watched the world move on without one another?" Heather asked thoughtfully. "Better they become friends and he's stuck with a case of unrequited love, you know, than never being free to care for another person. Has he ever been interested in a wolf?"

"Heather! He's an Ulfyr that's temporarily stuck in a wolf form. He can't shape-shift to his human form. Ever. He's scared of taking his true form, but he's not interested in any animals."

Heather crawled into the back seat to change into her work clothes. "What, he can shape-shift like you? So what's to stop him from doing it?"

"We were warned by Tyr," Joshua said, shaking his head. "For some reason, it's extremely dangerous for him to do so. It's been like that since before he could first change."

They pulled up in front of the café, and Heather got out of the back seat on the driver's side, smoothing out her café uniform as best she could. Semi-satisfied, she leaned over at the driver's window.

"That is horrible. He can never look human nor take his true form. Wait a minute, human isn't his true form?"

Joshua glanced at the café's front door, shaking his head, and pointed. "You're going to be late."

Heather kissed him quickly and crossed the sidewalk waving goodbye.

*   *   *   *

The night was cool, and Theresa slept soundly. Her room was fragrant and just cool enough to make cuddling up in one's blankets a thing very conducive to pleasant dreams. She awoke with a start. Quickly glancing around, she noted that Heather was still sleeping soundly next to her. Gently, she rolled over and swung her feet out over the edge of her bed, her feet coming softly to rest on the thick, off-white carpet. Her steps soft and light, she moved around the bed to the door and opened it. Stepping out into the hall, she glanced up and down the hallway. Just down the hall, she could see the door to her parent's room, as well as the room being used by Joshua. She turned away to the right and made her way to the staircase. Descending the stairs to the main floor, she moved on into the foyer, in which was housed the front door and what they all referred to as the weather closet, a large closet utilized to hold boots, rain gear, and heavy winter coats according to the season. She threw on a coat and a pair of boots, which she didn't bother to zip up, and opening the door quietly, she stepped out onto the front porch.

She moved over to the swing that was located to the left of the door and sat down, pushing off gently with the toe of her boot, and she sat there, swinging slowly. She stared out into the street, observing the quiet of the neighborhood to her front. She sat there quietly, examining all the little details, the house lights, and other various surroundings and wondering consciously what had awakened her and induced her to come out on the porch. Normally, she was a deep sleeper. Her mind slipped gears, and she found herself reflecting on growing up here and her fears of what tomorrow might bring, not only for her but also for her hometown.

"As if I might use those things to distract me from what really worries me," she whispered to herself. There being no answer leaping to mind, she pursued the thought.

"What are you really afraid of then?" she asked herself.

The answers came unbidden. "Who am I, where am I going, what am I going to do with the rest of my life? A plan would be nice, one to face the wide open world out there with all its wonderful and vast possibilities, all of which are just as great, as are the opportunities to fail while living."

"*Is that really what concerns you?*" a voice asked softly in her mind.

"*I'm not even human,*" she replied in Rynspeak without thinking. "*I've lived a lie—I'm a monster. It's not as cool as I thought. I can't even do whatever it is I'm supposed to be able to do yet, except for some minor handling of fire, learned by accident. Yeah, one might say I'm a bit concerned.*"

"*So?*" said the voice in her head.

"*What do you mean, 'so'?*" Theresa asked, suddenly angry as she lunged to her feet.

"You've seen your friend Jack. Do you fear him, do you hate him, and do you cringe at his presence?" the voice queried.

"No—never!" she almost spat the words aloud.

"Then do not hate yourself. When the time comes, embrace who you truly are."

Theresa became alarmed. *"Who are you? You're not John!"*

Suddenly, Theresa bolted, running down off the porch and out toward the front gate. She slid to a stop as flames erupted on the sidewalk out to her front, flickering away toward the street. The flames danced along the sidewalk and passed through the gate, leaving it totally unharmed. Pausing on the sidewalk just outside the gate, the flames swirled about as if waiting for her to join them.

She opened the gate, and the flames swirled madly, taking on the forms of small children dancing all about and slowly moving out into the street, their flaming bodies illuminating the formerly darker areas of the roadway. There came a burst of brightness, and the flaming figures became larger, older, more mature, and far more detailed. They were now a group of flaming adults in regal gowns and uniforms, prancing and pirouetting about as if in attendance at a great ball—a great ball complete right down to the masks they held up to their faces . . . and then all was quiet.

It started to rain, and instinctively, Theresa raised her hands to protect her hair, but a huge gust of wind swirled about and seemed to gather the water, which then blended with the wind itself and became large creatures of the air, like hunting hawks perched on the boughs of the trees alongside the street. When the last had settled into the trees, they all sat quite still, watching her. Stones pushed up from beneath the earth alongside the road, rising through the neatly trimmed grass and were quickly transformed into stone golems. They stood there, huge and powerful, with their arms crossed, and they stood surrounding and watching her and the dancers.

Theresa grew uncomfortable as all of them locked their eyes upon her, watching and waiting for what she could not have said. Then suddenly, they all bowed to her, the male forms kneeling to one knee, and the females performing graceful curtsies. Theresa reached out, wanting to protest, wanting to stop them, and as she raised her voice to do so, it was cut short. A slim, black-furred hand, armed with long and deadly claws, reached around from behind her, took her hand, drew it back gently to her chest, and, without pause, did the same with her other hand. This caused her no fear, no dread, and all she felt was warmth and safety. Somehow, it was so very natural with how the totally familiar body drew so close to her. The voice in her mind came again.

"It was so said, 'Gather, all ye children of Ryn. To the lands of Found Elders. To the village of Festival's Hill, upon which the crown of Kinguard sits on Love's new brow.'

"Our lives seem so out of control, but if we accept and embrace what we are and live regardless, then we are boundless, simply because we then are one."

Theresa looked down at the slender black-furred hands and saw they looked more like gloves than actual hands, although it was quite clear that they were, indeed, hands. Above the black edging at the wrists was deep red fur and its soft caress was most welcome. She reached up around behind her and could feel the muzzle of the creature's face, and it felt familiar, as familiar as if it was her own flesh. A small smile touched her lips fleetingly; the muzzle ended in a slightly cold nose, brushing lightly against the nape of her neck. Though she couldn't turn to look back, she could feel its slender neck and the softness of its features.

"What am I?" she asked softly.

The body suddenly withdrew, and Theresa felt weaker as if a great part of her had been torn away. She whipped around. The groups of fire beings were illuminating a tree in the middle of the street, a tree which hadn't previously been there. She looked up into its upper boughs but couldn't clearly see into the darkness of the upper reaches of what looked to be a large oak tree.

She saw a shape, a tall, slender form, with a long, seemingly furry tail that swung about lazily. The sleek form seemed to be clinging to the oak's branches with consummate ease.

"We are the tricksters, the joyful, the loving, and the grieving. We are free, we are alive. The rest? Meaningless details, details meant to limit us. So what are we, Theresa Bok?"

"Vulryn," Theresa said, briefly feeling whole once more.

"All hail the Kinguard, marked so by the love from a prince of the former crown."

She woke up. Sitting straight up in bed, she looked about wildly.

* * * *

Lorelabs was quiet. The security guard was half-asleep at his post. Suddenly, there was a buzzing at the door. The guard rose with a hand on his holster and looked at the monitor, only to see it was Theresa in her pajamas, waiting outside and shifting back and forth restlessly from one foot to the other, much more than just a little impatiently. The guard buzzed her in, and he came out of his cubicle and around to the front of his post, a look of concern clear on his features.

"Are you okay?" he asked as he glanced around outside. He turned to hear her response, but she was already gone. He rushed back around the corner to where the hall led to the elevators and was just in time to see one of them closing. Theresa was standing inside, facing him, her hair falling down in front her face.

"Hmm," he thought. "I couldn't see her all that well. Best warn Tyr of a possible intruder, just in case."

* * * *

"Tyr!" Theresa cried out as she rushed out of the elevator.

The doors on her left, which she had never seen open or ever used by anyone, stood wide for the first time she could remember, and Tyr's imposing form filled the opening. She moved quickly toward him as he stood shaking his head and watching her approach.

"Young lady, what are you doing out of bed at this hour?" he asked. "John wanted to follow you, but he had to watch Heather for me. You took a huge risk coming here on your own." He wanted to say much more but couldn't. He was, for the first time in decades, speechless.

Theresa stood in front of him, pushing her hair back out of her face.

It wasn't the fangs clearly showing in her partially parted lips nor the fact she had elongated nails, which were clearly not nails but were definitely claws that grabbed his attention. No—it was her eyes. They had golden rings about them—luminous, golden limbal eyes.

"Tyr, are you my father?" she asked softly, not demandingly but more like hopefully.

Chapter Five

A FRIEND NO MORE

Tyr's eyes grew wide in surprise. Theresa stared at him, her fangs slightly visible and her claws as yet extended. Her eyes shone bright even in that well-lit hallway.

"Wait here just a moment," he said and left her standing there in a state of great agitation.

She watched him disappear into the heretofore secret office and quickly returned with a photograph and a silver ring in his hand. He laid one hand upon her shoulder and extended the other out to her, with his palm upward containing the two objects.

"I am not your father. This is the only photo we've ever had of him. I am sorry. We never got one of your mother."

Theresa snatched the picture from his grasp and simply stared at it for several long minutes. The photo showed Marcus standing beside a man of Asian descent. They were both glancing away, off to the side of the camera, as if something had interrupted the taking of the photo. An obviously abused large gray wolf was in a cage close at hand. The animal's hair was matted, with old scars running along his body. One could also make out a great many stitches that one might presume were the result of relatively recent surgeries. The Asian man had been smiling even as they were interrupted.

"You said he was abducted, but he was smiling," she said to Tyr, looking up with tears starting to trace freely down her cheek.

Tyr moved closer and brushed the dampness from her face, his touch as gentle as his gnarled hands could manage.

"Theresa," the older man said quietly, "your father figured out how to rescue us. He saved all those who survived. He is the hero I can only dream of being."

Tyr gazed down the girl before him as she struggled mightily, trying to choke back her tears.

"Then I am all alone. I was hoping that, for my own protection, you had hidden the truth from me—that you really were my father, like, like in some movie or novel or something. I was hoping I wasn't really all alone to deal with what I am."

Tyr smiled gently as he squeezed her shoulder. "We are all alone and yet not alone. These are our struggles—struggles we all go through no matter how trivial or important they are to us or even to others. They are real—in that, we are truly alone, for only we who suffer know the extent of our differing struggles and strife. However, there are those who would wish to console us, to help us along the way, to hold our hands, so to speak, as we struggle along, and in that, we are also never alone!"

With his free hand, he handed her a ring. "This belonged to your father. It is inscribed with runes to hold his power in check, but I don't know how well it will work for you. You seem to be far more powerful than he ever was."

She looked down and saw something written on the inner band in Korean. Translated, it read, {*It doesn't matter what guise you wear. It only matters that your soul be fair.*}

"I had to look up what it said. I think he liked that saying because he wasn't human, and it didn't matter to him. If only humans were not so trivial."

She clutched it in her hand and looked back up at him.

"You want more proof you're not my child," he asked with a wan smile, "but are instead a true hero's?"

Tyr led her over to the office sink. It was equipped with a small mirror and a cabinet on either side. He pointed to the mirror. Her eyes followed his pointing finger, and she gasped as she saw her eyes were not only golden and luminous, to the point of glowing, but also vertical, not round. They looked like gold-ringed cat's eyes.

"You have your father's eyes."

*   *   *   *

It seemed like the entire town was busying themselves with preparations for the high school's Halloween dance. You could hear the preparations simply by walking down the streets, almost in any street. From house after house came the sounds of laughter and childish, happy voices. That happiness which is, of course, the very best kind. Only Christmas could top the high spirits seemingly running rampant through the town. The town seemed to almost exude happiness and laughter as parents got their children ready for the party and dance that was the second biggest event in the lives of the younger set of Fairmount. The younger ones were, as always, getting under foot, while the older ones, like the visiting Joshua, were also making ready for the big night. Although he had earned a GED diploma during his military service some two years earlier through the US Army, he had been invited to the big Halloween dance by a young woman for whom he cared a great deal.

"Thanks for allowing me to come back to your hotel room," Joshua said as he moved from the bedroom to the living room. "So I could get dressed away from the house. I didn't want to run into her accidentally before the appropriate time."

"I hate this," Sara said as Joshua walked out fully dressed in a dress suit, holding a ball mask in his hand.

"Oh, we are not going over this again, are we, Sara?" he asked, looking at her.

"You are so stupid sometimes, Josh," Sara replied, moving up close to him as he glanced wearily down at her, obviously tired of the debate, as she reached up and started to undo his tie.

"You made it a mess—again."

"Ah," he muttered.

"So, if I understand my role correctly, I stay outside the perimeter and warn you if anyone spots anything suspicious?"

"Well, as I hear it, the police are to remain off the dance floor and have only a minimal presence inside the school. Most of them will be on the rooftops. If someone is planning something, it'd be tonight," Joshua said, feeling a bit awkward because of Sara's close proximity. Just friends or not, she really was beautiful.

"Even with all the protection, I am hoping her abilities will also keep her safe. This could cost the town many lives if it goes south," Joshua said ruefully. "Of course, John is going to be there watching things as well," he said as he turned around to examine himself in the mirror.

"How is John supposed to be able to do anything?" Sara queried. "He's stuck in his wolf body. At least, you could change into an Ulryn if the need arose."

He glanced in the mirror at Sara's reflection and smiled a bit before recovering. "He can use his heightened senses all the while we're there. My abilities are limited in any form and so much even in my true form."

"You sound almost resentful, Josh. What's up?"

"As Tyr told you, I am the weakest kind of Ulryn. I'm cursed-bitten only, you know, still human. We've both seen my mentor, Alejandro, in action. He's dangerous. My power is barely more than smoke and mirrors by comparison."

"Unless, of course, he gets within reach of your Umbrage," Sara replied, perhaps a bit grimly.

"Yeah, but he knew my weakness. He knew how to beat me by keeping away. He used my limitations against me."

Seeing his tie was repaired, Joshua pulled away from Sara, and he headed for the bedroom door.

"The mere sight of an Ulryn caused that Savryn to flee from you in terror. It won't dare face you or bother Heather when you are close to her."

"True, but that thing was so terrified . . . such outright fear? It makes one wonder just how powerful one is, who is a direct descendant of a Ryn. What are Ryn?" he murmured thoughtfully as he left Sara to head out for the dance.

*　　*　　*　　*

"Okay," Heather murmured to her friend. "That's it. It's now official, I am too hot for this school."

"Sure, Heather. You've been saying that ever since we started getting ready. It's really going to be some dance."

Heather stood in Theresa's full-length mirror, looking at herself in critical appraisal. She was dressed in a long, black, silk gown, and she was being accurate—she looked absolutely stunning. The string straps supporting the top of the gown were completely hidden by her long hair. The back was open, almost too far down, and the slit on the side permitted the occasional viewing of her long, brown, nicely-toned legs.

Heather turned to see Theresa opening her window seat storage chest set in the hollow of the bay window. The minute it was open, Theresa was throwing objects about, looking frantically for something. Heather couldn't help but laugh.

"What are you looking for?"

"I can't find my silver clutch purse. I've kept it in here forever, then the one time I need it, it takes a vacation—crap!"

She slammed down the lid loudly and plopped down on the well-padded seat in a huff, seemingly on the verge of tears.

"Theresa, why's it so important?" Heather asked, not so sure she should be laughing.

Theresa looked up at her friend, and Heather could see the girl was in a state of near panic.

"What am I doing . . . I'm popping out fangs, claws, and glowing eyes? I shouldn't go, this is too much pressure. God, I swear, I'm scared half to death."

Heather smiled and knelt before her friend. She took her friend's hands into her own and started to smooth out her long black hair.

"Sweetie, first of all, I've got silver around my own eyes, which I will admit is less noticeable, but far worse? I'm a blood sucking vampire that dug her backside out of a grave and then wandered about lost like some dizzy loon. Then suddenly, I'm reunited with Joshua, the love of my life, a man whose bones really need to be pounced on badly by yours truly."

Theresa started to laugh and wound up choking upon hearing Heather's words.

"All right, all right, that's just plain gross. You trying to make me sick so I can't go?"

"Not hardly. My point being this—I died. I was somehow given a second chance. I don't care if I came out looking like Princess Kate or like some crazed albino with a Furry fetish. Either way, I'm going to go ahead and live. You've never been through what I have, so let me give you some advice, okay? Quit fretting, and just—live! We've got great memories of the past, and we are going to make a great many more in the future. I have no idea what tonight will bring, let alone tomorrow, or decades down the line, but I know I want to live. Rich, poor—I don't give a damn. I'm alive right now, so screw tomorrow until it gets here!"

Theresa couldn't help but smile at her friend's determination.

"You are so beautiful. You know that?" she said with a wan smile.

"Damn straight I am. Now let's get you all 'fudged-up so I can be the Belle of the Ball, as, of course, I should be. Remember, we have contacts to hide the limbal rings."

*   *   *   *

An hour later, Heather stood looking at her friend's attire cutely, faking a sneer as best she could.

"You look . . . eh, okay, I guess."

Theresa twirled in her red silk dress. She wasn't as tall as her friend, but the dress made up for it, in spades. The front was somewhat low-cut, and the gown had long sleeves that draped and hung from her lithe limbs. There was no leg revealing slit to entice the eye, but the gown had a layered design, and all the hems were laced with gold. Her back was low-cut. but not so much as to show the scar on her lower back.

Heather turned to look at her back in the mirror, frowning slightly as she saw how toned and muscular it was as compared to Theresa's, which was soft and rather petite.

"You look so pretty, like some damn doll or something."

"Was that a compliment, Heather?"

"More likely, it was the result of outright jealousy," Heather replied, smirking.

Theresa laughed and hugged her best friend.

"How many times have I tried to be there for you and failed, only to see you bounce back, not only alive but also so strong. You're my life support, Heather."

Heather hugged her friend tightly.

"The strength of my limbs will never come close to the strength of your heart, Tee."

Theresa pulled away and saw tears in the corners of Heather's eyes. As she wiped them away with her fingers, the two started laughing aloud.

*   *   *   *

Both Joshua and Jack looked nervous, looking up the stairs.

"They're laughing. Is that a good thing?"

Joshua shook his head. "No chance in hell, Jack. By the way, you two official or something?"

Jack looked down, frowning. "We're just friends. She figured Steve would come with Elizabeth."

"But she's already graduated."

"Yeah, but so have you."

Joshua stood silent for a while before the upstairs door opened, and the two young women stepped out into the hall and made their way to the head of the stairs.

The men simply stared in awe as the two slowly descended the stairs in single file, although the stairway was easily wide enough that they might easily have descended side by side.

Joshua stepped forward, taking Heather's hand as she took her final step to the floor at the base of the stairs. Jack attempted to do the same but was just a tad too late and missed his opportunity. The girls, a bit self-conscious, started to laugh as they stood smiling at each other.

Jack caught Joshua's silent cue, a simple nod, and opened the door. Once outside, the girls found Amber waiting for them in a convertible. She was wearing a blue, rather short dress. She sat with the door open, facing the walk and her approaching friends. She sat with her legs crossed as she waved her left hand extended outward, making a sweeping gesture and indicating that they should all take in the beautiful convertible. The car had "Happy Halloween" written in fake blood on the back door and on along the side toward the car's rear.

"You are very old fashioned," Heather remarked as the group entered the car. A blanket had been laid across the back of the rear seats so the four could sit atop as if they were in a parade.

"No cheap. I spent every penny I could save for this dress. My dad suggested this is what his parents did for him. It sounded kind of neat, ah, traditionally speaking."

"Going stag, Amber?" Theresa asked, a touch of concern in her voice.

"Hell, yes, like I'm going to settle for any one guy at my age," she said, laughing as Marcus and Tara waved goodbye to the "kids," shouting for them to have fun.

As the car pulled away, Marcus placed an arm about Tara's shoulders and, turning away, headed back inside. As they passed through the front door, he fitted an earpiece into place in his one ear. He spoke into the tiny mic that was attached to the earpiece.

"LL Security, this is control. Okay, verify the following. Three snipers on the schools roof, four more across the street on the two flanking buildings, and several more operatives, who have 'volunteered' to serve drinks and act as hall monitors while the dance is going on. All units in place and verified. Good. Has John arrived? He has her scent, right? Good, keep me informed as to any changes."

*   *   *   *

The high school was brightly illuminated and spirits were high as the dance was winding up, starting the night's festivities. Young couples entered the building hand in hand and arm in arm. The singles entered, mixing in with one group, only to merge into others yet. The first broke up, drifting away to stand waiting by familiar lockers for their fellow single friends, hoping for the locker's users to provide congenial company.

The dance floor was the usual cafeteria/theater converted for the dance. The stage that was utilized for the auditorium functions on one end would house the live band to do their thing. The music made many of the adult chaperones cringe, but the students all started cheering and jumping around out on the floor as the music began to reverberate through the gym.

Outside, John walked the perimeter of the school, constantly sniffing the air in hopes of catching the scent of the Savryn who attacked Joshua, which would be unique and easily distinguishable from any human's.

"*Nothing yet, Josh,*" John's voice murmured in Joshua's mind. "*Enjoying your time with Heather?*"

Joshua walked out to the floor with Heather next to him. Theresa was already looking for Steve and his older girlfriend. Jack looked on, his features very dour. He sighed as he turned to the drinks.

"*You should be in here enjoying a dance with Theresa,*" Joshua replied openly. "*I remember you telling me you've been dreaming of it.*"

"*It's nice to dream and hope when you're young,*" came John's reply via Rynspeak. "*You feel anything is possible. As we grow and become adults, we give up on dreams and settle on the hopes.*"

"*Be serious, John. Hopes realized are simply our dreams coming true.*"

John snorted and shook his hackles. "*Best I get back to what I'm supposed to be doing.*"

Joshua sighed, and Heather took his hand and pulled him to the floor. He saw her smiling up at him. She leaned back a bit in his arms and started laughing out loud as she looked straight into the steel rafters and the bright lights shining down on them. Shouting and smiling, she pulled him tight up against her and held him close.

He could feel her heartbeat, and his skipped. Holding her close, he suddenly felt very protective of her.

"I wish Theresa would give up on Steve. She was chasing him long before I even came to town," Heather observed, watching Theresa look for Steve while Jack did his best to drown his sorrows with punch. Joshua continued to hold her close to him as they slowly turned in circles while everyone was dancing to the current number on the band's list, Heather continued, "She's been after him since third grade. She's really hopeless. She waited around for him to break up with every girl he ever dated, all the while hoping it would be her turn."

"I love you," Joshua stated plainly, not at all interested in Theresa's history with Steve.

Heather snuggled closer to him and smiled. "I know, Josh. I knew the year after I came to town."

"I should have done more for you then, Heather. I'm sorry."

"That's stupid. You had your own issues. Hell, I figured I could least wait for you to get over whatever your hang-up was. I was just like Theresa waiting for Steve."

Suddenly, a thought occurred to Heather, and she pulled away from Joshua.

"Heather, is something wro——"

Heather glanced toward Theresa, and then her eyes flicked toward the doors that gave access to the dance. She smiled broadly.

"Okay, that's it. Everyone's waiting for someone else to make a move. I owe John so much. Thanks to him, I feel like a human being, and I am dancing with the guy I've been wanting to be with forever."

Joshua looked a bit confused as he smiled slowly.

"What are you planning for those two?"

"I just think it's time we gave John a hand with his wish," Heather murmured coyly.

"*You heard us,*" Joshua said in Rynspeak, a look of surprise on his face.

"Please, when it comes to me. You let your guard down like it was never there."

*   *   *   *

John continued to walk the perimeter. Unknown to the men, the large Malamute-looking dog was an intelligent being, often listening in to their sometimes rather crude comments about their own high school dances "back in the day." He shook his head in disdain, turning his attention away from them as Joshua again touched his mind via Rynspeak.

"I need you to head to the props room, John. I want you inside and close to us just in case," Joshua said thoughtfully.

John didn't respond but merely started to run toward the entrance. A young couple arriving late opened the door to see the large Malamute run inside as they yelled at him to stop. The young man gave chase, but John quickly outdistanced the boy as he searched for the props room. Having seen the diagram of the school earlier before he left, he knew well the locations of just about every hiding spot in the school.

"What the hell?"

John's ears perked up, hearing Theresa exclaim aloud from the very room he was headed for. Bolting inside, he ran into Theresa just inside the door, causing her to stumble backward losing her balance. Moving almost as quick as thought, he not only recovered himself but also leaped under her falling form so that she landed on his back. Just as he caught her, he heard the door close behind them and the lock turning. He was too preoccupied with the door to pay any attention to Theresa sprawled across his back, trying to scramble off and regain her feet.

"Will you wait a second, John?"

"Oh! Oh yeah," he responded in Rynspeak.

The moment she was safely off his back, he moved up to the door and rearing high, placed his paws on the door handle.

"It won't open. I think we are locked inside here."

"Damn it. Heather . .," Theresa said flustered; pausing before continuing.

"I am sorry you're stuck in here with me," Theresa said, grinning.

She walked over to the door as he dropped back down to the floor, and she laid her hand on his neck just behind his ears.

"It's not you. I don't mind you, really. Heather just doesn't want me to make a fool out of myself," the girl responded, shaking her head.

"How could you possibly ever do that?" She could feel his desire to be helpful.

"I have this thing about this guy, Steve. I been working for him since Heather had committed suicide. I've had a crush on him for a long time, but he's dating an older woman. Think about it, before he even graduated, he's out on his own, and he already owns a café. It's the best in town, you know."

"The Witch's Cup and the Cauldron Café. I've been there before."

"Oh really!" Theresa said, somewhat surprised.

"Once or twice as I moved about through town."

Theresa walked away from the door and settled down in a chair that was located close by.

"Ah. All the comfort a girl could ask for. I guess I deserve this. Poor Jack. I wonder if any of this was his idea."

"Pardon?" she thought she felt *jealousy*.

"Oh well, I like Steve, and Jack kind of has a thing about me. I like Jack too, just not in that way."

"So you have no idea what you are even here for?"

"The dance, of course, why? Do you have some other reason? Is there another reason?"

"Of course not," he mentally sighed so heavily Theresa rose up off the chair, reaching for her back, her face scrunched up in discomfort.

"Your feelings. You are so hurt, John. What's the, uhh, matter?"

John saw her discomfort and snarled quietly in agitation.

"I've got to get you out of here. I'm hurting you."

"I just can feel your pain so strongly. Did I do something to hurt, uhh, you?"

John started to back away from her, but knowing it was futile, he just lay down, putting his paws over his head.

"I'm sorry. I am so sorry."

Theresa gasped, and suddenly, she felt more alive than she had ever felt. The pain was there, but there was this somehow mournful bliss that touched her very soul. No pain could conceal this feeling she felt from another. It was light. It was life. It was the very reason for being. She was swooned as if touched by a lover. The feeling was gentle, caressing her mind and putting her at infinite ease. She had felt this happy only a few times in her life.

John could see tears forming, and it made him cringe until he heard her laughing lightly. He glanced up, and she was sitting on the floor, and in-between a little "Ow" now and again, she was laughing and smiling. John regained his feet and slowly moved over to Theresa, his head close to hers as he looked down into her face from slightly above his. She gingerly lifted her hand to his muzzle and gently caressed it and moved behind his ears. Her smile put him at ease, and all he could do was smile back, happy to see her like this while looking at him. If only this one time.

"You are in love," she murmured softly.

John bolted back, cowering away from her. His claws scratched on the floor, and suddenly, the room became pitch-black, and she could hear the crackling of fire all around her.

Theresa started to panic. She could see his sliver eyes climb as if he grew in size.

"I can hear the fire, but I can't see it . . . and I can't get control of it!" she said wildly.

"This fire is mine and mine alone. This is how the Umbrage manifests itself to me. I do apologize—I was startled, and I reacted defensively. These flames answer to no one but me. They will not harm you. They would never harm you. No more than could I."

Theresa heard the fires burning all around her and reached out and understood why she couldn't see. The black fire *consumed* light and burned all around her, and yet when she touched them, they were warm like a summer's breeze and as harmless.

"You couldn't harm me with these flames. That's interesting."

"I thought you would be terrified of my flames."

"Oh no, John, quite the opposite. You see, Heather told me some of the details as to what happened between her and Joshua. I just didn't know yours would not be mists."

John sighed heavily, and his breath came quicker. Theresa stood slowly and started moving cautiously toward the sound. His breath came even quicker.

"John, are you in love with me?"

Nothing but a slight gasp and a following silence was her answer.

"I can't see a lot going on around me just now. So many things I am worried about. Family, friends, the town, I'm sorry I didn't notice before. We hadn't really had time to be around each other."

"You have nothing to apologize for."

"Yes, I do, John."

"Don't come closer, please. I am an animal, just a beast. Let's leave it at that."

"I can't return your feelings the same way, but I still care abo—" she fell silent and then suddenly stopped dead in her tracks when her outstretched hand touched something hard. Her hand moved over the hard surface out in the darkness before her, and she could feel that it was a muscle. She couldn't believe how toned the wall of the chest was as she felt it under the thick and solidly haired surface where her fingers moved through. Slowly, she moved her hand upward over a heaving chest, with the heart beneath it beating so fast. Her hand then found the thick, finely haired neck, and as she raised her eyes, she looked up into two silvery ringed eyes staring back down at her.

"Or can I?" she murmured more to herself than to anyone else.

"Huh?"

He could hear her giggle in the darkness. "Hold on. The contacts are being a pain, and its dark," she said cutely.

Suddenly, he saw a pair of golden eyes looking right back at him. "I'm not human either, and for the first time, my beast, I'm glad."

*   *   *   *

"Damn it. Why isn't Theresa using Rynspeak, Josh? We're only getting half the conversation. Thanks for the intel by the way."

Heather and Joshua started ascending the stairs after Heather locked the door behind John, mischievously giggling all the while to herself.

"Clever Heather, using John to remind her she isn't the only *beast* in this world. He's so nervous we can hear his half of the conversation. He doesn't even notice he's broadcasting it to everyone who can use Rynspeak."

The two stopped at the top of the stairs and looked back down toward the door concerned as the hallway further down went dark, and they could clearly see the tell-tale signs of the Umbrage, John's flames licking the edges of light just beyond its reach.

"It's not like yours, Josh. Yours were like a mist compared to them. Why are his different?" Heather asked, staring as the flames continue to burn nothing, except the light trying to penetrate into their midst.

Joshua slowly walked up to the flames and gingerly touched them and smiled, "Of course, he has full control over his Umbrage. Well, according to what Tyr has told us, each manifestation of the Umbrage tends to be different with different people. He says it's weird how every different individual views something we believe to be all consuming. The first few days after I left home and lived in the dormitory at the barracks, the mornings were foggy. It was so thick I thought the mist beyond my window consumed everything including my home. For John, he must have seen the forest fires on the TV or some such. Maybe a fire broke out when he was young and saw how dangerous the fires were."

"Maybe we should get clos—" she started when the two of them heard laughter, and they listened to the conversation from John's end.

Joshua slowly walked up to the flames and again touched the fringe. He smiled and gestured to Heather to do the same. She was shocked. She didn't know exactly what it was she had expected, but it felt warm, nice, and comfortingly warm!

"It's so warm. Like your feelings for me, Joshua. His feelings are so sincere."

"He is far more powerful and much more in control of his Umbrage than I am, Heather. If he wasn't, the entire town could have been devoured by these flames easily by now. I saw it tested at the labs. It's a sight to behold and one to dread."

Heather's hand touched the edges of the flames and smiled.

"How wonderful Theresa must feel right now to know such honesty from another's heart," she thought to herself. Suddenly, she pulled back and placed her hand over her mouth half-smiling, almost on the verge of laughing. She suddenly yanked Josh's hand away.

"Give them some alone time, Josh! God, they are so sweet!"

The two of them, smiling, continued up the stairs, and glancing upward, they saw Karin at the top, looking down at them. Joshua and Heather glanced at each other as they communicated via Rynspeak.

"Josh, keep people from going down there until the darkness recedes. I'll see what Karin wants."

Karin watched the two of them exchange kisses, and reluctantly, Heather parted from Joshua as she walked up to meet Karin. The two stared at each other, Karin not moving as Heather gestured toward the girl's restroom just up the hall.

*   *   *   *

The two went around and entered the women's restroom. Heather started checking in the stalls, going as far as looking over the doors to make sure they were alone. Satisfied, she turned to speak, and Karin slapped her hard across her face.

Heather could only look at her in shock, not only because she was slapped but also because it had actually hurt.

"What the hell, Karin," she started, and Karin slapped her a second time.

"I told you to befriend her—and cause her grief. Four years—four years and nothing," Karin said, walking back and forth, biting her thumbnail, and looking angrily at Heather as she did.

"What the hell are you talking about Kar—" she started to ask again and was slapped again for her trouble. She didn't even see Karin swing that time.

"How?" Heather asked, eyeing the blood in the hand she had put to her mouth.

"You forgot everything after I prepared for this very moment?"

"Mom?"

"Mom? Mom! I wanted her broken! I wanted Theresa Bok to be brokenhearted, and even your own stupid suicide didn't work. I thought you knew what you were doing, but no, oh no, you couldn't even die right. You are worthless to me."

"Mom, why do you look like Karin?" Heather asked in confusion.

Karin walked to the mirror and admired her handiwork.

"I was so ignorant of the world when I was only known as Matoaka. How many years did I waste trying to please the males in the tribe while living in England? I blame them for everything that's happened over the last four centuries."

"Mom, how is it you look like Karin?" she asked again. This time, her question came from trembling lips because she already feared the worst.

"What? Oh, I took her blood. We learn most of our skills instinctively, but some can only be learned by trial and error, like our invisibility and like taking the blood of another to assume their physical form. It's a gift unique to the Aluryn of the Savryn race. Though her blood . . ."

Heather walked hesitantly up to her mother, her entire body starting to quiver out of fear for her friend.

"You know I killed her, so why ask? I had to see if you were sticking to the plan or not."

Karin turned around and walked away toward the door.

"I need results, Heather. The time is fast approaching when I wish to let Fenri—"

Suddenly, Heather wheeled and grabbed Karin by her hair and flung her to the floor, pinning her there.

"You killed her! She was my friend! I was doing this so you'd stop hurting people! You got to stop this, Mom—your hatred of men. No, this town is stifling, horrifying! You are even killing women now. I didn't want anyone hurt anymore! Not women, not men! How many, Mom? How many people have you killed and not told me to get revenge for Dad?"

Karin smiled as a bone-white tail whipped up and around Heather's throat. The girl started choking.

"Hundreds, thousands? I've long since lost count, baby girl."

She lifted her, still choking her daughter off the ground.

"Sweetie, let this go. Just do as I say, and we will both be free of men—all men. After this? I might even be able to let go of your father's smile."

Karin released Heather, and the young girl landed heavily on the floor.

"You can't do this. I won't let you." She gasped as she coughed up more blood. Her throat repaired itself quickly.

"Sweetie, sweetie, I see I need you after all. Such devotion, how much will they miss you now? I guess you failed me in life, so the least you can do is die and be of use that way!"

Heather changed instantly and struck at her tormenter, only to find her mother suddenly beside her. She stared into her mother's cold eyes and looked down to see her mother's arm, with her elbow deep in Heather's side. Slowly, she looked up at her mother one last time.

"Huh, weird. I never noticed. You don't even have your father's eyes."

Chapter Six

A NEW THERESA

A horrible scream filled the air. Joshua wheeled and ran up the stairs. *That had been Heather's voice*, was the thought that screamed in his mind as he rounded the corner, running full into Karin. His eyes flicked over her, her clothing was torn, and her shoulders were injured, seemingly as if she had been clawed.

"Some white monster attacked me and Heather! You got to save her," she said, screaming.

Joshua let go of her, stunned by her words, and turning away, he ran toward the sound of a slight whimpering that only he could hear due to his unique hearing and which he knew was being made by Heather. He burst into the women's restroom, slamming the door back hard against the wall. He actually choked as his eyes took in the scene before him. Falling to his knees in the doorway, his upper body leaned upon one side of the door frame.

"Drink," he all but screamed at the ravaged girl. "Take my life, please," he said, tears falling freely as he overcame his shock.

Heather's broken body lay on the floor, her body black and purple all over as if she suffered from multitude of fractures under the skin's surface, the bruising focused on what appeared to be where she had been grabbed by her assailant. He crawled up to her, taking her in his arms. Noticing a gaping hole in her side attempting to close.

"If I did that, I would be no better than my mother, a-a monster," the girl replied through gritted teeth.

Joshua eyes grew wide in horror as realization washed over him.

"She did this to you? Please, Heather," he pleaded. "Take my life. Take anyone's life here. I don't care anymore. Live, please. Just don't die," he all but cried as he held her close.

He continued to hold her and could sense her body feeding on itself, trying to survive.

He knew, without doubt that with no substance to feed on, her body would consume itself, trying to sustain her and ultimately die.

"No, Josh, I would rather die without resorting to becoming a murderer. Please, Josh, just hold me. I'm scared. Oh, I thought myself so fearless, but now in your arms? I just . . .," she said faintly, struggling to extend her hand up to his tear-streaked face.

He gently pushed the blood-caked hair out of her face. Her body grew too thin and too small. Her bones and ribs showed through and continued to wither as, with a supreme effort, she raised herself with her last bit of waning strength to kiss him gently one last time. As he laid her back down on his knees, Joshua reared back, and wiping his tears away, his Rynspeak reached out to Jack.

"Jack? Jack, it's Heather, in the girls restroom. Close it down. Hurry!"

*   *   *   *

"Okay, everyone, stay back. Back, I said—back!" Jack was yelling as security from Lorelabs came swarming in from the outside perimeter in full riot gear. The young adults started pulling out their phones to make calls and to photograph what was going on.

"That's it—everyone, out! Now! The dance is over," he yelled to everyone. The small megaphone he carried made him easily heard over the multitude of moans, groans, and other forms of obvious disappointment.

A loud bang occurred from somewhere around the corner, and everybody was both startled and amazed to see Theresa rounding the selfsame corner at a dead run, closely followed by an impossibly huge white wolf. Everyone in a position to do so turned to try to get a picture of the wolf as the two made for the restroom door, but a thought from John, as he hurtled along after Theresa, made the lights in the gym and the hallway suddenly flicker and go out. No one seemed to notice the black flames surging across the ceiling overhead, engulfing the fluorescent bulbs and absorbing all their light and devouring the bulbs.

Jack felt someone push past him, and he could tell by the person's scent who it was.

"Theresa, don't——" he tried to stop her, but she was already past him and gone. Suddenly, light poured into the hallway as the restroom door momentarily opened. He could hear Theresa screaming as the door closed behind her.

Jack saw flashlights and cell phone lights flaring here and there as the security volunteers made their presence known and quickly recruited the adult chaperones and began to move the crowd out toward the exits. Nodding to himself, he moved as quickly as possible to the restroom door, and throwing it open, he saw Theresa standing over Joshua who was still seated on the floor, holding Heather's body. John was right by her side, looking up at her patiently as if waiting for her. Theresa's small frame occupied space, but her screaming had ceased. Jack started to reach out but immediately dropped his hand, not knowing how he could even begin to comfort her after losing her friend yet again. He could see her hand shaking and then become tightly clenched. She turned and left Joshua still holding Heather, and the large wolf followed her into the darkened hallways of the school.

"Joshua," Jack said as Joshua turned to him with eyes that raged in controlled fury.

"She died once," Joshua said slowly as though tasting each word before spitting it out. "This might be temporary, like a warning or something from her mother to all of us. But I don't know enough about their kind. I told Theresa this, trying to calm her down. I am trying to keep it together, but it's so hard holding her in my arms looking like this. I think . . . I think Theresa's going after Heather's mother. You've got to stop her, Jack."

*　　*　　*　　*

Turning away, Jack bolted back out the door and down the hallway, yelling for Theresa aloud in Rynspeak, but she did not respond. The lighting around the corner was still working, and he caught a glimpse of Theresa and John exiting the back doors near the back of the gym floor. As he passed out the doors himself, he was shocked to see John attacking her. The beast bit deep into her lower back, and he could see flesh tore from her back. Jack charged forward and made to tackle John, but John threw him easily off his back. Jack rolled to his feet as he purposely ran for a tree to abandon his human guise to face John as a Cynryn.

Suddenly, a huge gust of wind temporarily caused him to take a step back, and when he opened his eyes, Theresa was nowhere to be seen. Jack looked down at John's bloody jaws and took a step toward him when he heard a terrifying scream coming somewhere from the direction taken by Theresa. Jack stopped and looked up, ready to take off after Theresa, but John stepped in his way. He looked angrily down at John, but he saw only compassion in him.

"*She wanted to do this. She wanted her father's inheritance. This was her choice. What you heard was her rage, the furious cry of a Vulryn.*"

*　　*　　*　　*

Heather's mother took flight and escaped easily enough. She dropped her disguise and only had to kill one sniper on a roof, which she did simply out of frustration. After all, he was a male attempting to stop her. Later, on the edge of the town heading for the woods, a sonic boom right next to her caused her to free fall to the ground, slamming hard into a street leading out of town.

Slowly, she stood, but she couldn't feel her left wing. She turned and was shocked that she was covered in her own blood, and her wing was missing entirely.

A disembodied voice queried, *"How could a mother do this to her own daughter?"*

She turned around, looking for the source of the Rynspeak, but it was a fruitless attempt. Suddenly, another sonic boom shattered her eardrum, and she slammed into a tree face-first. She could barely move at all as she coughed up blood, pushing herself away from the tree. Slowly, she slid down the trunk and stared into the street and saw a car drive by some thirty feet in front of her, and she could have sworn she saw something across the street under the pale of the headlights as it went past. She could sense a few animals nearby and started to draw the blood from their bodies. The animals, unable to resist, fell to the ground and died, bringing her the nourishment she needed to recover from her injuries.

"That hurt, Theresa. I never figured you to be so cruel, so vicious." She smirked as she rose her wings, fully restored. Suddenly, two sonic booms occurred simultaneously next to her. She screamed in pain as she fell to her knees in agony. Her wings were again blown clear off her, and her bones shattered.

"How? How can you do that?" She gasped as she started to crawl toward the road.

Suddenly, the ground started to swallow her up, and she cried out, trying to claw herself free. Once more, she drew on the animals nearby and started to heal, but even fully healed, she could not pull herself from the earth's grasp. It was as if the earth were a living thing and would not see her free.

"When I transformed, I learned how to do a great many things. They just flew into my mind, and it was as if I had always known but had some kind of amnesia. Maybe why my kin are called nine tails. To control the four elements and the five senses. But here's the thing, you start out thinking science. I am a senior after all. Air compression. I can control wind. Hmm, wind is only moving air. I can move and manipulate the wind. What if I compress the air . . . how much I can compress, I wonder."

The Savryn felt the earth stop trying to swallow her, but its grip felt absolute, and she couldn't break free no matter how she tried, when suddenly, a shimmering ball of air descended near her head, dripping from condensation around its invisible surface.

The disembodied voice sounded yet again, *"Come to find out. I am quite capable."*

Flames erupted on the road to her left and right all the way to her immobile form. On the other side of the road, she could see a silhouette of a tall and thin form walking toward her with a single large and bulbous tail.

The orb of compressed air stood guard as Theresa walked out from the edge of the woods. The Savryn could hear cars stopping and people yelling what was happening on the other side of the wall of fire, but Theresa ignored them as she came into the Savryn's view, the flames keeping others from also seeing her true form.

She walked onto the paved street with confidence, sauntering toward the trapped Savryn with all the arrogance of one in complete control. Theresa wasn't human-looking any longer. Her form was feminine and slight but tall standing around six foot compared to her previous five-foot, two-inch stature.

She was naked, but remnants of clothing clung to her form. It mattered little since her body was covered by rather luxurious, soft, red hair, except for her hands and her feet, which were covered in silky black hair, giving one the impression that she wore gloves and boots of some kind. Her tail, red and equally as luxurious as her beautiful coat, ended in a full white plume, which waved lazily about as if she had all the time in the world. The white fur from chin to groin finished the visage of this "werefox," or more accurately, Vulryn.

The Savryn could only cringe, seeing just how arrogant Theresa was. But it was her face that was most disturbing. Her foxlike face was all smiles, her teeth showing small razor-sharp fangs twisting her otherwise beautiful foxlike muzzle.

"Is this the real you, Theresa? You disappoint me," she said, smiling back.

Theresa walked across the street down into the other side of the road, standing before the Savryn.

"Oh? You won't be disappointed for too much longer. Just bear with me. How does the saying go? Oh yes, this is going to hurt—A LOT."

"So you're going to kill your own mother, Theresa? Go right ahead."

For the first time, cracks showed on her face, and the ground rose suddenly, lifting the Savryn so that the two could see each other eye to eye.

"That won't work. You are NOTHING like me," Theresa said caustically.

"'Course not. Heather took after me. You took after Joon," she said wryly.

The ground crumbled away, and the Savryn landed free.

Theresa took a step back in total shock, and the fire dropped off on the street.

"You finally see it. You two weren't just friends. You were sisters. My daughters. You are mine and Joon's pride. I came back for you. I put you through all this to free you of your father's control. In time, you'll forgive me. When that time comes, come find me. I'll be waiting."

Smiling, the Savryn turned to leave when suddenly, she stopped dead in her tracks. All desire to leave or even move left her when suddenly, she heard the cries of the people in the streets. She turned her head toward the people crying out, and they were again hidden by flames, but these were ebony flames of darkness.

"The Um-Umbrage," Theresa's mother murmured hesitantly as if to ward off the power.

"So you know. You can actually sense it. You have sensed this before," another disembodied voice asked.

The Savryn nodded. "Long ago, the dark one fooled me. Never have I seen an infected one wield the Umbrage, but you . . . this power . . . I do not doubt nor will I try to flee from it. There is no escape once you touch me with the Umbrage. No running, no fleeing, just my death."

Theresa, completely out of it, took no notice of the conversation, but just as she was about to faint due to shock, John was suddenly there, catching her in his arms. He was a beautiful white wolf-like man holding the lithe form of the fox woman. His form was massive, something over seven feet tall. The Savryn remained frozen, her back to them, not daring to move.

"You are the Malamute from the school I saw roaming outside? Wait, why is an Eluryn of the Golden Eyes pretending he's an Aluryn of the Silver?"

The two of them stared on as the Savryn quivered in absolute terror, their cold silver- and gold-ringed eyes staring at her as the Savryn felt her legs giving out and tumbled unceremoniously to the ground in fear for her life.

"*Savryn, your name?*" John demanded.

"Autumn Blackfeather. Mother of Theresa and Heather."

"*YOU DARE?*" John snarled at her as she cowered in the face of his fury.

John saw her glance back at him over her shoulder, and somehow, he knew, though not how, that what she said was true.

John stared back and forth from Theresa to Autumn and hugged Theresa that much closer to him.

"*Of all the things that could—go. To Lorelabs. I have your scent, if you—*"

"I know full well what an Aluryn can do, even if it's an Eluryn playing house."

*   *   *   *

The dance was shut down that night. The word of Chrissy's death, Heather's twin, was making the rounds. Steve and Elizabeth saw Jack, and Amber approached them in the parking lot outside the school, concern and distress etched in their faces.

"You neither?" Amber asked, looking over her shoulder, as if she thought she might be attacked at any moment. The others shook their heads.

"Such a public display. In a high school, of all places," Steve spoke softly, holding Elizabeth close to him.

"I-I saw Theresa run out of the school," Jack said quietly. "We need to go to her house and see if she is going to be all right."

"I should go," Amber interjected. "Outside of Heather and Chrissy, I am her closest friend."

Jack's brows furrowed, but he nodded. Steve smiled at Amber thankfully, while Elizabeth, the Wiccan high priestess and the only outsider of the foursome, nodded her approval.

"Let me drop you off," Steve said suddenly as they and several others near them stop and look about when they heard a loud boom just outside of town. Everyone kind of ducked, wondering if the entire town was being attacked. Suddenly, another two blasts sounded off in the same direction, causing car alarms to go off, and everyone started to scatter, heading for their cars and leaving the area in general.

"Oh my god—was that thunder or what? What the hell is going on in this town," Amber said aloud as she started to run to the car, with Jake close behind her. Steve and Elizabeth tarried in an effort to help the Lorelabs security and local police, who had arrived on scene and were attempting to get people to their cars, directing them to leave in an orderly fashion.

*   *   *   *

In a very short time actually, the entire parking lot was empty, save for Steve's SUV and the ambulance that came for Chrissy's body. Steve and Elizabeth could only stare as they watched the ambulance EMTs wheel out a body with a bloodied white cover, with Joshua walking close beside them. Steve could see Joshua's eyes were swollen. He had always thought nothing could move that man's heart and felt ashamed of having thought that now. He turned to Elizabeth and hugged her tightly, kissing her on the forehead.

"I cannot stay," Elizabeth murmured softly. "My coven will want to gather and discuss what has occurred and the possibility that perhaps something spiritual is going on. You know, curses or whatever."

He opened the door for her as he heard sirens going off all over town. He nodded to himself; only now had the local police been notified. *Strange*, he thought to himself as he closed her door and moved around to the passenger side, making ready to leave. He paused as he noted that he had just received a text on his phone.

Elizabeth watched as he sat in the car, holding his phone, reading the message.

"Is it Theresa?" she asked calmly.

"I'm sorry, Liz," Steve said absentmindedly. "Take the car, I need to see her. You know how she feels about me. She needs me to comfort her."

"I understand," she said as he kissed her quickly before exiting the vehicle. She left him in the parking lot, as he moved off afoot in the direction of The Three Cs.

*   *   *   *

Steve crossed the street and eyed his café ahead and went off to his left. His eyes slightly flicked over to the right, and he smiled somewhat wanly as looked upon the Kissing Tree. He sighed as he arrived at the store and turned down the alley as far as a fire escape ladder would allow him to access the roof.

Gaining access to the roof, he stood quietly for a few moments, and then he lurched into motion and moved off toward the center as he pulled his cell phone out of his pocket. He paused, however, as his mind was touched.

"*I needed to see you. At least one more time.*"

Steve almost doubled over as tears blurred his vision and started to trickle down his cheek. He clutched his chest for a moment before involuntarily straightening and mumbling, "It's more intense than I thought."

"*I'm so sorry. I forgot you can feel what I . . . I will go.*"

"Damn it, Theresa. Stop running away! Even though you've changed now, all you want to do is run! You never needed this form to be strong. You always were if you would have just believed in yourself once in a while."

"*You . . . you know?*" she asked in surprise.

He turned back and forth, looking around the roof and trying to locate her, but saw nothing but the usual vent ducts and debris keeping him company.

"Freshmen year. Marcus thought I would start seeing you someday, so he told me your secret in case I saw it firsthand. I know you are different. I heard it's like magic what you can do now and that with this magic, you have to be different-looking from other humans. I am not going to betray your feelings for me. I am in love with another woman, but I am still here for you—as a friend."

He stood alone, with only silence for a companion.

"Theresa," he called gently.

Suddenly, he saw an animal-like creature, slightly taller than himself, seemingly appear out of nowhere, and he was taken completely off guard. The creature looked to be a humanoid female fox. Her features, at least what he could see of them in those first few seconds, were soft, and as she walked up to him, he could see Theresa in its every footfall.

Slowly, he moved toward her and looked up into her slightly illuminous gold-ringed eyes. Her features were animalistic in every respect.

"You're still little Theresa in there, in every gesture, in every movement. The way you look at me, the way you walk. Even as your thoughts entered my mind, it was distinctly and intimately you, and you alone. How the hell did you think I wouldn't be here for you?"

He raised his hand and ever-so-lightly touched her head and then gently pulled her forward, bringing her head down upon his shoulder. He could hear her starting to sob so very softly, whining out amid her tears and whimpering. Like perhaps a fox caught in a trap, every once in a while, she emitted an actual yelp. It hurt his ears being so close, but he bore it for her without pulling away.

"I felt I lost everything, Steve, all over again, when Heather died—again!"

Steve gently nodded. "I thought that was Heather. No idea how she was still alive, but I simply counted my blessings that she was still there for you."

She threw her arms around him then, and the two held each other for a long while as she sobbed and grieved for her lost friend.

Below, sitting on the café's break table in the alleyway, John was in his Malamute form, listening to the entire conversation. He sighed heavily and started to run toward Lorelabs and to the person who had stolen Theresa's friend from her.

*   *   *   *

Autumn flew low to the trees in the dark of night, and she could see the glow of the illuminated Lorelabs grounds ahead. She flew over the gates easily and landed among the security personnel waiting for her. The guards closed upon her immediately and placed specialized cuffs on her, and she eyed them coldly, scoffing at them briefly.

"So they kept these after all this time," she murmured.

The doors opened and a large barrel-chested and scarred man stepped outside, wearing a kiltlike garment about his waste. Although nearly naked, he was like her, immune to the chill of the night despite his obvious age.

She started to scoff at him too, and then she caught sight of his golden limbals. Instead of scoffing, she suddenly bowed her head and actually shivered visibly.

"I'm not John's human form, if that is what you're thinking, Autumn. Matter of fact, I knew you quite well from the last time you graced us with your terrible presence."

She glanced up once more to see his face then lowered her gaze to avoid his.

"I don't remember you," she mumbled.

"How about now?" the man with the golden eyes asked.

She looked up, and her eyes grew wide in shock.

"Tyr!" she said his name with a great deal more respect than she intended.

An aged and terribly-scarred great, gray wolf stood before her now as the dust from his human form still bellowed about his paws dissipating.

"*What have you done? Mate of Joon Bok? Mother of two wonderful children, one of who, this night, died by your own hand?*"

"You don't even know me. Joon was *my* only salvation. His death was mankind's damnation. I came back to see it come to fruition."

"*What happened to you, Autumn? Why this horrid murderous change?*"

"You never lived a human and very mortal life, Tyr. I've lived for over four hundred years, aging little, and seeing how much man has changed and seeing what change they did was really only to hide their sins the better. The more that is exposed of their crimes, the more of them they keep ever hidden. They grow like parasites. Man will destroy this beautiful world that Joon once lived in. I will take it from them before that. I will leave it to everyone who isn't a man, and they will never again be in the position of power again."

Autumn heard an ambulance coming up the hill toward the labs. Tyr gestured for the security to open the gates, and the ambulance came in, closely followed by Marcus and Tara.

The ambulance team off-loaded Heather's body and started to take her inside the building. Joshua, having ridden in the ambulance with Heather's body, was now walking alongside the gurney. Tyr looked at Autumn and saw how crushed and defeated she looked.

"It was all for nothing," Autumn muttered.

"What was, Autumn?" Marcus asked, walking up with his wife.

"Why? Why did you kill your own daughter, Autumn? What hate do you bear so badly you'd kill yours and Joon's own child?" Tara demanded.

Doing another about-face, Autumn almost chuckled.

"It must be nice to live in such a fantasy land with all these fantastical ideologies, Tara. I was, however, born in the 1500s thinking I was a human female. Mind you, I don't have all the details since I was beaten and worse so much my brain was a bit scrambled in those times. You weren't traded off to some European as a toy to be displayed in London for all to see and play with and then only to be discarded the minute they broke their toy. I lived in the 1600s, in the slums, using my body as a means to eat. I found someone disagreeable and was finally murdered. Seriously, thank my ancestors and their gods I died. Oh, how he suffered before he died. But what the hell, I thought. Why stop there? So I killed and killed. I made sure it always looked like an accident. No evidence of vampires, or some such nonsense, clean, precise."

Autumn stood there in her Savryn form, smiling as if lost in some blissful memory. It made everyone cringe in disgust.

"I was every man's shadow, then World War I broke out, and I saw how glorious it was—men killing men! I was among those fields watching all these men die. I was in heaven—at least, I was until it stopped. Then World War II came along. The war to end all wars, but you can believe I tried to keep it alive. I spent so much effort in setting up things so they would fight until they annihilated each other. Then these lovely bombs dropped. While they ruined the fun, I decided I had to have them. Then I got, what, distracted? I met this Asian man trying to save the Koreans from the Japanese at the time. I heard of this hero of the Korean people from among the Japanese, and I had to find and kill him."

Tyr sat on his haunches and shook his head.

"That had to have been Joon."

"He never resisted. He let me stab him over and over. I killed him endlessly, for days on end. He came back with every morning to start anew, and I grew exhausted. Then I found out he created the illusion with his power. He was a pacifist. He thought I was hurting and needed to find something fulfilling. I couldn't kill him, but he created the image of me doing so whenever I felt the urge. He suppressed my desires and eventually crushed them. I forgave man—for a time."

Autumn glanced off toward the place where Heather had been carted off to and taken inside the building, and she grimaced. Reaching up, she clawed her own neck, gouging it deeply. No one moved to stop her.

"I fell in love again. I tried to show him he didn't love me, but his love was a bottomless well. For over thirty years, I wouldn't let him touch me. He actually desired me after a while. He wanted me, but I wouldn't have any part of him because it was the only thing I could do to torture him, but he waited and waited. He waited for me. Then, around nineteen years ago, Theresa was born. I was pregnant with Heather when I fled Lorelabs."

Tara looked away. Marcus walked over to comfort his wife, knowing she still loved Gregory, her first husband.

"The loss of Joon triggered a resurgence," Tara said choking back her emotions.

Autumn smiled. "I was going to use his children to avenge him. To set his daughters on the path to release the great beast under what you call the Kissing Tree. Then Heather, who thought I was here to avenge her father's death, wanted to protect you, those I feel who betrayed us and left Joon to die. I loved him more than anyone, more than my own children. She not only betrayed me but also her own father. To bring ruin to our plans to avenge him—I simply cured her of her ignorance."

"So you killed your daughter, an extension of your dead, beloved husband. Congrats on betraying his memory. He would hate you," Tara said venomously.

Autumn's eyes widened, and she screamed as she launched herself at Tara.

Suddenly, she shrieked in terror and fell to the ground, and everyone could clearly see black flames flickering and leaving a terrible, long scar along her back. Autumn whimpered in pain as she rolled around, trying to smother the pain she felt.

The group turned from Autumn to see John the Ulryn walking toward them. He looked truly majestic. He paid the security personnel and the others no mind, and his eyes were for Autumn and her alone. His long, white, mane like hair blew back in the wind as he drew nigh. For the first time anyone could remember, they saw not his bright and friendly countenance but that of a huge, white wolf like man, one that was deadly serious.

"You will not hurt anyone," he said in Rynspeak as he vocally growled, being unable to speak himself in this form. *"Let me be clear on this. This is my mother. She is as precious as Theresa to me. You try to harm either or my father Marcus and you will end up less than ash in the wind. This is your one and only warning, Autumn, regardless of the fact that you are Theresa's mother."*

Autumn started to laugh, clenching her teeth against the pain. Theresa and Jack shocked to know who John's parents are.

"You all think I'm dangerous? You—ha, ha, ha! You all have no idea! He is about as deadly as what resides below your feet, and yet you would call me a monster! There's the real joke in this!"

Tyr changed back to his human form, wrapping the kilt around him as he did so. He walked up to Autumn as he gestured for the security teams to lift her as he spoke.

Marcus caused the security to pause as he asked, "What do you mean by that exactly, Autumn? Let's not be cryptic about this."

"It makes sense now," the Savryn replied. "You weren't a total failure, were you, Tyr? You couldn't command the Umbrage, but you can create those who can. Don't tell me that you accidently bit Tara while escaping that night, did you?" Autumn started laughing hysterically.

Autumn continued, "So were they—those bastards who sought to hide him from any as might seek to release him. They were trying to control and use him themselves! Below the ground, he resides still, the father of all Ulryn! He who was the fabled hater of man. He who was the supposed child of the Egyptian god of the dead."

Tyr came up and started to choke her.

"You will remain silent about this," he almost snarled.

Her eyes brightened, and she smiled broadly. "You knew, and you didn't tell them how dangerous their child is. How dangerous is he who even now starts to stir? What I set into motion will free him, and only my still living daughter can stop him! Kill me and you will *never* learn how to stop either of them! I will take it to hell with me!" Autumn said, spitting in his face. She fell silent for a moment as though gathering her thoughts then continued, "You filthy pig. I liked you better when you were their toy. How you've thrown your life away to walk like a man, dog."

"Take her away," Marcus ordered as Tyr released her, and the security teams started to drag her away even as she started to laugh hysterically again.

Everyone watched her being hauled away. The silence was nearly unbearable, and then John spoke. *"Tyr? You told me never to take human form. Is that why? So I don't become what lies below?"*

For a moment, Marcus and Tara stared at John and then brought their blazing eyes around Tyr; their mouths agape in shock.

"Explain yourself—NOW!" Marcus demanded furiously.

"You are telling me my son could have been with his family this entire time," Tara said, nearly screaming.

"Since I was thirteen years old," John said while looking disappointingly at Tyr.

Tyr responded simply, "I know what lies below, the same as what could be above."

*   *   *   *

Autumn was hauled into the elevator. She was only too well aware of the fact that she could kill her guards as she might wish. At any moment, she could be free of them, but John would kill her within a couple of heartbeats after that, and right now, emotions were running far too high to risk his wrath. But distractions do cause one to be—what, oh yes—distracted, and she had to only wait for an opportune moment. The doors opened, and she crossed the floor of the cubicle section of the offices to the door Tyr had previously left, and as they opened, they revealed another elevator.

Again, they descended, and at the bottom, the doors opened into a single long room with several holding cells. One was equipped with all the amenities one would need to live in a single cell comfortably— its single bathroom and shower being next to the elevator. But what was most disquieting for her was to see Joshua already there, setting up a table and pausing long enough to point to an empty cell. Autumn was tossed roughly into the indicated cell, and the door immediately slammed shut. It was the exact same cell she was in before, long ago when she had been held here. She approached the cell's clear, see-through cover, watching Joshua's activities. He finished up his final preparations and left the immediate area, heading into the nearby bathroom.

She continued to wait briefly before he returned with Heather's body still covered in bloody sheets. Her face was suddenly the pinnacle of dread.

"Wait, what are you doing to my daughter's body, you cursed dog?"

Joshua remained silent as he gently laid Heather's body onto the table and strapped her to it, removing the bloody covers and replacing them with a fresh one to cover her now cleaned up body.

He turned to Autumn and changed. The Umbrage formed a mist and hid his change as it subsided, showing his jackal-like werewolf form. His long ears made him all the more menacing as he stared at her with his slivery ringed orbs.

"*Theresa changed, and she had golden eyes. She is an Eluryn-Vulryn,*" he said in Rynspeak.

Autumn's eyes widened in mute surprise.

"Tyr knew my training in military would make me more level-headed and suitable to watch over my family and know how to deal with any issues that might arise. He told me what Aluryn means in the Ryn's language. One being half-Ryn, and Eluryn means full-born Ryn. He told me many things I never shared with my mother Tara or my half-brother Johnathan."

Autumn's mouth simply dropped. Their relationship had completely escaped her.

Joshua smiled, showing his teeth in the ebony face that was a mask of death.

"It occurred to me then that Heather might not be dead—not really dead. She might come back yet again as a full born. Like her sister."

Autumn stared at Joshua, her eyes flicking nervously back and forth between him and the hidden form of her dead daughter, covered by the now pure white covers.

"If she wakes, I want you to be the first thing she sees."

Joshua turned away and left Autumn alone with her thoughts. The lights clicked out, and then she was alone and in the dark.

* * * *

The streets were quiet. The town's previous excitement had turned to hush murmurs and fearful glances about. Everyone, quite literally, was in one way or another discussing the recent events. But time being such as it is, people slowly settled down, and with the quiet came sleepiness, and many settled down into slumber.

Alone in the streets, the happy couple was dancing together as they spun away toward the Kissing Tree. The two of them drew nigh the tree. Both were wearing long coats and hats covering their heads and ears in the chill of the night. The two came to a halt and stood quietly before the tree. They looked at each other lovingly.

"Should we?" he asked her as he held her close. She only smiled as she kissed him standing there.

Nearby, however, was a lone figure watching from the vantage point afforded by the roof of a closely adjacent market. The watcher lifted his foot to place it upon the raised edge of the roof border. The foot was a cloven hoof. The owner of the cloven hoof peered over the side of the building, watching the couple. A clawed hand absentmindedly came to rest upon an old chimney stack close at hand. The creature was wearing tattered clothing that hung loosely on his frame. The beast's golden limbal eyes, slit from side to side, peered down at the couple. Its goat like head, with its sloppy and oily hair clinging to it, lowered briefly into the diffused light, peering more closely at the two before it backed off again into the darkness. The creature straightened and walked away toward a nearby tree that seemed to move its upper branches to the beast's location and thus quite gently aided the creature in lowering itself to the ground. The creature smiled to itself as it withdrew and left the couple and the town behind.

Chapter Seven

ENTER ALEJANDRO

Kala walked down the familiar halls of Fairmount High, the same ones Theresa, Heather, and Chrissy had walked. Now, two of them are dead, and Theresa hasn't been in class for four days. Usually experiencing a special excitement on Fridays, she was, on this Friday, filled with dread. Nothing changed the moment she entered her class. Amber sat in her seat, eyeing the place where Theresa sat every day and obviously contemplating her fate. Kala stepped inside and moved to her desk near the back, looking as unobtrusively as possible at Amber who sat near the window, close by the space occupied by Theresa's empty desk. Jack was the next to enter the classroom, and as he did so, several students congregated upon him and started pummeling him with questions. It was his first day back as he was just returning to classes.

The entire class was up crowding around, plying him with questions, but the homeroom teacher asserted control and broke up the crowd, ordering them to take their seats. Kala could see Amber was anxious, but she had remained seated. Jack seemed somewhat relaxed for someone who had just lost another classmate and had yet another who had not shown up for the last four days.

"Okay, class, let's begin," the teacher said, her eyes playing over her students.

*   *   *   **

The cafeteria was abuzz with the news of the death of yet another classmate but tried to curb their curiosity whenever Amber was near enough to overhear their conversations. Kala saw Amber approaching her, and their eyes met for a moment. She could see the obvious pain in Amber's face and indicated with a slight jerk of her head that she would like for Amber to join her. Amber nodded somewhat stiffly and somberly seated herself and began eating in silence as Jack entered the lunchroom. As he tried to seat himself and partake his lunch, he was set upon by a bunch of girls who seemed to both want to question him and ask him out. He waved them away as gently as he could, and he took his meal and joined Amber and Kala at their table, his action giving him respite from his fellow students.

"I thought it would be a cold day in hell before I would ever see you two sitting together again. Then again, it's pretty cold outside right now!" he said, giving the two girls a wan half-smile. Seeing his humor, such as it was, was falling on deaf ears, he just stared at his food and sipped absentmindedly at his drink.

"Does it take another's death to get you to tolerate my presence, Amber?" Kala asked gently as she continued to eat, not quite daring to look at Amber, and waited with bated breath for her answer.

"You want to bring that up now, Kala?" Amber asked, appalled at Kala's question.

"I was ousted before Heather's death, and yet you turned to me for comfort! Now we've lost Chrissy. When will I be forgiven—never, I am to assume?" Kala stated as she put her utensils down and looked directly at Amber.

Jack continued to eat in silence but was listening intently to their conversation.

"If that is your only concern, Kala, I guess we never were friends," Amber said, continuing to eat between her responses but without ever looking up.

"A lot of things concern me," Kala said irritably. "My mistakes never being forgiven, for one. However, the point I was trying to make is the very thing you are clinging to so hard. These high-end morals you hold so dear are now tearing you apart. By putting eternal blame on my actions and bearing everything on your shoulders, for another. You need to share the burden, or become one yourself."

Amber lunged to her feet, slamming her hands on the table, causing almost everyone in the cafeteria to look their way.

"You may be certain I shall never be a burden to you, Kala," Amber said coldly. "As for the eternal blame, it has been levied by the Wicca Council, not me, and for good cause!"

Suddenly aware of the fact that everyone was looking at them, Amber inhaled deeply, as a wetness started to be manifesting at the corners of her eyes. Turning away quickly, she left her food tray, the only thing left to indicate that she had even been there, and walked away; her back straight.

Jack watched Amber walk away, as did everyone else. Kala resumed eating her food.

"What the hell was all that, Kala?" Jack almost growled, like many others unable to pretend not to have noticed the exchange.

"You are nearly as foolish as she is, Jack," Kala said, her words bringing his face around. His brows furrowed his eyes hard.

"I'm foolish, while you sat there brow-beating a girl obviously overwhelmed with grief, and the only thing to come out of it was that you were feeling sorry for yourself and you were blaming her! You were the one who was caught trying to use forbidden magic. You're the one who is responsible for having been kicked out of your conclave. She is still a member, and you're being shunned by all of them—which is also not her fault. She honored your silent request to join you at your table, and you know damned well she shouldn't have, and then you quite literally attack her! You can be damned glad Theresa wasn't here or any of your former coven members. I'll take being foolish over being a first-class ass anytime!" he said caustically.

Kala smiled. "You haven't been acting your age or even as one older than the rest of us, insofar as how you are going about handling this. Something is up, and you haven't told Amber. Well, let me tell you something, Jack. I know Chrissy was Heather. I also know she still has her soul. She isn't dead, no matter what supposedly happened to her."

"Oh, you do, do you? Just how the hell would you know any such a thing? You know nothing, and nobody cares what you believe. You're not a Wicca royalty anymore, and nobody's listening to your premonitions, or what, visions. You need to get a life and quit trying to force your way into the lives of others!" he growled in an unusual display of anger.

Flustered, Kala responded, "I have no idea how—I just know. Heather is like a caterpillar right now." Kala placed her utensils down and held one of her hands over her chest with her other hand.

"I feel something," Kala said, her face a study in puzzlement. "She'll be back, and it will be soon. When she wakes, she will be the most beautiful and dangerous thing you've ever seen. I-I see wings so black, a heart so white, and a terrible inner conflict. What will she embrace? We can't know. She will need love, and lots of it. I hope she has family nearby, a real family."

"She does. But that's none of your business either. What do you propose to do, protect us all from your terrible visions? One does not insert themselves into another's life, or death, uninvited. People were grateful for your input when you were of the Wicca, but you had better get it through your head. You're not one of them now." Jack fell silent momentarily, and then Kala continued, much more quietly, as though thinking out loud, "One is very hateful, cold and dark. Another is very much full of love for everyone, including her." Jack said nothing, taking in what Kala had said.

"Personally, I think you take too much for granted, not to mention placing way too much store in feelings you can't explain about other people's lives and heartaches. You had no business talking to Amber that way, and again, if Theresa, Heather, or Chrissy were here, I can guarantee you, you would have regretted it a lot—a hell of a lot!"

Kala smiled. "Now who is talking mysteriously? Hmm, she has a loving family and friends. She should be fine then, in time."

Kala took his hands into hers, and he jerked away.

After a moment, he said, "You would have led the conclave, Kala."

She shook her head. "No, I wouldn't. I already know I won't be around here for much longer. Change is coming—big changes. Not today, not tomorrow, no, but they're coming."

"Now who's talking mysteriously?" Jack asked, shaking his head as he got to his feet and, taking up his tray, moved away in the direction Amber had taken.

*   *   *   *

Without knocking and bursting through the door at the Jones', Jack hurried into the midst of the few assembled there, surprising everyone. This certainly was not the Jack that everyone knew.

"Where's Joshua?" he asked, his manner very agitated.

Upon noticing that it was Jack, Marcus and Tara instantly went from shock to smiles.

"Jack, sweetie, what are you so excited about?"

"Someone told me that Heather was still alive. I mean it sounds crazy, but she already came back to us once! We need to find out if she is still alive for sure. We have to have someone there and wait to see if she wakes up!"

Marcus came up to Jack and placed a hand gently on his shoulder.

"Well, you'd best go tell Joshua what you've heard. He's with Sara back at the hotel."

"Thanks," Jack said, quickly turning away and departing as he had entered. He hurried out, excited, thrilled, and just a bit unsure as to the veracity of Kala's information.

*   *   *   *

"You are holding something back, Josh, I know it. I know you," Sara said as the two walked in the hallway.

"I told you. We are close to finding that Savryn. When we do, you can have an update to the report you're sending in about the Lorelabs investigation."

Sara grabbed his arm and turned him to face her as she stood near the elevator at the end of the hallway.

"If I don't report soon, my dad will become concerned. I can hold him off only so long with texting and polite conversations. You know he suspects you being special. Marcus gave you that silver ring so you could hide your true self. You couldn't use your powers no matter how much he hurt or angered you. It's worked so far." She paused a moment then continued, "Like he would ever physically hurt you," she added angrily.

"I wonder sometimes," Joshua countered, "the General's daughter likes me a lot." He smiled at her.

This caused her to smile brightly before she caught herself. "That-that's not the point."

At this point, the elevator doors opened, and Sara could see that the occupant was Jack standing inside, obviously quite excited.

"Josh!" he called out without ceremony.

Joshua turned to face him in the elevator and smiled at Jack while Sara's hand dropped instinctively to the gun at her side for a moment before relaxing.

"Josh! Heather is alive!"

*   *   *   *

"How would she know? How can she know all this? As far as I could tell, she is just a regular, human girl," Joshua said as he paced the floor. Jack remained on the edge of the bed where he had sat as Sara pulled out a PC tablet and started typing away in the hotel room.

"Here we go. Kala Geralt, seventeen years old, black female, an ex, very promising high priestess before falling out of favor for using black magic, reputedly in the form of a love potion meant for Steve Thomson. Elizabeth is the current high priestess and was originally runner-up to the position behind this Kala."

Jack stood and gave Sara a bewildered look. "Sara? How much do you know about the people in this town?"

Sara glanced up from the tablet for a moment before continuing her work. "If they are close to Heather, I study up on them. Kala was more part of the group before her falling out. The fact that she was, at one time, a very probable suspect for what happened to Heather, did not escape me. Too many odd opinions on her about town made her a suspect."

Sara lowered her tablet to the bed and stood. "We need to know more about her. You think you could talk to her? If she has some sort of power we are not aware of, then Josh's presence might seem intimidating. Perhaps it's some sort of precognitive ability, you know, able to actually see ahead in time or something like that."

Jack glanced at Joshua then back at Sara in dismay. "But she might know I am also like Josh."

Joshua placed his hand on his shoulder. "We trust you. Besides, you've been around her off and on for a long time. Being in the military, Sara and I coming up asking questions might just spook her. We don't want to put her on her guard."

Jack walked over to the room's window and peered out. "Okay, I guess I can do that. It's just . . ."

Josh and Sara stood next to each other waiting for Jack to finish his sentence. The sun, now low on the horizon, shone through the window and brightly outlined his body with the rays of diminishing light shining through.

"This entire business—it's changing our lives so much. Before this, I would have given anything for my life to have changed from the boredom I've known. But now, I'm with Theresa. I hate the change."

*   *   *   *

Kala was walking in the late evening near The Three Cs. She stood looking into its large window frame. She stood there as if in deep thought when a rapping on the window brought her with a jolt out of her thoughts and back to the here and now. Jack was waving at her to enter. She walked around the store to its entrance as Jack ran out, casting glances over his shoulder every once in a while.

"Ah, um, I need to talk to you after I get off work," Jack said. "I should be off in two hours. Would it be possible to meet up to talk afterward? It's kind of important."

Kala looked down briefly then back up at Jack and only nodded.

"Thanks," he said as he left her alone in the street to return inside. She stood there in the cold and watched him disappear inside and, after a few minutes, resumed her walk. She crossed the street to where the Kissing Tree occupied the center circle, and then she was rounding the corner, and in the act of crossing from there to the other side, a disembodied voice asked, *"Curiouser and curiouser? I wonder why?"* Kala stopped for a moment. She felt and experienced the strength from the speaker, and then she gave a tremulous smile and continued to walk, sensing the lack of wicked intent owing to the transparency of Rynspeak as it was fully used.

"Why? Why would you care why I was talking to him?" she asked no one in particular, still glancing all about, her voice a bit shaky, although she tried as best as she could to control the slight bit of panic rising in her throat. Regardless of the feelings from the voice, it was more than a little unsettling, to say the least. She was walking toward the alley, catty-corner across the street, an alley that was rather well hidden in deep darkness.

"What do you want?" she almost shouted. She was not used to being played. She had usually been the one controlling the game whatever it was. "Why are you contacting me? Who are you? You must want something. I can sense that you are not of a mind to kill me, at least, not right at the moment!"

"You are perceptive for a high school girl," the disembodied voice stated in Rynspeak.

"Now I . . . I am even more curious. It's not too awfully scary to have someone speaking in my mind. I don't know everything that's going on in this place. I do, however, know that something is off, out of kilter, so to speak. I just don't know what."

"You have gleaned this from personal experience . . . or is it something else?"

"Huh, mostly personal experience, I guess. However, with your words, your feelings also flow into me. I sense I need not fear you, again for the moment, so I . . . I will continue this conversation. As I said, I sense that something is amiss in this place, yet . . . yet I know not what. There is a terrible danger here, but I cannot divine its source. I sense it's not you, nor some others, whom I sense are different than most of the sleepers here," Kala said as she walked over to the wall and slid down it to the ground, seeming just as relaxed as if just hanging out with some friends.

"*Sleepers?*" the voice asked, a note of amused puzzlement accentuating the word.

Kala smiled at the sound. "Really, a lot of things are beyond my senses, but it would seem there are few I need fear. I can sense, if not define, what is around me—like you and everyone. One thing I can already sense for sure, however, is that you are not asleep. It seems you are awake to what you are, although possibly not who you are."

"*I am El Diablo, Satan, Lucifer—I am the evil incarnate!*"

Kala laughed nervously and smiled to herself.

"You think so little of yourself. Why is that? What could have happened to have you come to believe such a thing of yourself? I sense a noble soul. What could have made it so jaded?"

"*I was born over four hundred years ago, girl. I am well aware of myself. I am wicked, corrupted, and most certainly not to be pitied by some child.*"

"I hardly have any powers, Satan. I can sense things but have no means to defend myself from the vast power I can sense in you. You could have already killed me many times over, and I could do little, save only die. So it is that many perceived as satanic are misunderstood. No wicked being, or indeed 'evil' creature, would pass up the opportunity to strike out and do serious injury to me as I stand here, alone, in this dark alleyway."

"*You purposely lay yourself open to harm, for an opportunity to engage me?*"

"You are likely a great many things," Kala said thoughtfully, a small portion of her normal arrogance surging momentarily to the fore. "Still, the only thing I sense, mostly, is regret, resentment, and . . . perhaps sorrow. Would you care to talk about it?" Kala asked as she paused and looked upward, her eyes seeking to penetrate the darkness overhead. "Or you could stay concealed up—up there on the roof."

"*You are able to track my mind to my location?*" the voice noted with obvious, if somewhat amused, interest. "*What are you?*" the voice mused. "*Certainly, you cannot be a simple, high school girl.*"

"I have my gifts and have had them for most of my life. I've never used them to intentionally hurt others, but I am afraid it was often the end result when I tried to help, unfortunately quite often."

A large, dark shadow pondered this, as his highly sensitive ears caught the sound of footfalls ascending softly to the roof on the metal rungs of the fire escape ladder, which gave access to the roof from the alley. As the huge shadow watched from his secluded vantage point, Kala stepped over the edge of the roof and off the fire escape. The huge shadow moved slightly, making itself barely visible to the girl's searching eyes. The shadowy being was now partially visible to her eyes and proved to be quite large, somewhat hunchbacked, and seemed to be of rather strangely proportioned but still not really visible, insofar as any real details were concerned. *Evil creature indeed*, she thought.

He stood hunched over, his form mostly in the shadows, and his head hidden in a deep, somewhat raggedy cowl. The only other thing that she could make out were his horns. There were actually slightly curved horns protruding from within the darkness of the cowl and out into the dim light provided by the streetlights below. His clothing was also somewhat raggedy, as far as she could tell. He stood watching her as she continued trying to make him out. With her old arrogance again manifesting itself, she spoke in almost amused tones. "You look like Baphomet. Without breasts, of course. But still, a lot more like it than the horned one."

"Who are you girl? Be warned, do I think myself insulted, such an involuntary reaction would strike you long before your sensing ability could alert you to the change in my attitude and the danger you had invoked. I am not to be toyed with. I've been alive far too long for that."

The young black girl swallowed hard and smiled wanly, as she replied, "I am Kala, Kala Geralt."

"I think I might have need of you, Kala Geralt. It's hard to investigate those I observe, but perhaps you can sense what I cannot see. I have traveled far, keeping an eye on them. I have never seen them display any sort of power or with money enough to be of any import. However, a vampire-like female was in contact with them only recently."

"Perhaps I can help you, and I am willing, but after that, I want you to help me. I want to regain my place in the Wicca coven," she said softly. She gazed upon the beast with beautiful brown eyes ringed in gold as he moved slowly more out into the open.

"You look at me as if you think to look into my very soul. Very well, I will assist you, after we have gleaned the information I seek, a bargain struck. Come, follow me," the beast said as he started walking away from her. They moved to the edge of the building whereupon a slight nod brought the branches of the trees in the street below stretching up and out to them. The extended limbs gently encircled their bodies and lowered the great beast down gently to the street. Kala marveled as she found herself being likewise conveyed to the ground and deposited at the shadowy creature's side.

*　*　*　*

They were at the local hotel near the outskirts of town. Kala walked alone toward the hotel-office building and upon arriving there continued inside. The desk clerk sat, peering at her over his desktop on her right, smiling broadly and bowing to her.

"My dear Kala, the security camera is off, and the master key is at your disposal. Fret not, this fellow shan't remember a thing."

Kala's eyes widened in surprise. "I wondered why I felt he was asleep and yet not really so. You are controlling him, aren't you?"

The desk clerk took a sidelong glance at her. "Ah, what do you mean by that?"

"Never mind," Kala said as she and the desk clerk, who gave his name as Craig, started walking toward the elevator.

"There are people who I feel are asleep. Most human beings are, but you—you were the first."

"The first," Craig pressed, still smiling.

"You are the first whose eyes are wide open, and golden, I have ever met. I have no idea what it means."

The elevator opened, and Kala entered while Craig remained outside, looking a bit cautious.

"I hide my eyes from your sight, girl," Craig said, staring at her.

"Now you know why people think I am bit odd. It's like an aura. It's around you—it is *you*! I cannot explain what I sense . . . exactly. All I know is that I can 'see' *you*! That's about as clear as I can make it."

Craig slowly entered the elevator, and Kala pressed the button while he continued to stare at her, and suddenly, his eyes widened. "I can't quite reach you. I can't control you!"

Kala looked directly at him, a bit shocked. Suddenly, she recoiled a bit, saying, "You were actually trying to?"

"I've never met anyone I couldn't 'reach' except those with golden eyes like mine."

She took a step toward him and started blinking at Craig. "Want to gouge my eyes out and see if I am wearing contacts, or maybe they're supposed to glow in the dark?"

"You've been walking to a hotel at the edge of town, girl. Your eyes did not glimmer nor illuminate the entire distance. That much is true, and yet you are the first human I can't control." The controlled Craig said, leaning back and watching as the last few floor numbers came and went.

The elevator dinged and the doors opened.

"Well, maybe I am human, maybe I am not. I'm not like you, and that's for certain. In the end, how much does it change things?"

Craig thought for a moment and smiled as he stepped off the elevator, joining her.

*   *   *   *

The two moved along the hall until they came to the door number they sought. Craig knocked gently.

"Room service," he called out and fell silent. They listened intently for sounds from within the apartment, but none were forthcoming.

"As I observed on the video tapes earlier, the couple hasn't returned yet," Craig said, opening the door. Inside, the room looked like any other shared by a couple. The normal furniture for a regular room was there, the dresser with the TV on it, a single bed with two nightstands, one on each side, and a space heater located near the widow, which gave out onto the parking lot below.

"Odd," Craig said, walking over to the wall, touching it.

"What is it?" Kala asked curiously, standing beside Craig.

His hands ran along the wall, stopping and going as he went, "New, old, old, old, new! Hmm, this section of the wall near the window has been replaced. The carpet was recently laid. Something happened here and has been repaired rather sloppily and recently!"

Craig turned toward Kala. "See if you can sense anything, I will check other things. Oh, hand me those items I gave you earlier."

Kala removed a packet from her pocket and handed it over to Craig. "What are those, anyway?"

"Well, government investigators are allowed to use GK31 if absolutely necessary, but their use usually requires a warrant. So unfortunately, this isn't exactly legal for me to use if we find any OSs made in the United States. If they have OSs made out of the country, they might require an outside government to get involved with their versions of applicable GKs."

Kala looked a bit perplexed. "GKs, OSs? I don't understand."

Craig smiled as he started looking for any electronic device that required operating systems.

"GKs are gate keys, sanctioned keys, which access the backdoors to any US operating systems. OS is simply a shortened term for operating system. We can use them, but the codes to the OSs aren't included, so we can't see what dirty laundry they're protecting."

Kala glanced down at what Craig had in his hand and then turned to look around the room, and Craig turned to look for a tablet or smartphone.

The two continued to turn the room inside-out, and after a while, something turned up.

"Damn!" Kala exclaimed as she dropped something on the floor. Craig turned to see a very old Bible land on the floor, flopping open. Kala recoiled from what fell out of the hollowed center. A single, mummified, gray, clawed finger rolled onto the carpet.

Craig walked over and went to pick it up but froze. Kala was suddenly motionless. She stood staring wide-eyed, her breath coming in great draughts. The Beast-controlled man calling himself Craig had no doubt; she was having a vision, although he could have expressed no opinion as to what it was that she was seeing. For Kala, it was only all too clear what she was seeing.

Fleetingly, she saw desolate landscapes, corpses of men, women, and children, strewn about as far as the eye could see. She could hear screams in the distance—horrible, terrifying screams. The land roundabout lay in utter ruin. There were no trees, and all life was gone—not even insect life was in evidence. As for the flat and barren landscape, where only the ruined, jagged, skeletons of destroyed buildings seemed to touch the murky clouds in dying supplication, it only added to the horror that was the place she was seeing. Suddenly, a green flame came up from the charred ash that was the ground, and she screamed as it reached out, seeking to touch her flesh, and suddenly, she was back in the room. She wanted to vomit.

"So much hate, so much hate . . .," she uttered the words over and over as a terrible fear clawed at her heart and mind.

She felt herself being lifted and thrown onto the bed by Craig, screaming his head off, saying the same thing over and over.

"I will kill them all—all of his children, every last one of them!"

Kala struck him with everything she had, full in the face with the nightstand's lamp, square in the face, and he roared, grasping his face and rolling off her, landing on the floor hard. She heard someone banging on the door, asking if everything was all right in there. Kala leaped to her feet and made a run for the door, but Craig grabbed her by the pant leg, and crawling upon her again, he tried to bite her leg. She reached down to push his face away, and as she touched his face, he suddenly let go. Kala bolted to her feet again and raced to the door, and as she stood there leaning against it, she looked down at him and realized it was the real Craig looking up at her in shock and amazement.

Barely coherently, he mumbled, "What am I doing here? What . . . what's going on?"

Kala turned as the door opened, and she was thrust away back into the room.

"Put your hands on your head. Do not move—both of you!" Sara ordered tersely as she leaped through the door in a low crouch, her side arm arching slightly back and forth between them, making it quite clear she was in no mood for any frivolities whatsoever.

Kala did as she was told but seeing the mummified finger on the floor, up underneath the edge of the bed, she moved quickly to make a grab for it, only to be brought to a teeth-shuddering stop as Sara slammed her foot on Kala's hand, keeping her from the object she sought.

"I said, do not move! The next move will be your last!"

*   *   *   *

After everything had settled down, Kala was checked quite thoroughly by Sara to make certain she hadn't sustained any injuries at Craig's hands. Sara and Joshua released Craig and spared him the night in jail, at Joshua's behest which made both Sara and Kala do a double take. Sara said that she was dropping any and all charges. Finally, having bid a thankful farewell to Sara and Joshua, Kala too took her leave. A short while later, as she was walking again toward town, she was suddenly stopped by the beast on the side of the road.

"*What happened?*" the creature asked Kala who stepped up into the roadway. "I touched that thing, and then suddenly, I saw desolation and death. I felt so much hate. I take it you were overwhelmed because of the sensitivity inherent in your powers?"

"*I became lost in this endless sea of hate. There was no end to it. I was drowning before your touch yanked me out of it. Whatever that was, never touch that thing again,*" the powerful creature said.

Kala removed the finger from her pocket. "It must only affect your kind like that. As for me, I had the brief image and the initial wave of hate and then that was it. Nothing more after that."

"*What is it?*"

Kala raised her hand high enough so her ally could see she held it using a bit of plastic wrapping meant for a candy bar. "Because I knew you couldn't. I saw such horrible things. What would you have seen?"

"*My nightmares I would see nightly, regardless, like my many, many sins, not to mention the social handicap of being born to an Aztec mother in a newly*

Spanish world, raised back then in the newly created country called Mexico. Then there's coming to the United States to make money after my mother died at the hands of some Spanish humans.

"*My first sin was falling in love with an American woman, having a beautiful Catholic wedding, which was only to end in ruin when we were attacked in Malibu by thieves on our honeymoon. I had protected her. However, she saw the real me. She called me El Diablo, Satan, and Lucifer. I never felt nor thought I was anything like that until that day. She became a nun and renounced me and our marriage. She's an old woman now, I tried to visit once, but she screamed and had a stroke that nearly killed her, and I haven't visited since.*

"*My second sin was in joining the US government as a black ops operative where I would, hopefully, die, but I always fought back and always managed to survive. I am caught in-between my desires and my faith. I want to die, but I cannot simply give up. I must fight and not purposely die, or its suicide, but still, I want to die. I cannot give in to it, I am trapped in a living hell of my own making.*

"*Then the third sin is, being mortal and ever flawed, I spent the night with a woman. She was discovered afterward with child. She wouldn't let me be part of their lives. But I sent them money. She loves me, as does my son. He doesn't understand, of course, but she was right. I simply can't risk their lives. I am a killer, quite literally a murderer. My child lives his life as a bastard, although he has a living, loving father, one who hasn't visited him since he was ten.*"

Kala held her hand over her mouth a moment before lowering it, saying softly, "I'm so very sorry."

"*Piece by piece, he collected me, where you abandoned things-.*"

"What?" she asked as she resumed walking back into town.

He took her up and placed her upon his back, and suddenly, they vanished into the woods, gone like a deer running at full tilt.

"*Nothing,*" he responded absentmindedly. "*Still, if they had known this, then I am sorry. We must find them first.*"

"I might have an idea where they are," Kala said, smiling as she held on tight.

*   *   *   *

The two of them entered the city where they remained amid the plentiful trees that lined the sidewalks. Then they took to the rooftops as they came to the downtown area where trees were less numerous.

"They frequent The Three Cs. If they are not there, they might likely be—yep, right there," Kala said, pointing across the street. The large bay window clearly showed the couple enjoying their meal.

"*What is your story? How are you so, so perceptive?*" he asked as they crouched lower down, closer to the rooftops to keep an eye on them without being seen.

"Like I said, I've always been like this since I can remember. I was the odd girl out, you know, a black girl in a mostly white town. They treated me all right, I guess, but it was hard not to feel like the odd one out most of the time because, well, really, I wasn't white, not to mention what I could do. I found a coven and thought my calling was becoming a Wiccan, and that was my real purpose in life. It certainly felt closer to what I thought I was meant to be."

"*But it wasn't,*" he said in Rynspeak openly and absent-mindedly, his attention on the couple in the window.

"Nope, it was close, but not quite there. It's hard to explain. I seem out of time and place sometimes. Like I should have been born long ago, and then I have feelings as though I've seen the future. Although the future thoughts or sensing only started occurring recently. It's really weird."

"*These glimpses into the future, what were they like?*" he asked, continuing to watch the couple closely.

"It's really odd. This town, every trace of its existence, was gone. It was like it had never existed! Nothing but a small lake exists here, and the only part of the currently existing area still showing above water is Humphrey's Hill. Where Lorelabs is located," she said confused as to what she was sensing quite clearly indicated in her words and attitude.

"*Then it would have been called Humphrey's Island,*" he said, standing as he noticed their quarry finishing up.

"I suppose it might be called that," she said, standing herself.

Just then, the couple left the café, and the creature nudged Kala to follow them.

"What should I call you, by the way?" Kala asked as they continued on the rooftops as the couple came up to their car; a 1977 Cadillac Coupe DeVille down the road.

"Cynryn is fine."

"Look," Kala said, touching his arm and pointing as the car started to leave. She grabbed around his neck, and with one hand, he reached around and held onto her bottom.

"Hey, stop with the grabby," she said, slightly embarrassed.

"As you wish," Cynryn called out as he suddenly leapt into the air with such force she almost lost her grip.

"Grab me. Grab me!"

* * * *

The two came across the car a few miles east out of town near Proctor Brook.

Kala was lowered to the ground, first looking for people near them and gave the all clear. The Cynryn lowered himself to the ground, and just as he started to cross the road, headlights came up over the hill, and he backed off into the woods until the vehicle passed.

The two came up to the couple's car and started rummaging through it.

"I can't believe I am doing this with you. But why are they even here? They went into the woods as if they knew where the coven was."

"Wait, the coven is within the Proctor Brook's woods?" he asked, the tone of his Rynspeak felt very concerned.

"Yeah."

"We must go there—now."

* * * *

The woods had a path that few could discern unless they were practicing Wiccans or hunters. Deeper in the woods, there is a natural clearing, which had been utilized by the Coven of the Mystery. Elizabeth is the high priestess, and Amber is her second-in-command.

Both they and the rest of the coven were asleep and bound to trees. The couple checked on their condition and for some re-administered a drug into them, forcing them back into a deep sleep.

The woman in a long tan coat knelt, checking the girls, while the man continued preparing the large altar where rites were performed by the coven. The slab of stone on a cut down stump of a tree was large enough to hold a regularly sized woman on it.

The flowers that usually was abundant around them were withering or dead. Blood was already spilled, and animals apparently meant for sacrificing had already been done.

The many protective talismans were broken or burned away to ash long ago.

The middle-aged woman with red hair stood, and apparently satisfied with her end, turned to the man with striking brown eyes. "So we grabbing this artifact? We need it to wake him, right?"

The man looked behind him and toward the redheaded woman. He wore a leather bomber jacket and a gray knit cap with blue jeans and tan hiker boots. His look was completely different from his aristocratic friend.

"Honey, please do. These girls will make fine sacrifices to the son of Loki, under Yggdrasil's roots."

Kala and the Cynryn looked at each other, and he motioned for her to stay while he started to enter the clearing.

The couple heard a noise and pulled out guns and pointed them out into the woods when suddenly, the gun was shot out of her hands, and the man threw his away.

"What the hell?" she asked and then sighed. "Jack, when did you become full Aluryn?"

The man walked up, and she began back-peddling, and the man struck her down. Her coat fully opened where she landed hard on the ground. She was dressed in a short red dress and had jewelry around her neck and wrists. The man stood over and stared down at her, "How do you know who Jack is, or more importantly, *what* he is?"

"You're not Jack. Damn it, who are you? His long-lost father or something?" the woman sneered, as the man controlled by the Cynryn grabbed her by her hair and jerked her to an upright position.

Her heels caught her coat, and she was forced to discard it and stood bare armed in the cold night.

"As a matter of fact, I am," he said, striking the woman hard once more, causing her to stagger and fall yet again.

"You were going to do something to these young women, and I want to know what. NOW!" he demanded, looking venomously at her.

The woman stood laughing. "Heather's mother told us about this place. What happened nearly twenty years ago? We came to avenge our fellow brethren! The last remnants of Loki's Brood will free Loki's son, and we shall reign over all as it should be!"

*   *   *   *

Kala heard rustling behind her as she whispered to Cynryn, hoping his ears could hear even her. "Hey, someone is coming up the path!"

The man Cynryn controlled looked behind him as the trees lowered their mighty limbs and restrained the couple. Leaves and limbs contoured around their bodies and held them to the trunks as the man went limp, as if unconscious, and the woman tried to scream until the branches muffled even her cries.

Kala saw the flashlight and knew the person would arrive on-site soon as she started to run through the woods. She didn't get very far as suddenly, a tree blocked her. But with a single touch, the branches returned to their place, and she ran through only to be tackled by a rather large form. She fell to the ground hard, and she yelped as she turned around, only to see a gray-skinned and horned, "Jack?"

Jack backed off suddenly as he exclaimed aloud, seeing his classmate beneath him. Kala could see Jack's true form. Gray-skinned with deep red hair, his already handsome features were sharpened even more so. His chest, now chiseled, and his arms well-formed, she couldn't help but admire him even in the near total darkness that was illuminated only by the candles that the couple had placed on the altar. The horns were the most minor thing about him as at waist-level, and below, he was truly a beast—with thick red fur that ended not with feet but cloven hooves. Suddenly, the figure with the flashlight came into view and pointed at the girl, only to holster the weapon.

Jack looked at Kala still in mild shock and then at Sara as she walked up to the tree and leaned against it with her arms crossed, smiling. Jack looked on confused but then became furious.

"Damn it, Dad! Just show yourself now!"

*   *   *   *

Sara frowned and said suddenly, "You're no fun, son!" Sara suddenly wilted and then collapsed, unconscious like the man before. A large beast form came into the range of the candlelight by the altar, giving a hellish look to his form.

"She can't know I was here son. Her more so than any other. Joshua would think I came to check up on him, which I did in conjunction with another j—OOF!"

Jack tackled his beastly father to the ground and started to hit him repeatedly.

"Where, Dad? Where the hell have you been all this time? I've seen you before, you know. Skulking around during the day and at night. Always fleeing when I approached you? Why, Dad? Why weren't you *ever* there for me? It's been nearly seven goddamn years since the last time I saw you!"

The creature saw the angst in his son's face, but his goat like appearance gave no sign of caring.

"Your mother surely explained. It's not like I could write to you based on my lifestyle. Besides, you've been living a mostly human life up to now, right? How could I take that away from you? Endanger *su madre*, or *mi hijo*, I don't think so."

Jack backed off, and his father rose, his hood falling behind, showing the fully horrid features of his head that looked exactly like a goat with two great horns on its head. The only thing different is the fact his limbals glowed golden with flecks of red around the horizontal iris.

"Yeah, it was explained that my father was some bounty hunter for hire, working for the government," he said caustically.

"I told her never to lie to you once you were old enough. I am not going to offer any excuses. I don't regret a damn thing I've done. My son is looking good and, from what I heard and have seen recently, is happy and healthy. I'd do it all over again to give you that kind of life, *hijo*."

*   *   *   *

He walked up to a nearby tree, touched it, and stepped into it. What came out on the other side of the now decaying tree was a medium-sized man. He wasn't as tall as his son. The handsome Hispanic man looked over his shoulder and raised his arms as branches provided him with leafy coverage for his naked body. Leaves formed a nice, almost kiltlike garment, covering him from his waist to just above the knees. The man was as fit as any athletic human could be. His features were as sharp as his piercing golden eyes, and for the first time, Kala noticed that the pain she felt when he first used Rynspeak with her was clearly showing in them.

Then Kala noticed that Jack didn't share any of his features, and Jack continued to stare at his father while answering the question in her head.

"Dad has a lot of knowledge in his head about what he is and the others. His mother was a child of the first Cynryn. Whenever a child is born, it doesn't necessarily need any human genetic information for the child, save one or the other. I guess you could say I took on the faux human appearance of my mother albeit male while my true form is that of my father."

"So your parents can be of any human race, and you won't necessarily look like one of your parents at all?" Kala asked, rather taken aback by this revelation.

"Yeah, you got it," Jack's dad said as he walked over to the couple and stood there, with a huge grin.

"I could get information out of them, but you kids probably wouldn't like it. You should leave, taking the ladies with you," he said, suddenly turning around and shaking Kala's hand.

"*Niño dulce*. It was great to work with you. These are the two are who I have been hunting. Hopefully, I can get information on what their part was in Autumn's plan."

Jack lifted Elizabeth into his arms, and he glanced back as he started for the woods, "Autumn's?"

Kala started lifting one of the girl's, but it was a bit more difficult for her than for them.

"Sorry, I was preoccupied. Yeah, about Autumn? Wonder if that would maybe be the name of Heather's mother they spoke of?"

Jack stopped and turned around, concern on his face. "Autumn Blackfeather?" Still holding the sleeping Amber in his arms, Jack's father stood there for a moment, his mouth agape.

"You know of her?"

"She was arrested and placed in a special holding cell at Lorelabs. She killed Heather. We found out from her that Heather and Theresa are sisters," Jack explained.

Kala gasped, overhearing the conversation. "'Gather, all ye children of Ryn. Gather in the lands of Found Elders. There in the village of Festival's Hill, upon which a crowned Kinguard sits on a new brow. The Hateful False King fears only the Prince's Queen at Yggdrasil's womb.' I see. I see . . ." Suddenly, Kala collapsed.

"Kala," Jack said as he lowered Amber down on the altar and raced to Kala's side. Jack looked around and saw Elizabeth at a tree's base, sleeping soundly as other priestesses began to wake.

* * * *

Within the cellblocks below Lorelabs, Autumn was using a single small light over her cell's bed to read a romantic novel. She flipped the page when she suddenly caught something. And she paused her reading to listen intently.

There it was again. Autumn closed the book and tossed it aside, listening intently only to hear again what she thought she'd heard.

She was sure this time she'd heard it right, the sound so clear she couldn't move, and she wished she couldn't even breathe—the terror was so intense.

"Mom."

Terror's grip did not allow her to move her body at all, but she found she could move her eyes, and slowly, she did so. They came up and locked upon a pair of golden eyes staring at her from beneath the covers on the tilted medical bed. She closed her eyes in absolute horror, and her body started to shake uncontrollably. She looked up again, and the eyes were gone—as was the body.

She couldn't move. She could only shake. She hated herself for thinking of the first time she realized she was going to die so long ago. She thought she could accept it this time. She thought she could live with dying for her cause, but now, all she wanted to do was live. All she could hear was her own breathing. Suddenly, she saw younger versions of her own arms wrapped around her. She tried to move out of their grasp, but they were not only holding her in place but also broke several bones in her body in the process. The sound of snapping bones was worse for Autumn than the pain as she understood how much stronger her daughter was now. She was an full-born Ryn—an Eluryn.

"Ssshhhhhh. It's all right, Mother. I'm here for you. We're together. I will never let you go," Heather could be heard saying behind her.

She could see the light from Heather's golden eyes reflect off her shoulder and hair as her daughter started to giggle softly in her ear. Autumn knew full well one of her kind was not really themselves when first they wake. She was going to die, a death from which she would not be coming back from. Knowing this, Autumn started to cry.

*   *   *   *

The drive to Lorelabs was a pleasant one for those coming up the path. With forest to the left and right of the drive, the turning of the trees at this time of year gave a golden hue to the entire woodland, which would serve most aptly as inspiration for paintings or some such. The drive was a few minutes from the main road, running alongside the town, hugging the large hilltop on which it stands, smack dab in the middle of the map of the town and its surroundings.

At this hour, nary a creature stirred in the hushed woods. Something had long since been sensed by the woodland critters that normally occupy them. Within the gated property, a lone guard walked casually out of the gate, rummaging through his pockets as if looking for something.

"Okay, does this require a key? Maybe just a button," the guard asked himself as he looked back toward the door and continued to pat his clothing, looking for something.

The guard stood still, turning around when suddenly, he felt what he was looking for.

"It's frigging figures, damn it," he murmured curses under his breath, suddenly cursing in Spanish as he walked back inside. The gate suddenly opened outside, and a tall, dark, looming figure was lowered to the ground, lowered by the trees, whose boughs the figure had been hidden in until that very moment.

The Cynryn started walking toward the gate. The beast was covered in tattered remnants of cloth that caught even the slightest movement of the wind, making him look almost spectral as he came through the gates, his visage hidden by its deep cowl. Jack's father approached the doors, which suddenly beeped, and the guard returned to open the gate.

"Welcome back, Mr. Demon slash Satan," the guard commented, smiling broadly. The guard tipped his hat as he returned to the desk and sat down, hunkering as if to take a nap. The creature went past the guard station as the man nodded off. The creature turned to the corner when suddenly, the guard woke with a start and looked around.

"Oh hell," he said, checking the cameras, his keys, and keycards. His eyes stopped abruptly on the camera that looked out upon the *open* gate, and his eyes widened in shock.

*   *   *   *

The elevator doors opened, and the being who called himself a Cynryn stepped out into the cubical area. He flipped the light switch on the wall beside the open elevator doors, and everything was illuminated around him. His large, dark form stood out in strong contrast to the bone-white walls, enclosing the many cream-colored cubicles that literally filled the entirety of the available floor space. He made his way through them, arriving quickly at the enclosed office set against the far side. The wooden door was locked, and then suddenly, it wasn't.

The door to Marcus's office opened quietly, and the Cynryn walked over to look down upon the desk, upon which rested Marcus's PC. He leaned forward and placed a device behind it. He hit the start button, and the computer's screen lit up momentarily, and then the screen went blank for a few moments before completely starting up, bypassing the unit's security and making available the entirety of the computer's files for anyone to peruse. His fingers played lightly over the keyboard and suddenly, files started to download. He watched for a long moment, and then finished, walked out of the office and followed the wall to another smaller, private elevator which accessed the room. He pressed the button and waited for the door to open. The door did so, and the Cynryn entered, even as he heard the larger elevator he utilized prior in coming down starting to rise, being summoned from the floor above.

*   *   *   *

The elevator stopped on the chosen floor, the doors opened, and the Cynryn saw a surgical table in the middle of the room slanted toward one of the many cages in the room. One of the cages seemed to have been retrofitted, merging a few cages to becoming a living room and bedroom for whoever resided there. But the creature was relieved, seeing nobody was under the covers on the table. He turned toward a lone cage of a middle-aged Native American woman sleeping on a cot in some tattered remnants of what was likely an evening gown. The woman stirred and opened her eyes. The illuminous golden limbal eyes of the hooded figure made her eyes widen—limbal eyes that were as luminous as her own.

"Death, I assume."

"Is that not what you have been seeking all this time, Autumn?" the creature said in Rynspeak.

Autumn stood and ran to the translucent wall between them. "You! You made us run from you over and over. Every time, we'd lose you, and every time, you always manage to find us again."

"I never lost you, not once. I have other obligations that occasionally caused me to pause my pursuit. I have time now, since I am actually here for another reason."

He glanced back at the surgical table and then returned his cold eyes back to hers.

"Your own daughter? I would like to say, as a parent, this is going to be a pleasure."

Autumn could feel the pain coming from him. He was deeply hurt that her own daughter died at her hands.

"Are you so sure, demon? This place is home to a great many things. Some which will make you rethink everything. Power resides here and secrets far beyond anything you've ever faced before," she said spreading her arms wide smiling.

"Still? Even now, you speak like some poor dramatization. Drop the act, and tell me what you know. How could they capture you?" he asked.

The two turned around, hearing the elevator descending.

"Looks like you are going to see firsthand," she murmured.

*　　*　　*　　*

The doors opened up, and the creature's eyes under the cowl widened to see another set of golden eyes glare back at him. The large scarred man stepped through and stared at the creature under the tattered clothing.

"Who are you?" the scarred man demanded.

"So, Cynryn? Ulryn," jack's father calling himself Cynryn asked. His muzzle could be seen. It was smiling dangerously—the smile of a creature ready to die, *wanting* to die. Tyr felt sorry for him.

Tyr stepped away from the elevator door, which would not close.

The creature looked toward the door and then toward Tyr. The Cynryn's eyes widened, and he stood in front of Autumn as if to shield her, his arms spread wide.

"*I need her*," he started, when suddenly, they heard a large boom from the top of the elevator itself. He stood his ground and braced himself when suddenly, he heard Autumn cry out, and he turned to see black flames engulf her, and she fell to the floor of her cell, screaming aloud. He suddenly turned to see Tyr also engulfed in the same black flames. The beast's eyes widened because he couldn't believe the control and the power.

Suddenly the entire elevator was engulfed in the ebony flames, and he heard something dropping into the flames.

"*They are under my protection*," a voice said firmly in his mind, as an unscathed large, white werewolf-looking beast emerged from the flames. The Cynryn felt no malice from him.

"This is a manifestation of the Umbrage. You are protecting friend and foe alike, huh? So you are like a Kinguard," Cynryn said, pulling his hood back, revealing a hideous goat like head and scraggly unkempt hair that grew past his shoulders.

The fires withdrew from Autumn who was still wailing in terror and Tyr who simply brushed himself off, nodding at John.

"How do you know of the Kinguard? I barely heard of it myself from my previous captors," Tyr asked, curious for the moment, now that John had arrived.

Before the Cynryn could respond, he could hear a familiar voice call down the elevator shaft. "Is everything all right? Did John make it in time?"

The goat-headed man started to laugh, a sound which was cringe worthy in itself, to say the least. Tyr and John stared at him while Autumn looked like she was laughing to herself.

"*Joshua? Is that you? Is Sara there? You have been failing as of late to report on your findings, and I am starting to see why. I assume you always knew of them and that they are friends of yours*," the one calling itself Cynryn said in open Rynspeak. They could feel both the mirth and sadness coming from him. It left everyone more than a little perplexed about his complicated feelings.

"DeSantos? You've got to be kidding me!" Joshua exclaimed from somewhere well up the elevator shaft.

Suddenly, another large form landed, holding Joshua in its arms.

"Theresa, you have got to learn humans are not as durable as you when it comes to dropping several floors," Joshua said as the large female fox humanoid lowered him to the floor. She was wearing an expandable white jean jacket and an expandable skirt that adjusted to her change in forms. Tattered remnants of hose and a blouse hung from her legs and chest respectively.

The one Joshua had identified as DeSantos, who had been formerly calling himself Cynryn, looked upon the Vulryn with reverence as she glanced behind him and briefly looked down before she started to climb up the shaft. DeSantos ran to the shaft, past everyone, and looked up to see the Vulryn disappear. He only caught a glimpse of her tail as she exited the elevator shaft.

* * * *

He turned back toward the empty surgical table and cocked his head sideways. *"Why was the Vulryn so upset?"* DeSantos asked, curious to her reaction.

Joshua frowned but started to walk up to the table when he noticed nobody was there. Suddenly, Joshua ran up to it, and DeSantos backed off as the Umbrage was suddenly manifested around Joshua. *"Everyone, stand back. I've seen him like this before."*

By the time he was at the table, he was fully transformed into an infected Ulryn. He threw the covers aside, and seeing nobody upon the table, he demanded.

"WHERE IS SHE?" Autumn could feel the absolute desire to kill her right now.

His fury barely contained, he turned to Autumn, who simply stood staring at him with no visible emotion.

"You really do care," she said thoughtfully.

Autumn's cage was enveloped by the Umbrage as Joshua walked toward her.

"You have NO RIGHT to even live! Much less to speak other than to answer my question, and what I asked you, bitch, is—where your daughter is! NOW!"

Autumn smiled and started to walk toward him, causing him to smirk with evil intent.

"That's fine by me . . . burn," he triggered his Umbrage but was shocked as it withdrew, backing away from Autumn's person.

"That's funny, I mean, that you don't know, but your Umbrage knows me, regardless! How much of the Umbrage is you? How much is it part of something bigger than the both of us, my love?" she asked as she walked up to him, the Umbrage continuing to part for her as she enfolded him in her arms and slowly, gently held him close.

John and Tyr could only watch in dismay and shock as they saw Autumn hold Joshua close. Then suddenly, Joshua was returning her embrace, holding her even closer to him.

"You are so cruel, Heather."

"It took my friend's death to learn this trick. Still, I found out how from my mother before she departed from this world. And yet that lone act is also why I can't be with you," she said, pulling herself from his arms and backing off.

Joshua was so hurt from her pulling away that he was speechless. Taking the opportunity, John spoke. *"What happened to your mother, Heather? What did you do to her?"*

Heather, continuing to look like her mother, moved over to a corner and pointed to a pile of ash.

"She couldn't feed off me . . . I was shocked. I was trying to give her my blood, but she couldn't make use of it. Her powers were far weaker than mine, apparently. She was so fragile, the poor thing. Then I got so hungry myself. I mean, she was dying anyway," she said, licking the tips of her nails with a soft smile.

"This isn't you," Joshua said as he reached out and suddenly saw a part of his Umbrage hadn't dispersed—it had, in fact, clung to her.

"What? Why hasn't it disappeared?" Joshua asked, bewildered.

"Who knows? Maybe it's a manifestation of your love for me. You protect me, even now that I'm a monster!"

Suddenly, the Umbrage expanded and grew across her body, devouring the tattered remnants of the clothing she wore and draped her in a long, black, evening-like gown like she had worn at the dance. She appeared to have returned to her human form but then started to grow a bit taller and with markings on her arms and hands like tattoos made of the Umbrage. Her gown had a hood that hid her face, but her long black hair flowed out of it, and one could see the glowing golden eyes illuminating from its depths. Suddenly, two huge black-feathered wings erupted from her back.

"I am a killer, Joshua. I am not the Heather you knew. I'm not innocent or sweet. I woke up and killed my own mother. I don't even feel like I need to ask forgiveness. When I came to my senses, I was scared, but I'm not scared any longer. I will help you whenever I can, but I can't be with you—I'm tainted," she said, stepping back away from him as he reached out to her.

"I have no idea what you've been through. I have no idea why my Umbrage will not disperse and has become a form of clothing and protection for you. But I will respect your space. Just please come back to me. I love you, Heather," he said using Rynspeak, smiling.

While he spoke, she started to float off the ground to everyone's amazement. She then started drifting backward and passed entirely through the wall.

Joshua watched her pass through the wall then turned back toward John. *"Are you tracking her, John?"*

"I can't, Josh. I'm sorry, but I cannot mark anyone who is apparently an Eluryn," he said as he started for the elevator with Tyr and DeSantos.

"An Eluryn's power cannot *directly* affect another Eluryn," DeSantos and Tyr said in unison.

Tyr and DeSantos looked at each other for a moment before DeSantos spoke. *"How do you know so much about the Ryn, Tyr the fake?"*

"I beg your pardon," Tyr said as he jumped on DeSantos' back so he could be borne up and out of the damaged elevator shaft.

"We will make repairs as soon as possible. Next thing on the agenda is, who's the goat?" John asked, smiling as they ascended.

"How can you be so jovial after what just happened, John?" Tyr asked, looking back down at where they had previously been.

"Heather is alive, regardless of her feelings or her actions as she woke and took her vengeance on the one who killed her. She wasn't herself. You told me yourself that when a Savryn first awakens, they are confused and starving, not really themselves. Likely, she blames herself for the actions she remembers even in that state. I trust her. She'll be back. Theresa will be upset when she finds out she missed her again, though. On second thought, maybe I shouldn't be so jovial."

Tyr started to chuckle and smiled. "Josh? You know this DeSantos?"

"He taught me how to fight in Ulryn form. He's also Jack's father," Joshua said, smiling at his former mentor.

"He's also an Eluryn-Cynryn," Tyr noticed, taking in everything said up to this point.

DeSantos spoke up at that point, saying, *"My name is Alejandro DeSantos. I've got some things I need to talk to all of you about. Joshua, let's meet upstairs and get Sara. She needs to sit in on this."*

Chapter Eight

SISTERS

Kala woke and assisted Jack as best she could in moving the girls into more comfortable positions in the coven clearing while looking back at the captive abductees, which Jack could not imagine how his father had ever come to be involved with in the first place.

"Well, this coven has gotten a lot more active since I last occupied this space," Kala mused, smiling to herself.

Jack moved Amber next to Elizabeth and the others as she slowly started coming around.

"Oh hell," he said excitedly as he looked around in confusion, having no idea as to what he should do. Kala started to hand him a sizable tree limb, which he almost took in his hand before he caught on.

"Really, Kala," he said, laughing aloud.

"Hey, I'm just suggesting. A lot has happened since the blowup at the cafeteria," Kala said, tossing the limb aside and shrugging, her hands up in the air.

"You know, I was right. You were being an ass," he said, running to the nearest tree.

"What are you doing? She's almost awake," Kala asked as he started to reach out to the tree.

"Changing back," he said in an obvious tone.

Kala crossed her arms, looking down at Amber then back at him.

"By all means, put on a show, but I am assuming you cannot regenerate your clothing, or am I wrong?"

Amber started to come around and slowly opened her eyes.

"Uh-oh," he said as Amber stared at the sight of him, his hand still extended out toward the tree.

"A . . . a messenger of the Horned God!" she said, her eyes growing wide with shock.

"No, Amber. I . . . um . . . dressed like this in . . . in . . . er . . . a tribute to your god and goddess," Jack said, trying to save the situation while Kala slapped her hand to her forehead while shaking it.

Jack whispered, "What?" Suddenly, Amber scrambled to her feet, quite angry, "You mock our god and goddess with such attire! You insult us in our own coven. We have enough ridicule and disrespect from most people without being mocked in our own sanctuary!"

Jack turned and started to approach her, his hands outstretched pleadingly, "Amber, let me explain—no—Amber, wait—I said wait a damn minute, Amber!"

Amber started tossing whatever came to hand near her, starting with her shoes, throwing them at him, when suddenly, a tree limb stretched out and took the shoe away from her. She turned, amazed by what the tree had done and knelt before him.

"You are trying to keep this secret, and I was rude, messenger of the Four Corners and the Elements. Please forgive me," she said, bowing in reverence.

Kala started to laugh aloud as Jack quickly ran to her and lifted her to her feet. Amber could see the cloven hooves of his feet being all too real, and she felt faint being held by an actual satyr.

"Amber, I am not a messenger of your god or goddess. I'm not even an satyr! I just look like one. I'm a Cynryn. Look I need to go okay?"

"Cynryn? You're leaving already? What's going on?" she asked, glaring at Kala who was waving at them with one hand as she continued to lean against the tree.

"You think he's cool? You should see his dad," Kala said, smirking.

*   *   *   *

Sara saw the doors open to a white room with little in the way of decor to be found among the many cubicles. She stepped out and was cut off by Joshua who was smiling mischievously. Sara gave him a look as he softly said, "Heather is alive, Sara. Not only that, but guess who the first one to tell me was?"

Among the many standing about, she couldn't decide. Theresa was not present, but both Marcus and Tara were, as well as Joshua-now returned to his human form and John in his Ulryn, which took her by surprise. There was one among them, however, who stood out more so than the rest. Tyr nodded behind him where a lone Hispanic man, in rather tattered clothing, was sort of lurking behind the others.

"Alejandro!" she said in surprise.

Self-conscious, he smiled as she closed the distance between them. Coming up to him, she tossed his hood back and gave him a kiss on his cheek, hugging him firmly.

"You're here! Guys, you have no idea how many times he saved my father's life when I was a kid. He's a little too 'old' to be a bodyguard like he used to be, but he was so involved with Joshua's upbringing. He's like a second father to Josh and me."

"Wait, you're saying your father knew what he was?" Marcus asked, a bit more than mildly curious at that point.

Sara shook her head. "Oh no. I caught Josh and Alejandro training. Josh and I were still kids, but I thought they were like, you know, superheroes with secret identities. I've kept both their secrets from the General all this time. I've even played lookout for them on a few occasions, though he suspects something is still up with Lorelabs after all these years."

She released Alejandro and stood beside him happily, her arm still wrapped around his.

Joshua stood and moved to the center of the floor.

"As I told Marcus before, Alejandro discovered what I was soon after I turned thirteen. He had his ex-wife and son move to town recently back then. I wasn't even conscious of what the change meant at that point and was thinking of having Mom keep me in a cage at the time to protect myself and others, but he had an idea what to do. He knew what I was the moment I met him when he came to make sure his son and wife had moved in without incident. He soon found out Marcus and my mom knew about me and asked to teach me. Our training was brutal."

Everyone seemed to wait for him to continue the story. Joshua moved closer to Alejandro and tried to stare him down, only to break into a smile.

"He completely *beat* me down. He kept reaching out with his mind. He kept trying to find me inside the beast. He eventually did after I quit resisting. After he broke the beast and got me free from its wrath, he then designed a special training program to teach me how to fight with the strength and claws I had. With a combination of *Baguazhang* and *Krav Maga* training using my claws on my hands and modifying it to use my legs as an extension of *Krav Maga*, I learned how to fight with deadly efficiency using my whole being. *Baguazhang* for nonfatal takedowns and *Krav Maga* for fatal encounters."

John looked down at his clawed hands. *"I failed so hard at learning Krav Maga when you tried to teach me what you had learned from him."*

Joshua walked over to his massively larger half-brother who towered over him as he stood there, staring down at his claws.

"Bro, you were always more of a pacifist than a killer, which I thank Tyr for. That's why I am here for you. You couldn't turn your claws toward anyone."

"Unless our mother was endangered," John said in Rynspeak, remembering what he had done to Autumn when she lunged at Tara.

"What child would not protect a parent they love, John," Marcus said, walking up to the brothers and patting their shoulders, smiling. "I am proud of you two for what you do and don't do every day."

Alejandro smiled and removed most of his loose clothing that was meant mostly to intimidate his enemies. Underneath, he wore a rather large yellow shirt with Hawaiian flowers across the chest and back of it. His shorts were oversized khakis while his shoes were sandals. He set all the loose clothing across one of the cubicles and took his turn at the center.

"I had no idea about a great many things. First of all, that there were so many Ryn still existing in this world. I thought Joshua was a fluke. He never told me his origins, and since he was a kid, I never thought I could get an accurate story out of him, but now I see it. Lorelabs! It's history. I looked into it deeply before I came—the death of its former owners, how you turned this place around to be something of a support group for any known Ryn."

Marcus and Tara started to say something, but he raised his hand to stay their voices.

"Wait. I know it's not what I said, but it might as well be. Never have I seen such a concentration. Ulryn, Savryn, Cynryn, and what I assumed I saw was I thought impossible to ever see in my lifetime—a Vulryn!"

DeSantos spread his hands wide.

"I am eldest here among all of you, save mayhap the one formerly known as Autumn Blackfeather. I am over four hundred years old. My mother was the daughter of the first Cynryn, well over one thousand years before her untimely demise. What I say is by word of mouth. I know not how much of it is accurate, or biased, based on what I have seen at times as distain for some Ryn. However, after seeing you all here like this. I thought I would tell to you what was told to me so you can pass it along to others of our heritage."

*   *   *   *

The Joneses' house was silent and empty when Theresa returned home in her human form. Slowly, she opened the front door and looked inside, the darkness making her illuminous golden eyes stand out all the more. She entered, carrying a small bag with her that held an extra change of clothing. She walked inside and closed the door.

"Normally, in the movies, a young woman walking into an empty house is a death sentence. It's weird. Before, I suppose I would come in here with apprehension after all that has happened. But now, I almost look forward to danger. Have I changed that much?" she whispered to herself as she started to ascend the stairs. She came to the door to her room and, taking a deep breath, opened it.

Inside, she could see Heather as she had always known her, in the middle of stuffing a suitcase. She wheeled around, completely surprised. They stood there, staring at each other for what seemed like eternity, two sets of golden limbal eyes each staring at the other. The awkwardness caused Theresa to start laughing, and she charged across the intervening space to hug Heather, but she passed right through her. Theresa recovered immediately, stopping herself from falling onto the bed, and turning, she saw Heather, suddenly seeming solid by the room's door.

"I am not the Heather you once knew, Theresa," she said, staring at her friend cautiously.

"Right now, I want to know why you stopped me from hugging you. I've missed you, Heather, so much," Theresa said, sitting down on her bed, her legs crossed and her arms behind her, casually leaning back.

"Like I said, I'm not the same," Heather reiterated as she walked toward Theresa and once more passed through her as she grabbed the suitcase and passed both her and the case back through Theresa.

"Nice trick, sis," Theresa said, smiling. This shook Heather to the core of her very being, and tears started to form.

"I killed Mom," Heather said, trying to subdue her feelings of trepidation.

"The bitch deserved a lot worse than death at the hands of one of her daughters. She's killed a whole lot of people neither you nor I had any idea of," Theresa said somewhat sadly.

"But you wanted to know more about dad before she died," Heather said. "I'm sorry Tee. It's the reason I'm going to go. I woke up, and I was so hungry, but more than that, I was so filled with hate. What if I became like that toward you, or how about your parents or Joshua?"

"I guess I'd have to kick your ass," Theresa said, smiling.

Heather suddenly grew a bit taller as her black wings filled the room. The mark of Joshua's love, his "tattoo," was suddenly manifesting upon her arm, and her clothes fell through her as a long, black, hooded gown just suddenly appeared, covering her body.

Suddenly, Heather put her hand through Theresa's head. "If I wanted to—AHH!"

Fire erupted as she retracted her hand. Unsinged, Heather looked incredulously at her arm and hand before seeing Theresa smiling and standing and moving over to the window on the far side of the room. She opened it, letting the cool night breeze of late October blow in. She turned to face her wide-eyed sister.

The breeze crossed her body, and she grew and changed. Red fur covered her body, and claws grew from her hands and feet, ruining her clothing and shoes.

Theresa sighed, standing there in her werefox form, her tail swinging lazily about,

"*Damn it. More clothes out the window, so to speak!*" she said irritably.

Heather could only stare at her in wonder. "You are an Ulryn? Like Joshua?"

Theresa looked indignant, "*Hell, no!*" she almost spat the words. Spinning around, she gestured at her fluffy tail and the black socks on her hands and feet and the slit irises no wolf could ever have.

"A were- fox?" Heather asked with a looked of bewilderment.

"*Apparently, I am a Vulryn, and as I thought after you passed through me the first time, if you tried to pass through me again, I should be able to affect you. At least, I hypothesized I could.*"

"It seems like when we changed, we recovered from amnesia. Like we were always this way, and we instantly remember what we are and what we could do," Heather observed, looking at her form.

"*I want to know how the hell you got those clothes. I wish I had that trick,*" Theresa said with just a touch of jealousy.

"Long story. Want me to go over it?" Heather said, smiling for the first time. The two of them returned to their human forms and hugged, both bereft of any covering whatsoever. Theresa murmured softly, "Yeah, I think you'd better, sis."

*   *   *   *

At Lorelabs, everyone settled into the nearest seat to hear what DeSantos had to say. Marcus and Tara, being very excited about hearing of the possible origins of Ryn and the problems that might very well affect their children, including the one they'd raised since infancy, pulled extra chairs out of the surrounding offices into the larger room, which was actually the break room, the only place large enough for the group to gather. John stood behind his parents, as did Joshua who remained in human form. Sara stood between the brothers. DeSantos looked upon a gathering he thought he would never see in his lifetime. Moving his hand across his head he pulled his long hair back out of his eyes and took a huge breathe to speak of what he was about to impart to all of them.

"Well, it's hard to determine how old I actually am. While Aztecs were well known as to their understanding of time, theirs and ours are a bit different. That said, I do not know exactly how old I am. I appear to be in my late thirties or early forties, but truthfully, that doesn't mean much because as you know, we age differently than humans. I'm just not sure. I know the Aztec civilization was still a great empire when I was young. My mother was a part of that great civilization. She could remember the first of our kind so long had she lived, the progenitor of all Cynryn," DeSantos said as he paused to sip a drink from the large glass of water sitting on the long table in front of him. He glanced around the room, eyeing everyone just in case anyone had anything to ask.

"Well, for the most part, I only have information on the Cynryn. My mother said we were the weakest of the Ryn. I asked her what Ryn meant. She said they were spirits that could create a physical form. Any form. But like most intelligent beings, they tended to settle into a trend of preferring a given form over any other," DeSantos continued.

"As for her, her parent was a creature that was a goat like humanoid."

Marcus said, sounding a bit dubious, "Why would the weakest among the Ryn want to look like, well—you?" he said, raising a question toward DeSantos.

"Actually, I asked that myself, after I first change," DeSantos said thoughtfully. "I had no idea an Aluryn, like my son, could be a beautiful rendition of this form. Mother said because we were the weakest, we had to look dangerous and threatening to keep humans from trying to hurt our kin," DeSantos went on, as Marcus nodded, agreeing with the logic.

"We also have the most abilities," the elder Cynryn continued, "although nothing as terrible as, say, the Umbrage. We can communicate with animals. We can bend plants to our will, and we have the ability to see into the past, present, and future of the things we touch, including ourselves. I heard of twin girls living nearby who are detectives, born of another Cynryn named Glaistig, whom they are looking for. The one who sees the past solves murders, and then the one who can see the future focuses mostly on herself so she can see every attack angle, although she can be overrun by too many adversaries. But I digress. My ability as an Eluryn is the ability to take over the mind of anyone not a fellow Eluryn and control them from even great distances. I am a great negotiator and also a rather good assassin! I never sully my hands and can go into just about any situation unarmed and come away alive. I can also see the present, so tracking is far easier for me, no matter where one tries to hide."

"So that is how you beat me when I first brought out the Umbrage when we fought that one time. I am infected and not a true Ryn," Joshua stated, giving DeSantos a look.

"Well, I pushed a bit too hard, and I was sure I could handle it if you lost it, and you did," DeSantos said, shrugging his shoulders.

DeSantos paused before continuing, "Well, point is, we are descended from spirits that are not human but could create an Aluryn with a human partner. It's how we all came to be. We are descended from the original children and their chosen humans. Unlike humans, the child doesn't seem to need both DNA. A single sex is chosen from the parent's DNA, as is what race of Ryn or humans. I've been told that Ryn and human don't always have to match but almost always does, from what I've seen of others I've encountered in my long walk through this life."

"I did not come to be in that way. I was conceived as a normal human, but my mother became infected, which in turn infected me. I wasn't even born in a human form, but as a wolf. My dad had to bribe the doctors at the hospital to keep silent," John said somberly.

DeSantos's face went pale. "You can change into a wolf already . . . and your true form, have you ever been human?"

John shook his head, "I was warned by Tyr never to turn human, ever. My parents were furious about it. They could have had a son since I turned thirteen."

DeSantos shook his head. "Tyr, you know then why those two I pursued are here and why Autumn returned. You know the only other one who was born the same way and how he almost brought ruin to both mankind and the Ryn."

Tyr looked on as the others stared at him, and he in return glared at DeSantos.

"I have been protecting them for the last eighteen years. If you knew, what compelled you to tell them now?"

Marcus came up for air. "Tyr? What have you been hiding?" Others started to stir and ask questions, questions which Tyr could barely hear and respond to before the roar of anger and lines of questioning made him yell, "ENOUGH!"

Tyr watched as everyone quieted down and stared with anger and hurt in their eyes. He continued, "I am a failed experiment to be a controllable monster of Lore. This monster, according to those who were originally devoted followers of Tyr, was the killer of Ryn, including all but two of the true Ryn, whose spirits were source of our kind. He betrayed them all. They were almost completely wiped out to protect mankind from him, and would have been, if he hadn't been betrayed by his closest friend, the Tyr of Lore, or so I heard."

DeSantos spoke up. "He was bound and imprisoned for all time. To go mad was his punishment."

DeSantos walked around among them as he continued, "He was supposedly bound under a tree. The roots grew around this large boulder and held fast to both it and the beast. They never thought that with time, he would be forgotten because none who survived could ever forget, but as time went on, more and more children of the Ryn died. The two left alive fled or abandoned these children to carry on without them. A young woman told me before I left her where he had been imprisoned, here, in this town. But Tyr already knows that, don't you?"

He glanced over at Tyr as Tyr averted his eyes but then saw Marcus's face lit up as if something had just occurred to him, and whatever it was, it made him look as if he was about to be sick.

"Please, Marcus, it seems you've figured out his location for yourself," DeSantos said, quietly gesturing toward Marcus.

Marcus nodded. "Damn it. Had I known, I'd never have gone along with those sick bastards. I can only assume this, mind you." Tara looked shocked. He nodded toward his wife. They held each other as she reached out to Joshua and John. They all held each other closely.

"Yggdrasil," Tara said as if in a whisper. "The tree now called the 'Kissing Tree' was originally called *Yggdrasil*."

"Fitting, since it allowed the human race and what was left of the Children of Ryn to live because it held this monster in check," DeSantos said stopping his walking and staring at John and Joshua. After a moment, he again took up his story.

"The beast under the tree was the first Ulryn. Tyr was supposed to be a clone of him, I'd wager. You are the results of his existence, Tyr. Oh, and you, John," DeSantos said, walking to John and placing a hand on his shoulder. "You were born the same way he was. You were born the same way as the so-called son of Loki, the beast men once called Fenrir."

* * * *

Amber and Kala removed themselves quickly from the coven and started toward the road, avoiding what they expect questions from the high priestess and her coven as they woke being for the best after Jack left.

"Alejandro abandons us and Jack ran on ahead. His father had to carry those two to Lorelabs and lock them up. Thanks boys," Kala said as she walked back to the road with Amber.

"You think you can still return to the coven?" Amber asked casually.

"I don't even want to now. I've seen far too much to go along with the limitations of your coven. There is something greater in store for me, but I was being too petty. I was thinking small. I want to be bigger, like Jack's father, and make a difference," Kala said as they continued to make their way along the path.

"Still haughty as ever, I see," Amber said, brushing aside occasional branches as they continued down the path.

"Yeah, but you've seen, Jack. Do you really think he's the only one in town who's different?" Kala asked, smiling.

"How many people like him are there?" Amber asked, suddenly curious.

"I have no idea. But I think if I found others like me, we'd gather together. You know, safety in numbers and all that."

Amber flashed a strange look at Kala's back. "What would they ever be afraid of?"

"What is anyone afraid of, Amber? I mean, we live quite near Salem. How could you actually ask that question with a straight face? You think things like how man reacts to fear has changed? It's a primal instinct. Remember the saying?"

"What man doesn't understand—" Amber started.

"Man will destroy," Kala finished.

"This isn't the inquisition, Kala."

Kala stopped and then turned around to face Amber. Her look was stern.

"Instead of stating the obvious, which we are all quite well aware of, let's try looking at it from another angle. You thought you saw a messenger from the Horned God. Others could see him as a real life demon. Remember, in today's society, your gods are seen as pagan devils. They are these days, though not to be real, or worse, in league with the devil, or any number of other vile things, by the vast majority of the people. It's not like being different because you're overweight or of a different race or religion. It wouldn't be like someone with a stigmata to most people, not by a long shot."

Amber wanted to counter the argument but finding it sound, simply went silent, as Kala paused and turned to her.

"Not everyone is like that, Amber, but it only takes a few to fan distrust, and with the doubt can come fear, then sadly, hate! That's part of human nature as well. We fight it like we could hope to win against humanity's instincts. We need to accept our primal instincts, those in ourselves and in everyone. We need to come to terms with it, individually, if we are ever to hope to restrain it, instead of merely restraining each other. Hate is an easy way to deal with what we don't understand, but it always ends up being harder for—and on—everyone."

"True, but trust is harder. At least, with hatred, you know where you stand, and these days, trust is seemingly harder to count on," Amber said softly, absentmindedly giving voice to her thoughts.

"That's what makes hating so easy. It's simply easier to hate than it is to trust!" Kala said, nodding.

They continued on to the clearing near the roadside. As they approached it, they could not help but notice the woods closely adjacent had apparently been burned recently. Amber walked over to a burned section and saw that the ground had been violently disturbed; she also noticed black marks crossing the road.

"What happened here?" she asked nobody in particular.

Kala walked up to a singed tree and touched it briefly before pulling away.

"Uhh, I'm not about to look deeper. So much hurt, so much pain. It makes one want to die just to come close to such feelings. Someone was hurt here—badly!"

Amber glanced around the clearing but found nothing except for a single car. She assumed it belonged to the couple Jack had taken away and so moved to examine it.

"Any keys?" Kala asked, walking up to the vehicle.

"So far, no luck. Wait, no," Amber said dejectedly.

Kala tapped Amber on the shoulder as she turned to say something and spied an old man coming out of the woods.

"Uh-oh," Kala started to say and sheepishly looked at Amber as if to silently say, "Do something!"

The old man was rather small. He was dressed well, his wrinkled face contorted angrily as he addressed the girls.

"What do you girls think you are doing in my 77 Deville? Are you here to rob me? Do it. Like I care these days . . . damn kids."

Kala and Amber both started waving their hands toward him while saying in unison, "NO!"

"Sir, we thought some of our friends came here in this car and left their keys. We were trying to retrieve for them." Amber said while Kala gave her a dour look.

"He's never going to buy that," she said and was immediately surprised as the old man smiled.

"Well, if you are not going to kill nor rob me, get in, and I will take you two to town. In the back seat, girls. No one rides shotgun while I'm driving."

The old man gestured to the back seat, and the girls happily complied, not wishing to make the man angry again.

"Thank you," was all the girls could manage as the man clambered into his vehicle and starting it, nosed it back toward town.

Kala glanced at Amber and whispered, "Wish I could communicate like Cynryn. It would be easier to talk privately with you right now."

The old man glanced into the rear view mirror, "I'm sorry, miss, were you talking to me?"

"Ah, we were just curious as what your name is. Who do we thank for our ride?" Amber asked, fleetingly giving Kala a knowing look as she smiled at the old man.

"Oh me? The name is Thiess, young ladies. Thiess Kaltenbrun."

*   *   *   *

Inside the Joneses' house, a crash could be heard, accompanied by the unmistakable sound of giggling. The two girls, having returned to their human forms, had started having a bit of fun, imbibing a bit and celebrating Heather's miraculous return from the dead yet again!

"I am seriously not going to be concerned at this point, if you get hit by a bus, a train, or other acts of God, Heather. Why did I ever worry about you again?"

Heather started laughing. "Because you can't help loving your sister, sis."

Theresa couldn't think of anything to say in response, so she just started grinning and kicking her feet on the couch in pure happiness.

"Oh my gawd! I can't believe we are really sisters! Damn it, I swear I always thought you were like a sister, and now, to find out you really are!" Theresa said as she lurched to her feet and grabbed both of Heather's hands, in one of which she still held a drink and began to jump up and down in pure happiness which, of course, sent the drink flying. Making a half-hearted attempt to grab the drink, Heather knocked over the bag of chips sitting on the edge of the couch, causing the chips to fly everywhere.

"Oh hell," Heather said, clamping her hand over her mouth.

Theresa panicked and fell to her knees, looking at the formerly immaculate couch her adopted parents kept in said condition.

"Ah, could I warm it and wash it out with water? My powers are worthless for stuff like this."

Heather suddenly smiled. "Young lady, do you need my services?"

Theresa turned, giving her sister a bewildered look. "Why are you trying to sound like a gentleman?"

"Watch," Heather said as her hand passed through the couch and brought all the drink away, leaving the couch completely clean, and she did the same with the chips, moving them into a trash can without disturbing their surroundings.

The two plopped back down on the couch and started laughing.

"Okay, you're moving in here with us, Heather," Theresa said, grinning. "The Jones won't mind, and you get to do all the house cleaning."

Heather gave her sister a dirty look. "Like hell I am. You're going to pitch in too."

The two laughed a bit more as they began to relax and sat quietly for a long moment, staring at the blank TV screen.

"So how are you and John doing?" Heather asked Theresa as her sister glanced over at her, confusion clearly etched in her features.

"What? Oh, we're doing fine, but what do you mean by that?" Theresa asked, curious as to where this was going.

"I sensed at the dance how he felt about you," Heather said, smiling. Theresa frowned, staring down at her feet, wishing she had her tail at the moment so she would have something to do with her hands.

"You never reciprocated his feelings?" Heather asked in surprise, reading between the lines of her sister's silence.

"When you died, I called Steve, not John," Theresa said, frowning as she turned toward Heather.

"But you have to know how he feels! I mean, my god, I felt Joshua's concerns and fears too, but John's were so pure. No doubts, no concerns—he was purely into you. I can't even describe what he felt for you except that it was—innocent. Joshua's feelings did have some sexual interest attached, but John just wanted to be at your side and protect you."

"He was in the alley while I talked to Steve," Theresa said, now feeling ashamed.

"Oh, Theresa, you didn't . . ." Heather started as she saw Theresa nodding.

Heather got up and walked into the kitchen, and Theresa quickly followed behind her.

"I knew he was there, and yet I spilled my guts to Steve, though he turned me down!"

Heather turned on Theresa angrily.

"A lot of good that does! Now how will he feel? He's second choice, hooray. You've settled on him? He will revisit that little talk every time he turns around, not to mention feeling it whenever you happen to speak of it."

Heather took Theresa by the shoulders. "Rynspeak, now. John's name."

Theresa glanced down and looked away from her sister as she said in Rynspeak, "*Johnathan.*"

Heather threw her arms up in the air and sighed heavily.

"Oh, Theresa, I sensed your love for him, solid and sure. However, it's so overflowing with unidirectional regret, even toward yourself! He's going to feel like hell thinking you are just accepting him on the rebound!"

Theresa started pacing back and forth in great agitation.

"What am I supposed to do, Heather? Never speak with him again? I sure as hell don't want to hurt him, and I *do* love him! But I knew Steve all my life, and I only recently met John. How the hell am I supposed to become attached to him like we are longtime lovers?"

Heather turned on Theresa with her mouth agape. "Longtime lovers? Is that what you thought your feelings were toward Steve? Damn it, Theresa. You can *feel* his love. What did you ever feel from Steve, even once? He's not us. We can't hide how we feel if we Rynspeak directly to each other. He spoke to you, and everyone who had Rynspeak could feel it."

Theresa's mouth dropped.

"He's the sweetest damn guy I ever met!" Heather went on. "All I want to do was keep him for myself . . . er . . . and *no*, don't tell Josh I said that. You are so lucky, Theresa! He wants you! My god, *only* you!" the last part Heather said in a voice filled with exasperation.

"I know! I know," Theresa said, a bit flustered herself.

Heather let out a sigh, slapping her hand down on the kitchen counter. "Well you certainly can't talk to him in this state. He'd be confused, for sure."

"What do I do then?" Theresa asked. Heather rolled her eyes and sighed once more and shrugged.

"I haven't a clue. You are so screwed," she said, shaking her head.

*   *   *   *

Marcus stood, Tara following suit. The two looked at each other and then turned their eyes toward the others once more.

"You are saying we have a demigod buried under the town tree, and the former owners were using his blood for medical miracles?" DeSantos asked; one brow raised in question.

Everyone locked their eyes upon Marcus and his wife.

"When we were hired, all we knew was the tree provided some extraordinary healing properties. Tara and I tried to discern what made the sap so unique, other than its blood red tint. We couldn't find anything special about it outside some trace of animal and human DNA that could have come from bleeding near or on the tree and the birds who might have died and whose remains were absorbed naturally into the ground, which the tree fed on," Marcus said thoughtfully.

As he paused, Tara picked up the narrative and continued, "The findings were inconclusive. We wanted to study it more, but Garner and his team, who ran Lorelabs in those days, wouldn't let us. After we took over, we decided it wasn't safe to use, being that it was being gleaned from such a little known and poorly researched ingredient. We decided to pull the plug on it, even if that was the majority means for the town's prosperity. We had acquired quite a bit in that time and used the money we had gathered to help the town out all these years. That's why the town is in such dire straits today."

"Atrocious, they used his blood to make themselves rich. What is worse is they were descended from the servants of Tyr, who were meant to keep Fenrir's prison hidden all this time. I heard as much back then when I was still imprisoned," Tyr said as DeSantos stared at him.

"I was born as a normal wolf and was heavily modified on a genetic level to become a suitable clone of Fenrir, Alejandro. I thought I was just supposed to be a clone of a wolf they called Fenrir. How was I supposed to know I was an experiment to recreate a demigod?"

DeSantos once more took up the story. "My mother spoke of him. She saw him tear apart the Children of Ryn and actually looked on as he killed a Ryn, one who tried to offer him a peaceful resolution. He spread death to man and Ryn alike. She said he felt betrayed, and so he betrayed everyone. I do not know the details of that betrayal, however, since it was mentioned in passing more as a warning. I am sorry I forgot all the details."

The group took a breather to assimilate what had been said and really, to wrap their minds around all the new information. "Autumn is dead," Joshua said, leaning against the sink.

DeSantos walked around gathering his thoughts before continuing.

"The couple I've identified are the only ones left, at least, that we know of that has this knowledge, other than us. How much they know, I have no idea."

The elevator door dinged and opening, revealed Jack in his Aluryn-Cynryn form, walking in with the couple in handcuffs. "They've been processed. The special cuffs are on loan from the guards above. Where do you guys want them?"

Tyr rose and started to talk, but was interrupted as DeSantos spoke first. "You did good, son."

"Yeah," Jack said, passing his father without as much as a glance toward him. "Thanks."

Jack came up to the elevator shaft and looked over the edge and sighed.

Tyr came up to him and gently rapped his shoulder, smiling.

"The elevator is out. Most of us had no idea he was your father and thought he came to free Autumn."

"In their excitement, they really destroyed the elevator. Grand entrance, although not nearly so grandly thought out," DeSantos said, grinning somewhat roguishly.

"I know what it's like when someone doesn't think things through," Jack said as he returned to the elevator and left, leaving behind the couple still in cuffs.

Tyr was about to say something as the doors closed, but DeSantos shook his head gently as he touch Tyr's arm. "In many ways, he's a young man, but he's still my son first. He's hurt. Let's give him time to process my return into his life."

"Are you back, DeSantos?" Marcus asked with his hand extended. DeSantos looked at the hand for a moment before shaking it politely.

"For a time, at least. I was tracking this couple when I was told to check up on Joshua's progress if I found the time."

"Ah, so you are still a . . .," Marcus started.

"A bounty hunter? Yes, I am. The world needs people willing to do dirty work to preserve things as they are. They know what I will and won't do for them."

Joshua stood, a bit confused. "You are no longer in the military?"

DeSantos moved away, walking back toward the elevator.

"No, I'm not. I'm a freelancer, although I used to be exclusively for hire by the US Military. The odd jobs I do most of the time are as a bounty hunter. It pays the bills."

Joshua took DeSantos's hand and shook it. DeSantos looked curiously at Joshua for a moment before breaking into a smile, reflecting that of the younger man.

"You're welcome, just do me proud, Joshua."

The remaining elevator doors opened, and DeSantos stepped in. "I need to go see my son now. I'll talk to all of you later."

*   *   *   *

The door to the Joneses' house opened as Marcus and Tara stepped inside, closely followed by Joshua. They could hear the sound of snoring coming from the area of the living room.

"Theresa doesn't snore," Joshua said as he stepped past his parents and headed into the living room. The living room table was covered with assorted debris consisting primarily of chips and candy. A few empty cans of cola were in the trash. His head came back around the corner, and he was smiling brightly. Using hand signals only, he indicated that the others should hasten to join him. Theresa lay sprawled mostly on the floor, wrapped in a blanket that partially covered her sleeping form. Her one leg was still draped on the couch, on top of Heather's snoring form, where she lay on the couch, also asleep.

Tara laughed softly, and Marcus smiled as Joshua moved Theresa's leg off of Heather's person and gently lifted Heather from the sofa.

"Josh," Marcus said softly as Joshua turned toward him expectantly, "she's Theresa's sister. Keep that in mind."

"You can take her to Theresa's room," Tara said, giving him a bemused look. Joshua's nodded as he looked down at Heather's still sleeping form resting in his arms before moving toward the stairs to carry her upstairs.

Marcus gently shook Theresa, waking her, and smiled as she rubbed her eyes and queried, "Heather?"

"She's been taken up to your room by Joshua," Tara said looking over Marcus's shoulder.

Theresa slowly stood up, still wiping the sleep from her eyes. "Oh okay," she said sleepily.

Marcus and Tara stood holding each other, watching Theresa go up to her room with the door closing behind her as she went in. The two looked at each other and nodded. "You up for a night cap, honey?" Marcus asked, smiling as he ushered his wife into the kitchen.

Theresa stepped inside the door to her room and paused, leaning back against the door she closed quietly behind her. She stood watching Joshua nudge Heather's luggage aside with his foot before gently placing Heather on the bed. Theresa moved to the bedside and pulled the luggage off the far side and slid it under the bed for the time being. Joshua slowly stepped back to stand beside Theresa, and the two stood there for a couple of minutes, blissfully watching Heather snoring away.

"I always thought she would eventually end up being my sister. I just never knew she already was." Theresa whispered thoughtfully.

"Had that much confidence we would eventually get married, did you?" Joshua asked quietly, his eyes locked upon Heather, watching her breathe gently.

"You two love each other. I never doubted it," Theresa said, smiling and throwing an arm around Joshua.

"Well, you always wanted a little sister," Joshua stated softly.

Theresa looked at him oddly then started to point at herself, then at Heather, and then at Joshua, making a disgusted look.

"Oh, that's it," Joshua said jokingly as he grabbed her in a headlock and started to muss her hair.

A couple of minutes later, Joshua stepped out of Theresa's room, waving at her as he gently closed the door and walked over to the railing and stood looking down into the living room, where he saw his parents waving him down, holding up drinks. "Want one?" Marcus asked quietly.

Joshua smiled as he descended the stairs. A vibration in his pocket gave him to know that he had just received a text. He paused on the stairs to check his phone.

"Sara safely got back to the hotel?" Tara asked. Joshua replied with a nod.

"Yeah, just now, she said to say good night," he said as he continued down the stairs, closing his phone and putting it away as he did so.

"Hell of a night," Joshua said, sighing heavily.

Marcus leaned back and put his drink down. "Tyr held a lot from us," he said thinking aloud.

"You think he didn't trust us?" Tara queried.

"Possible, Mom," Joshua replied thoughtfully. "As much as you all helped him escape, it was the humans who made and tortured him," Joshua went on, staring down into his drink before meeting his parents' questioning eyes. Some time passed before he continued.

"One minute, calm, and then the next, all drama. Well, I'm for bed. Good night," Joshua said as he got up to head off to bed.

"Joshua, what you went through when you first changed . . .," Marcus said quietly.

Joshua waved it off. "I understand why you and Mom sent me to Jack's dad when I first started to change. I was out of control. Thanks to him, I was able to join the army, like my dad before me. It's okay, Marcus, really."

Tara played with her silver earring as she watched her son go upstairs and disappear into his room. Tara looked concerned as Marcus put his arm around her. She nodded, meeting his eyes, and the two followed their son upstairs, passing their children's rooms and heading for their own.

*   *   *   *

Amber, Kala, and Thiess drove slowly into town, and the two girls in the back seat noticed he was starting to tear up. Amber leaned forward and put a hand gently on the old man's shoulder.

"Something wrong?" she asked softly.

The old man looked at her through the rear view mirror and gently patted her hand upon his shoulder with his free one.

"No, miss. I simply miss my wife. We came here long ago on our honeymoon. It's beautiful to think back but painful at the same time. In time, even good memories become painful to remember. In the center of town, there is a lone tree which we kissed under."

Kala leaned forward, suddenly interested. "You two were the ones who were the source of the name 'Kissing Tree'? Was it you two?"

Suddenly realizing what Kala was saying, Amber leaned forward in her seat, waiting eagerly for his answer.

The old man smiled as they approached the downtown area that hosted the tree.

"Who knows? Maybe if we did, it was likely a 'common' name applied by the people who lived here after we left, certainly not before. Don't you think?"

The girls, laughing, said, "Yes!" in almost perfect unison.

The car pulled up across from the Kissing Tree and nosed into a parking place in front of The Three Cs. The three exited the car, and the girls came up on both sides of the old man and helped him cross the street. It was just a bit after midnight. They all turned and made their way across the street toward the tree. As they approached the tree, the old man smiled as if he was being reunited with his wife once more, or so the girls felt as his smile grew incrementally in direct proportion to the lessening distance between them and the tree. He stopped near the tree and turned to the girls.

"I can take it from here, ladies."

The girls both smiled and started to re-cross the street when the man stopped Kala by saying.

"You couldn't even see what is to happen, could you? You are nothing like them, oh, 'special' girl."

Kala stopped dead in her tracks and turned to see the man touch the tree and close his eyes.

Suddenly, he began speaking in another language Kala could have sworn was German. *"Ich bin hier, Sohn von Anris. Nimm mich als dein Werkzeug und deine Auferstehungsmittel,"* the words went.

The old man clutched his chest and collapsed at the base of the tree. The area his palm had touched was without bark and it seeped sap the color of blood. Kala ran back to him, and Amber wheeled around and returned hurriedly to their side.

"What the hell happened?" she asked.

Kala strained to lift the old man and, with Amber assisting, finally succeeded in lifting him and helping him to return to his car.

"I don't know," Kala said. "For once, I don't know!"

*   *   *   *

A large clinic for the well-to-do on Salem Street, near Oak Pond Village, was busy with accident victims near Newbury Highway outside Fairmount. Ambulances delivered the injured to the emergency room when the girls arrived. They left the old man's car parked in the lot outside as Amber was first out of the driver's side, yelling for help. Kala got out and opened the back door in an attempt to move the unconscious man inside. A couple of nurses came hurrying up to them and began to help them when some EMTs ran to give them assistance. Kala and Amber followed them in through the emergency doors where they were stopped by the registration nurse.

"Kala? You go on ahead and answer any questions you can. I'll fill out the paperwork," Amber said, glancing up from the papers the registration nurse had given her.

Kala nodded unconsciously and followed the doctors. She answered all the questions she could, but the information she had available wasn't enough, and they asked her to remain outside as they moved him to another room. She looked around, fretting, and saw chairs along the wall nearby and took one, grabbing a magazine close to hand in an attempt to occupy her mind, all to no avail. She flipped through the magazine and threw it aside in frustration.

"I wish my sister had more of an attitude like yours," a young, red-headed girl said, smiling, her accent thick and denotes her Irish origins.

Kala looked up and saw her through her tears of frustration.

"Excuse me?" she murmured.

"Oh, I didn't mean to be intrusive," the young woman said, standing there. "Would you mind if I sat here with you?" she continued.

Kala noted the frame on the girl was small but seemed firm and well-toned. She evaluated the girl and her posture for a moment, quickly realizing that the young woman was very likely one who exercises often.

"I'm . . . I'm sorry," Kala said. "You weren't being intrusive at all. I was just preoccupied."

The red-headed girl smiled brightly, her long, braided hair fell in a single neat braid on either side of her head, as she came to sit next to Kala. "It's all right. Name's Dawveen."

Kala took her hand into her own, shook it, and was suddenly curious as her head tilted over slightly. "Huh! You're awoken."

"What?" Dawveen queried.

"Oh. Um, nothing. That was pronounced, 'Dawveen,' was it?" Kala asked. "What brings you to the States?"

The young woman leaned back, crossing her legs in a rather masculine way, as she glanced longingly down the hall. Noticing that Kala was watching her, she remarked, "My sister. Her name is Aileen, which means 'noble' in the Irish tongue. Well, we've been touring America—actually, searching for our mother. We were on our way to Indiana when suddenly, the Grey Mutt bus wrecked. We helped those we could before we were all brought here. My sister's being checked out. She had some metal stuck in her. People got worried."

Kala's mouth dropped slightly. "You weren't . . . ?"

The red-headed girl smiled wickedly. "We're fine. A stupid piece of metal stuck into one of us won't stop us for long. Nope, we're made of sterner stuff like our mother. She's a tough gal, if what we heard of her is true."

"She liked to fight, I assume?" Kala inquired, finally glad to have something to occupy her mind.

"My mom? No, not really, like Aileen she is. But when she gets mad, oh boy. I've heard stories. Hell hath no fury and all that. No, she was a lady. My sister took that from her. Me? I honed my skills so I can protect them both. I took her fighting spirit. I'll right down kill anyone who mess with 'em, I will."

Kala, not knowing how to take that declaration, only nodded.

"Ah, here she comes now," Dawveen said as she stood and sighed, seeing her sister surrounded by doctors. She was redheaded like her sister, but her features were softer. She was in a hospital gown and sitting in a wheelchair. Several doctors were in close escort, doing their best to be of assistance to the attractive young woman.

"You're twins," Kala observed.

Dawveen smirked. "In the physical sense, we are. Just wait."

The young woman smiled and waved at them. The men fawning all over her made Kala want to roll her eyes. Aileen slowly rose to her feet, with help from a couple of the doctors, and she stood there in front of her wheelchair, seemingly still a bit shaky.

"Thank you so kindly, gentlemen. I am sure I'll be fine now, and I have my sister here. Please, there are others in far greater need."

Several of the young doctors laughed a bit nervously, and bidding her good-bye, they returned to the operating room. Aileen turned toward her sister, and hugging her warmly, she nodded to Kala.

Kala studied the overly polite young woman for a long moment, then glanced back at Dawveen.

"Told ye, girlie, we a wee bit different for twins, eh?"

Kala reached out to shake her hand, but Aileen ignored the hand, and coming right up to Kala, she gave her a gentle hug that reminded Kala of her mother doing that to her as a child.

"Strange. Your soul is young, *and* old," Aileen, said looking at her curiously.

"What?" Kala said somewhat startled, but before anything more could be said, Amber came hurrying up the other hallway, waving at Kala.

"Hey, Kala! Who are your friends?" Amber asked, smiling.

"Oh, this one here is Dawveen, and this is her twin sister, Aileen," Kala responded, gesturing to the two girls.

Amber smiled as she returned Dawveen's proffered handshake, only to find herself immediately being hugged ever so gently by Aileen.

"Hi. An elderly gentleman collapsed downtown, and we brought him here so he can get some help," Amber said, smiling.

"Sis here needed a piece of metal get yanked out," Dawveen said as Aileen glared at her.

"Oh my god," Amber said. "Are you all right?"

"Had to have been this long," Dawveen interrupted her sister's response, holding her hands some four feet apart.

Kala and Amber stared at the gesture then at Aileen who was walking around like nothing was or had been wrong.

"Ah . . . um . . . they've got really good doctors here, and it wasn't really all that big," Aileen gave Dawveen another dirty look. Her sister's only response was that her grin became even wider. Aileen sighed.

"Well, we've got to be going," Amber said as she again thanked them both for keeping Kala company.

"Yes, we cannot leave until another bus arrives, so we will try to help out by comforting those we can. Thank goodness America's Halloween isn't such a holiday as not to have the buses running," Aileen said, glancing about.

Kala and Amber groaned. "Oh wow, how time flies. Is today Halloween already?"

The twins nodded, and the girls looked at each other with dour looks. "We haven't even had time to pick out a costume."

"I can go as I am. A Wiccan," Amber said, shrugging. The young women subconsciously started to rub their hands on the front part of their heads.

"Yeah," the twins said nervously.

"I have no idea what I am going as tomorrow—err—later tonight," Kala said.

"Well, don't go as an angel. It doesn't suit you," Aileen said, deep in thought.

Kala looked at Amber with wide eyes and then back to Aileen who was smiling politely, "We be needing to go."

Amber and Kala waved goodbye to the sisters and went outside, looking around and kind of sighing.

"It's late, Kala. I really don't want to call anyone. Should we just sleep in the old man's car tonight? I left his keys in the glovebox," Kala nodded, and the two started for the old car.

Within the clinic, those involved in the bus accident was being flown out via helicopter while the less injured individuals occupied the third floor. The helicopter took another two survivors into the air from off the roof, and the doctors ran back inside.

"We only have four more critical patients to remove. How much longer before the next arrival?" a doctor asked, looking over the chart.

"Another twenty minutes," the nurse said next to him. "All right, what's the condition of the patient the two girls brought in?" he asked, flipping his chart again for the elderly man's information.

"No idea how or why, but he's still in a coma. They said all he did was lean against a tree, some 'Kissing Tree,' I guess. We'll have to do some more testing on him," the nurse stated with a confused look on her face.

The doctor continued to look over the charts. "We need samples from the tree. Maybe he was in contact with some biochemical pesticides? I wonder . . .," he murmured to himself as he entered the old man's room.

In the room he shared with another badly injured accident patient, the other man's wounds were meticulously wrapped, but blood could still be seen through the bandages.

Thiess stirred under his covers as if under the effects of a fevered dream. The doctor came up and took his arm to check his heart rate and was astonished how fast it was going. He immediately hit the call button and started prepping the man for a move to the emergency room.

"We need to slow his heart rate," the doctor called out as the nurse drew a hypodermic needle from her uniform pocket and pulled its cover off, exposing the slender, silvery needle as she handed it to the doctor. The doctor turned back to his patient and leaned forward to use it when suddenly, it burst into green, sickly flames. Thiess' eyes snapped open. The old man sat up and wildly looked around.

"What the hell? Sir? You need to—" the doctor said, trying to get him to lie back down, but the old man shoved the doctor hard, launching him across the room where he slammed hard into the wall. The nurse turned to run, but the old man was suddenly in front of her, snapping her neck. He sniffed the air about him and smiled. Stepping through the door into the hall, he slowly closed the door behind him. Screams could suddenly be heard out in the hallway, causing many others to respond, adding to the symphony of screams and howls.

*　　*　　*　　*

Theresa woke up and rolled over to see her friend fast asleep. She moved, as gently as possible, to get out of bed without waking her sister. Her feet gently made contact with the soft, off-white carpet, and she glided to the closet, trying very hard not to giggle.

"I've got to get used to these changes. I'm so quiet now," she said to herself, dressing hurriedly. She stepped out into the hall to the smell of breakfast being served, inhaling gratefully. She leaned over the railing to look down into the living room that lay directly below. She could hear Marcus and Tara in the kitchen, making breakfast. Tara asked something Theresa didn't catch, to Joshua and John who was in his Malamute form who were down below in the living room. The two brothers seemed to be staring at each other rather intently. She tilted her head with a trace of confusion, and then it dawned on her. "Oh, of course, they're conversing by Rynspeak. Duh."

She started down the stairs, and John, detecting her presence, suddenly moved into the kitchen to eat the breakfast set out for him on a plate on the floor.

She came around the post at the bottom of the stairs and joined Joshua on the couch, plopping down next to him ungraciously.

"What's the matter with John?" she asked, looking off into the kitchen.

"Oh ah, I was teaching him a new trick. John why don't you show her what I taught you to do?" he asked, giving a look at his younger half-brother.

John nonchalantly turned and came up to Theresa. He sat on his haunches and simply stared at her a moment.

"I was told I could give you a gift of sorts, as long as you're willing, of course."

Theresa flashed a glance at Joshua. He smiled and nodded at her, and she turned toward John smiling warmly in return. Joshua lowered his head, and black flames started to flow and flicker on his form. However, the moment the flames touched Theresa, she panicked and recoiled, and the flames instantly dissipated.

John shook his head and turned toward Joshua. "See? *What I have for her, she doesn't want. Satisfied?"*

Joshua, Marcus, and Tara watched John head toward the door, where he paused, glancing, and sighed. He turned and walked up the stairs, retreating to Joshua's room.

"I don't want? What is it I don't want again?" Theresa asked in confusion.

Tara came and set the plates down at the kitchen counter. "Pull up a stool, you two. Breakfast is ready."

Joshua and Theresa joined Marcus and Tara at the counter and started to eat in silence.

After a while, Theresa repeated her former question, to which Joshua responded, "He wanted to mark you like I did to Heather."

"You gave her a tattoo," Theresa said before they heard a cough, and they looked up to see Heather waving at them.

"Theresa, you are so damn dense sometimes," Heather said as she smiled at Joshua. Still in her pajamas, she lifted her arms into the air and lowered them over herself in a gesture like a magician, and suddenly, a black dress with a hood formed around her body as her PJs dropped to the floor. An aura or mist floated and dissipated into the air around her, and she started to descend the stairway and headed for the kitchen.

"You gave her your power," Theresa said, her mouth agape.

Joshua waved her thoughts away. "Seems that if both parties trust and love each other enough? I can impart her with a gift of sorts."

Theresa stood and started walking away. The group looked perplexed as she started to head for the door. "Theresa," Heather said softly as she passed her, briefly touching the black gown she wore. Theresa looked into the dark cowl and saw Heather's eyes glowing with a gold like radiance within.

"You look cool, sis, but me and John? I know how he feels. But my feelings aren't like a switch, no matter how he feels about me. I feel for him. I feel strongly, but that doesn't mean we are meant for each other like some fairy tale."

Heather started to say something but only watched as Theresa walked out the door. Everyone turned toward Heather, who looked perplexed as she shrugged. Just then, John bolted out of his brother's room and left through the door. Heather watched this unfold and everyone ran up to the door and looked outside.

"*Theresa!*" John called to her openly through Rynspeak. Theresa, on the verge of tears, staggered and clutched her chest. She put a hand out as if to say, "Stop."

"*Not this time, Tee. I love you—you know this,*" John said simply.

"Does it matter how I feel?" Theresa said, turning around, and he could see the tears flowing freely down her soft cheeks.

"*If only I could hold you like a man. But I am not a man. You are not a woman despite your preferred appearance. We are separated because we both can't be what we really are. Not without becoming freak shows to most of the human world. Isn't that how you feel?*"

"No, you are a Ryn, and I am a Woryn," she said, chuckling and coughing at the same time nervously. "You know, man and woman?"

"*No, we're not. I am sorry. Regardless, you're too guarded to open your heart to me,*" John said again in open Rynspeak, and it tore her apart, hearing the truth.

"*I love you, John, but not in the way you want. I'm so sorry,*" she said, crying.

John walked up to her and nudged her leg, and she started to pet his head.

"It's okay, really. I've never loved anyone, expecting to be loved back. It's enough to know how I feel about you, regardless. It hurts, but if nothing did, I wouldn't even be alive. I would like you to trust me enough for my love to afford you some protection."

"Even if that love can't be returned," Theresa said, kneeling down and hugging him.

"Even if you hate me, let my love help you," John remarked, and suddenly, he barked aloud, his tail wagging.

"You can't do this here," she suggested, and he shook his head. "Okay, back to the house."

Everyone inside the house bolted away from the door and returned to the table, seemingly totally preoccupied with their breakfast. Theresa and John stepped inside the house and closed the door. Suddenly, a gust of wind came through the house, though all the windows were closed, and Theresa grew in stature and form. Her clothes got ripped and torn for they were too small, but she didn't care. Her arms covered her chest and her groin despite the fur being long enough to cover her in those areas. John took on his true form; his black flames danced around him and engulfed his previous form only to grow, burning nothing as he stepped out in the form of the great white Ulryn.

The flames did not die out but danced around him as if in pure joy.

Theresa in her Vulryn form came up to him, and he held her in his arms, and briefly, a mark on her forearm appeared and then changed to look like the red fur had turned black on her arm, marking it with runes.

Suddenly, she found herself briefly covered in black flames, which turned into a long black gown with a trail long enough to hide her tail. Her chest and neck was completely covered as were her arms, with long sleeves that billowed somewhat at the snug cuffs. A slit in the gown allowed for freedom of movement, and a tiara formed over her head. She glanced at her dress and glanced up at the tiara and smiled.

"A bit over the top, don't you think?" she asked in Rynspeak, gesturing up at the tiara. John stared at her for a moment, seemingly perplexed.

"I thought the dress up, but I didn't add the tiara. I have no idea why it appeared."

The entire scene was interrupted by Joshua's ringing phone. He lifted his phone and swallowed hard before answering.

"Yeah, what is it Sara?" The family looked on as Joshua's face contorted and then became very serious.

"I've got to go," he said as he put down his fork and started for the door.

"What is it, honey?" Tara called out as he passed by John and Theresa.

"Sara said to meet her at the hospital. A hostage situation." he yelled as he left through the door. A gesture from Theresa sent a gust of wind, closing it behind him.

Everyone sat quietly, looking at the closed door, hoping everything would turn out okay. "I am sure he will be fine. He's Josh," Marcus said holding his wife close to comfort her.

Chapter Nine

OBEY

Joshua and Sara responded to an assist with a hostage situation located at the Oak Clinic, southeast of Fairmount, near Oak Pond Village. They came up to the circular drive leading to the clinic, only to see several police vehicles already on the scene. They were, however, all unoccupied.

"What the hell happened here?" Sara whispered as they drew close to the medical facility. The bright light of this Halloween day glared off the pale stone walls and the grounds surrounded by trees nearly as dead-looking as the scene before them. The windows of the three-story clinic were dark and the grounds seemingly abandoned.

Their SUV drew up to the scene, and they cautiously came to a stop near the gate where a sniper could not get a clear line of sight, just in case.

"This is crazy, Josh. The vehicles are abandoned, and there is a lot of blood and broken windows, but no bodies. None."

Joshua assessed the situation and nodded. "Agreed. Something is wrong. You circle around and see what you can find. Join me at the entrance when you're done checking out the perimeter."

Sara started to move and then stopped to look back at him. "What are you going to do?"

Joshua's eyes glared menacingly at the front doors. "I'll be going up to the clinic to say hi."

Sara started to reach out to prevent his departure, but he had already walked out into the open, and she did not dare be seen.

Joshua walked out onto the pavement leading to the circular drive that circled around to the clinic's front doors. His hands were held well over his head the entire time. "I am Special Operative, Joshua King, of the Special Investigations Unit, here to negotiate the release of the hostages."

There was nothing but silence as he stood clearly in view. He wondered if he was going to be shot when two additional police units drove and came to a stop near him. He looked back and forth at the both of them as they parked to block the entrance and cover Joshua.

"All of you, stay back. SIU, operating on Federal authority," he ordered, and the men complied but continued to watch the situation closely. He continued to walk up and repeated his attempt at negotiations, but no one responded.

Joshua moved around the circular drive, drawing closer to the darkened front doors of the clinic, as the newly arrived officers swiftly moved up to positions sheltered by the cars left behind by their previous occupants.

Suddenly, a head popped out, and it was Amber. "Get the hell out of here, Josh! We can't leave! You are all going to die!"

Joshua glanced up and saw Amber. His mouth slightly agape, he kept glancing at the front doors with his hands still raised and the window which Amber, seeming in total panic, had yelled out of.

The doors burst open, and the cops trained their guns on the entrance. Joshua could hear the sounds of large growling creatures still lurking in the darkness.

"All of you back off. Now, RUN!" he yelled as three infected werewolves burst out of the doors into the bright light of day and charged at Joshua. The cops opened fire but to no avail as two ran right past them, while a third tackled Joshua to the ground. Wrenching off his silver ring, Josh threw it violently away and staggered, irresistibly, to his feet.

The two others charged into the cars, knocking the men on their backs after being hit by the abandoned vehicles. One beast leapt onto the car—its mouth slathering seemingly with delight when a roar came from behind them, and a body of their dead companion came at them both. The bottom half of their companion hit the one on the right, and the upper half slammed into the one on the left. The two officers took advantage, yelling to each other and cursing as they attempted to unload their guns into the beasts as they struggled to throw the partial corpses of their fellows off of them; using their bodies as shields in the process.

They fired repeatedly but again to no avail as the creatures freed themselves and turned to them just as the one on the left had his skull grabbed and crushed, gore seeping out of its ears. The grateful officer looked up to see his savior, only to find another of the beasts standing over them, black as night. He struggled to put new clip into his gun as it leaped away from him and to the other car. The dark beast crushed the shoulder of the other cop as his companion started to fire to no avail. The infected opened its maw to bite his prey when Joshua, in his infected form himself, grabbed the other one. He lifted it into the air and threw it at its recovering ally who was regenerating its damaged head.

The two beasts tumbled amid one-half of their companions to turn toward the larger, more fearsome black beast. With slick black fur and elongated ears, he stood atop the cars and howled at them. The beasts groveled before him, whining and whimpering. The two officers slowly stood as their beastly ally held them back.

"What the hell are you?" one of the officers asked, helping his partner up.

"*They have a master somewhere, and I am your ally. SO RUN. NOW!*" Joshua said in Rynspeak.

The officers, never having been communicated with in such a fashion, were much shaken, as would be anyone who was not used to Rynspeak. The feelings conveyed were very strong. They felt his fear and anxiousness. They also knew from this that he was not like the other beasts, and they felt he was trying to protect them. The officers immediately started to run, only to find his fellow officer to instantly burst into sickly green flames. As the other looked in horror as their friend instantly disappeared in those sickly flames, Joshua turned and just brought up his Umbrage to protect himself from instantly being devoured by the far stronger green flames.

"*Obey.*"

Joshua felt a rage and hatred he had rarely known and was overwhelmed with a sense of bloodlust. What was worse is the other officer also doubled over. However, he was malformed and crazed. He tried haplessly to find Sara, but his mangled, deformed leg kept him from giving chase, and suddenly the poor creature burst into green flames. Sara's eyes grew wide in horror as she remained hidden.

Joshua was trying his very best to fight his instincts as a lone figure walked out, slightly limping. The old man started to walk toward Joshua. His instincts made him want to obey, to kneel and follow the old man's orders, and did just that. He was kneeling before the old man walking toward him.

Joshua could see the old man's silver eyes gleaming with power as he approached. The old man came up to the kneeling Joshua and sniffed the air, sneering.

"Despite your control of the Umbrage you're just a pathetic infected human. Kill those within. Suffer, knowing you killed them, and die. I will handle the rest of mankind," he said, smiling, and started laughing and coughing while he limped to his car, the door on the vehicle still open.

Joshua bowed his head and watched the old man leave. He turned, and slowly making his way inside, he sneered toward the window where Amber appeared, his mouth slavering. He walked inside and saw the clinic crawling with some fully infected but mostly disfigured humanoid Ulryns in various states of being. They all gave way, and he could hear human movements on the upper floors above, but just then, he heard Sara.

"*Joshua? Joshua, what the hell is going on with you?*" Sara asked in Rynspeak; still being connected to their mutual link. Joshua suddenly doubled over, and those near him looked on in confusion, but not for long as Josh opened his maw and bit his own hand off! He spat it in the face of one of the fully infected and then roared in defiance, finally breaking free of Thiess' control as his hand regenerated via a brief showing of mists healing his stump.

The entire hallway suddenly became engulfed in a black, misty fog, and the growls, whines, and roars from the other infected just as suddenly ceased. One such beast tried to escape but was engulfed, his fingers clawing the ground and pulling itself forward without the rest of its body. It tried to regenerate itself, but slowly, it withered and turned gray before becoming like ash. A pair of silver eyes could be seen within the depths of the ebony mists moving along the hallway. He walked among them, the more deformed making way for him, while the fully infected made a futile gesture of defiance.

Joshua ascended the stairs. Every creature that dared attack him met a quick and final death before his Umbrage. An infected leapt at him and a wave of his hand, the creature would become like the black mist itself and dissipate. He rounded yet another flight of stairs to see a disfigured infected trying to attack him, but its legs were horridly disfigured, its face was twisted, and its mouth was partially sealed shut with its own flesh. Joshua knelt as it feebly reached out, and Joshua's eyes went from cold to mournful. He caressed the pathetic creature and touched the beast's head. The mist quickly devoured the pitiful creature so it wouldn't suffer. He stood and looked above to his destination. A door barred him from the third floor, and he extended his mist and instantly removed the obstacle, only to find yet another normal infected launch itself at him. Josh grabbed its head and slammed it across the hallway and watch as it erupted into a black mist disappearing from Joshua's silvery sight. His eyes turned to his right to see a spectacle.

Down the hall, a young redheaded female was beating on a fully infected with a broken chair leg, stabbing it repeatedly until it turned to ash from being starved to death after repeatedly trying to heal. She was wounded. Her right arm was limp, and she gasped as more started coming toward her. The ground was littered with the corpses of men, women, and wildlife—corpses of two bears and a deer piled by the entrance to the red-haired girl's room.

"Ya gotta be kidding me." She panted, and bracing herself, she threw the broken chair leg away. "Bring it on, ya bastards," she cried out when suddenly, a voice spoke inside her head. A feeling of compassion and authority was felt throughout her body as the voice said, "*Inside the door, NOW!*"

She leapt back into the room as a black mist devoured the infected and the door sticking out into the hallway. Everything it touched also became a black mist, and just as suddenly as it came, it went, leaving nothing in its wake.

"What just happened?" the young redheaded woman asked from where she lay sprawled on the floor, her eyes flicking about, looking at what the black mist had done to her enemies. She leaped quickly to her feet, wincing in pain as she clutched at her right arm. She stepped cautiously out the door and looked to the left, down the long corridor to see a large, black infected walking toward her. Her violet eyes went wide in shock, and she looked back into the room and then back at the huge beast walking calmly toward her.

"Run, all of you!" she cried out as she charged at Joshua. He watched as she ran only toward him and saw another redhead, a twin, ushering two other girls away from him, one of them he knew all too well.

"*Amber!*" he said in open Rynspeak, open to all within range to hear.

The one escorting them stopped dead in her tracks, causing the other two girls to collide with her. The one closest to Joshua suddenly slipped and fell on her injured shoulder, crying out in pain. He knelt down and offered her a hand. The young woman simply stared back up at him in complete shock.

Slowly and gently, he lifted her, much to her surprise.

"Was that your voice in my mind? It was commanding but gentle, sort of soft, and . . . and hard at the same time. It was an odd sensation, it was."

"Yes. I came here to investigate, only to find there was a lot more than a simple hostage situation. Hold on," he said in Rynspeak as he went silent for a moment. He saw Kala, who he remembered seeing before even if he did not know her personally, and Amber running toward him.

"I knew it. First, a powerful, horned Baphomet-like creature and his satyr son, and now, a mist wielding werewolf. I just knew something was screwy with our town," Kala spoke as if she'd known about the strange creatures all along.

"Joshua!" Amber said, wide-eyed, her mouth agape and still partially in shock. Dried tears decorated her cheeks.

He simply stared at her a moment before he seemed to come back to the here and now. *"I need to clear a path for Sara to join us. You must return inside and wait for our return."*

The two Irish girls started to move the wide-eyed girls back into their room, making sure not to look inside the rooms where bodies and remnants of staff and patients lay about in various states of dismemberment from being fed on by those rampaging throughout the complex.

*   *   *   *

Sara heard the gunfire out front but had suddenly lost Joshua's thoughts. She tried to contact him, but his mind seemed to be fogged. It was hard to feel his presence. She peered inside through an emergency exit. Out back and through the darkness, she could barely make out the many disfigured infected. Having already placed a clip of .22 silver rounds into her gun reserved for Joshua, she started wounding the malformed infected to take them out of the fight. They roared in pain as they fell, unable to regenerate, and she discovered the malformed were not particularly life threatening—pitiful, even, in some cases. She stepped over them, continuing to circle the perimeter as she called out to him with Rynspeak.

"Joshua? Joshua, what the hell is going on with you?" she whispered into his mind's ear, and suddenly, his mind broke free. He was sharp, clear, and furious. The roars of defiance from the infected died

down almost immediately inside, and she could hear them whining and fleeing. Some rounded the corner, and she wounded them with nonfatal shots that grounded them. However, her actions were pointless as she saw Joshua walk past a large group of them as his mist brought death to anyone he came across. Sara had to withdraw as many infected in various states fled from Joshua's presence, and she hid in a room several hallways from him to get out of the infected ones' path.

She remained silent as many of them passed her without notice, but with no small amount of time, some fled slower and then remained in the hallways, they themselves feeling safe from the wrath of the great beast that had slain their comrades. She rested against the door to her room, but she slipped, and her heel caused a clicking sound that attracted them to her. She called out to Joshua in Rynspeak.

"Josh, help!"

The door was suddenly being beaten on, and she tried her best to keep it closed, but in less time than she had hoped, she was overpowered and thrown aside as a fully infected Ulryn burst into the room. The creature was salivating and walking menacingly toward her when a large black clawed hand palmed the beast's head, and suddenly, it became as the black mist itself. As it burst into mist, the black fog avoided Sara unnaturally, never touching her.

Then Joshua's large infected Ulryn form towered over her, and he reached down to take her hand. Sweating profusely, she took his hand, and he helped her stand. Already diminutive by most people's standards, she seemed really quite tiny by comparison.

"What's going on here, Josh? Has someone infected all these people?" she asked as she looked into the deep, darkened halls of the hospital, the only real light coming from the window behind her inside the room.

The light radiated off his black coat and his gleaming silver eyes as he glanced down at her for a moment before following her line of sight out of the room. *"I wish I could have said this was impossible."*

She reloaded her .22-caliber pistol with additional silver rounds, and pulling out a small flashlight, she held it, and the gun away from her as the light penetrated the darkness beyond.

The two made their way out into the darkness, and with purpose, Joshua started for the stairwell.

"*Did you find any survivors?*" Sara asked, meekly fearing the answer.

Joshua nodded as they started to ascend the stairwell. "Amber and Kala are here for some reason. I also found two Irish girls— twins, it seems. From what Kala was saying, they are here in this country looking for their mother when their bus got into an accident. The older of the two was injured, helping those from the bus and was being treated here."

"All these infected and now this. How do you assess them?" she questioned him as they passed the second-floor door.

"*They were attacked. Wounded. Not likely part of this. However, to have them survive this long and live? Are they simply this lucky? Premonitions, maybe?*" he said in thought as they closed on the third-floor door.

"Right. Well, we can ask what happened in detail when we get to them."

"*We are almost to them. They are around the corner,*" he said as they opened the door and set off toward the room where they had held off the beasts earlier.

The two continued toward the room. Here, a dim light spilled slightly into the hallway, marking the entrance in the darkness, which would have been invisible with only the light from the flashlight. They rounded the doorway, and inside, Sara saw one of the twins being tended by the other, wrapping her arm in a bandage that was apparently bleeding on the bedding. Amber and Kala were on the other side of the bed holding her hand. Amber saw Joshua and Sara come into the room, and the moment she saw Sara she almost fainted in relief. Kala marveled at Joshua as he reentered the room.

"Oh, thank God!" Amber said a bit too loudly as she ran up to Sara and hugged her. Her body shook violently in Sara's arms. Sara looked down at Amber and could see that everything that had happened to Amber had left her very stressed. Kala seemed rather comfortable for someone who was nearly killed by monsters, not to mention for a normal human in such a situation.

"You're taking all this well, considering the current situation, Kala," Sara said wary of the girl.

Kala smiled brightly. "They are a lot like Jack and his father, DeSantos. They risked their lives for us. Amber is just not used to myths being real, that's all."

"*You know DeSantos? That Jack is his son? What happened here?*" Joshua asked, concern very apparent as he walked over toward the two Irish girls to avoid being too close to the nerve-wracked Amber. Kala smiled, sensing his feelings, while Amber, not being used to being around such creatures and cringed into Sara's arms, who held her tightly.

The elder of the two sisters had fallen asleep while she was still being held by the younger sister. Her sibling yawned and raised her hand.

"Maybe I should explain what happened?"

*   *   *   *

A couple of hours earlier

"What is going on out there?" Dawveen said, looking out into the hallway, watching doctors and nurses heading down while some were screaming and heading for the stairwell.

Aileen came up to her sister, trying to look over her shoulder, but her sister gently pushed her back. "You just got out of surgery. You won't be getting any better until we get to the trees. The drugs need to be out of your system. You know they affect our kind."

They heard more screaming, and Dawveen closed the door and started to look for a means to lock it off. "If it was only made of real wood. Damn fake wooden doors!"

She finally found a mop and used it to help bar the door. "Aileen, what's going on?"

Aileen, wincing in pain, knelt to the ground and touched the floor. "You know I can't *read*. Not in this condition."

"Just try and give me a heads-up," Dawveen said as she put her back against the door, trying her best to ignore the screams mixed with some very animalistic roars.

"Oh no," Aileen said, slumping down and holding her side with a look of complete shock on her face.

"Aileen . . ."

Aileen looked up, tears in her face. "I . . . I don't know what has started this, but random humans are turning into deformed or fully formed werewolves!"

"You got to be kidding? Hawt, goat, damny-damn," Dawveen cursed as she looked back, wondering what was outside the door.

"We need to be silent," Aileen said, whispering. Her sister looked frantically back at the door, and Aileen nodded. "Yeah, yeah, I can do that. The blood I'm smelling is suffocating. They won't be able to smell living ones, but if they get close, they could surely hear our breathing. We are limited on what we can do. Damn it!"

Dawveen took a deep breath before continuing, "Okay. We need to leave and be hitting the trees nearby. I need to if I am going to protect you. Ya understand, right?" Dawveen was begging her.

Aileen nodded. "I understand. I will ride on your back, but be careful. I am a bit fragile right now," Aileen replied.

The two young women stood up and walked to the window and peered outside. Dawn was nearly upon them. If they did not leave soon, they could be seen.

"Ready, sis," she whispered, looking out into the parking lot and the circle drive that had the front gates and freedom.

"Always with you by my side, Dawveen of Glaistig," Aileen said, smiling.

The two girls opened the window and peered out from the third floor. Before them lay the parking lot, the circle drive, and beyond that, the front gates. The two took the sheets from Aileen's bed and the empty bed next to her, and they created a cloth rope that almost reached the ground floor outside. Dawveen ripped out the screen, wincing with the noise it created. Tossing the lengthy rope, she climbed out and flipped around so her sister could safely climb on her. They started to slowly descend when suddenly, Dawveen cursed under her breath.

"Dawveen?" Aileen asked as they almost reached the ground.

"Could you just overlook this one time, sis? We are in a bad spot," she mumbled.

"People alive nearby?" Aileen asked in her sister's ear, whispering.

They reached the ground, and Dawveen let her sister off her back, who winced in pain at the effort.

"Ow. Yeah. Weird, though." Aileen gripped her sister's hand tighter. "There may be two?"

"There is a girl near us," Aileen said, focused on the person in danger.

"All of us will be found either way once we leave here, so we escape and leave them to their fate, or we can attempt to save them and place ourselves at risk."

Aileen smiled, remembering an MMO game her sister used to play that would make her relax. "So what is the percentage chance of surviving? Do we Lenna this?"

"They are in that old boat of a car over there. Asleep, if you can believe it. They will wake up when we cause a ruckus, and then we live because they become a distraction."

Dawveen slapped her forehead, starting to shake off her fatigue. "You save them after I figure out something."

Aileen and her sister ran to nearby trees and stopped briefly before running to another tree and then once more before crossing the pavement to the lone car where the two girls were fast asleep.

Dawveen followed her sister to each tree, looking back to make sure they weren't seen. Dawveen started to sweat as anxiety started to grip her heart, unlike her sister who seemed completely unfazed despite the injury. It was then they could hear two deformed werewolves inside heading for the front doors of the clinic. Aileen started to run for the car, while Dawveen started for the door, crying out a quote from that same MMO game, "Let's do this! Lenna Jerky!" Dawveen rounded to the front doors, yanking them open as two infected werewolves came running full tilt toward her.

"This is Sparring!" she roared as she kicked the doors right into the infected ones that were struck with flying steel and glass, wounding them both severely, even as she quoted the movie exclamation. One of their necks broke instantly upon impact with the door as it gave, but her heel did not. One started roaring in pain, thrashing about on the ground until she kicked it away. Suddenly, the entire clinic went dark.

Aileen ran up to the car and opened the door, and she stirred the sleeping black girl first. The young girl remained asleep as if unconscious for some reason.

"Why won't you wake?" she asked curiously.

"Question is, how the hell do I get you two and ourselves out of here alive?" Aileen asked, looking up. Her eyes widened in horror upon seeing her sister desperately fighting off the two infected werewolves.

Aileen grabbed the two in the car and yanked them from the car.

"No time to explain. We need to return to the room if we want to live!" Aileen exclaimed as she grabbed Dawveen's hand, and the two of them, carrying the girls, made a break for the clinic wall. Aileen was groggy at first, but seeing Dawveen glancing fearfully back over her shoulder gave her the incentive to remain focused on their objective despite her injuries.

Dawveen was engaged with the two werewolves and seemed to be losing ground.

Aileen screamed in terror, which arrested the attention of the two infected beasts and brought them around to face the three.

"Damn it, girl!" Dawveen exclaimed as she punched one beast in the face and gripped the other in the groin area and squeezed hard. The one fell instantly, roaring in pain, while the other took the opportunity to clamp its maw into Dawveen's right arm.

"You want my arm? Have it, ya mutt," she said as she shoved her arm deep into its mouth, forcing it to let go or choke. Pulling her arm free, she ran toward a healthy tree and around to its far side as the beast she'd just broken free of charged at her again. The huge tree stood between her and the beast and in its frenzied state ran straight into the tree, slamming into it with incredible force. The snarling creature rebounded back into a car, smashing its head and one shoulder. It lay jerking and quivering as it tried to reform, a terrible task to attempt with a crushed brain. Dawveen grinned cruelly and ran for the bedsheet rope.

Dawveen smiled seeing her sister and the two girls make it to their room, and she grabbed on with both hands and started to ascend when her foot was grabbed by the second infected beast that had managed to heal itself but was starting to go raving mad from the hunger induced by its healing. He started to thrash her about while she hung on for dear life. The sun was just rising above the gap in the hills beyond as she yelped in pain. Her right shoulder crashed into the wall, injuring the limb, although not totally disabling it. She clung to the bedsheet rope for dear life as her sister stuck her head out of the window overhead. Suddenly, the infected beast, roaring in frustration as it released Dawveen, fell into the bushes.

"Give me both your hands, Dawv," Aileen cried out, reaching down for her sister. Her sister glanced at her injured arm then back up at her, a "duh" look contorting her face. Aileen gasped as she took her sister's other hand and pulled her up and inside. The two looked out of the window down on the ground. The creature wailed in pain and in hunger, twisting and flinging itself about the ground as it slowly starved itself to death, trying to heal from all the new wounds. Slowly, it became thinner and then stopped moving all together, its body turning gray as ash before falling apart into a pile of dust. The twins collapsed against the wall below the window and tried to catch their breath as they noticed that the black girl was starting to wake up and feebly trying to comfort her companion. Amber was starting to hyperventilate as she stood outside the room, seeing the dead bodies everywhere.

Aileen threw a worried glance toward the door, her eyes then flicking back to the girl comforting her friend.

"She must calm her down, or they will know where we are," Aileen said quietly to Kala. "My sister and I need to rest a bit."

Kala, frantically trying to wake herself up as she tried to calm Amber, nodded. "I know, I know! I'm trying, but she is freaking the hell out."

"I'll calm her arse," Dawveen threatened.

"Her name is Amber. I'm Kala . . . nice to meet you too," Kala stated glaring at Dawveen as she clamped a hand over her friend's mouth as best she could.

"If ye like a fight, I'll oblige ya," Dawveen said, rising to her feet.

Amber saw her standing and started to scream as Kala covered her mouth. "Amber, calm down. Calm down!"

Amber's eyes widened in absolute terror, and then suddenly, they looked tired as she slumped over, having passed out.

Dawveen sneered. "Oh, for Bog's sake!" she exclaimed, and their little refuge suddenly went silent. A moment later, they heard a door open out in the hall somewhere. Kala, Dawveen, and Aileen could only wait with bated breath for the potential threat to pass.

Dawveen paused in her reminiscence and stared off into space for several long seconds, and then her eyes flicked over to Joshua again, and she continued, "As you can see, we were shortly thereafter discovered, and I fought them off for what seems like eternity before your arrival," Moving a lock of hair out of her sister's face during which Aileen slept soundly by her sister's side.

Sara excused her and Joshua a moment and started to stare at each other off and on. Kala, watching them curiously, tilted her head slightly and then murmured, "Ah, the telepathy Alejandro and I shared!"

"*Okay, their story seems more than a little off,*" Sara surmised in Rynspeak.

"*She's a bad storyteller. The dead trees outside? The dead animals strewn about outside their door but unexplained, or the fact they referred to 'our kind'?*" Joshua asked indignantly.

"*They saved the girls, and if we start a confrontation right now, we could endanger them,*" Sara mused, glancing at the twins and then at Amber and Kala.

"*Right. What would anyone like me say to humans, not to mention law enforcements? Too many horror movies of what governments do to aliens and the like.*"

"Amber woke up, and I got her calmed down some, but it really was too late. You know her. Can you talk to her?" Kala asked, interrupting them while eyeing Amber who clung to Sara like a security blanket. Joshua turned to look directly at her, and she cringed before him, shivering.

"*I do not see how I can be of any help like this,*" Joshua said, shaking his head. "*I would need to revert back, and with my spare clothing down in Sara's SUV, not to mention the fact that we might still be in jeopardy, I cannot afford to do so . . . not even to comfort her,*" Joshua said, finalizing his thoughts, his brow furrowed in frustration. "Amber will have to deal with it until we get outside. After that, you can change and maybe talk to her. Perhaps you three should follow along behind Joshua, Amber, and me," Sara said as she led Amber out the door. The twins gave them a ten-second head start before following, ensuring Amber some piece of mind and their own close proximity should the three come under attack again.

"I have no idea what happened here, but my sister and I need to resume our search for our mother," Aileen said regretfully. "I do not see any real reason to hanging around here," she said, continuing to making their way toward the parking lot. Joshua moved past her and her sister following the girls. Helping Kala, the twins followed Joshua through the door.

Joshua glanced both ways, his silver eyes seeing quite well in the darkness. "With all that is going on, I cannot take the time to detain you. So yes, you can go."

"We're sorry for all that happened," Dawveen said as Aileen continued to coddle her, which irritated Dawveen to no end.

"I believe your story. There is no reason to apologize. You two saved our friends' lives. Thank you, Cynryns," Joshua stated as if that should have settled things.

The girls looked at each other, and Aileen started to laugh. "Cynryn? Well, that is the silliest thing I ever—"

"Do you feel more at home in your own body right now than as a human? When you first became what you truly are, was it like you had amnesia and the memories of how to be what you have suddenly came to be? Like you felt you should have always known this was the real you? I never felt that. My Ulryn brother did. He and my adopted Vulryn sister explained it to me. They said they seemed to awake as if they had been asleep the whole time. That being in this form was more natural to them than being human ever was as if they lived their whole life as a lie until that waking moment."

The girls turned to each other and seemed to share unspoken thoughts between them.

"So we are not human. Cynryn? Is that what our people are called?"

"From what I've been told, that's what you are. We are children of the Ryn, an spirit race of some kind, apparently. You are what's called half-born, or Aluryn. I also assumed you are wearing contacts. I've no idea what Cynryn means, but Ryn apparently means spirit, so you would be like the spirit of a Cyn, whatever that means."

"I have a feeling it means something like pestilence!" Aileen blurted out without meaning to.

"So you are infected. What does it mean, 'infected'?" Dawveen asked as they entered the door to the stairwell and started for the ground floor.

"My mother and I are both infected Ulryn. What Ulryn would mean, I wonder." Joshua glanced down, fearing the answer he already felt deep inside.

"Death!" Aileen blurted out, again without thinking.

Dawveen glanced at her sister, her attitude one of scoffing. "Yer saying we are descendants from the four horsemen of the bible?"

"*Savryn*," Joshua said in Rynspeak expecting the sister to respond, knowing full well exactly what they would fit in as among the horsemen.

"*Famine*," Aileen stated flatly as her sister shook her head.

Dawveen looked between the two, guessing what they were saying in Rynspeak. "Ya two be nuts as a hatter, you are."

"But that cannot be true. If so, we are missing a child of the Ryn," Joshua said as they exited onto the ground floor door and started to make their way to the entrance.

"War," Aileen said, agreeing.

"Where are you pullin' this from, Ali?" Dawveen asked, stepping out the ruined entrance seeing Kala, Sara, and Amber heading for the SUV.

"I see the past, right? The names triggered a response, is all," she said, looking up at Joshua who stood towering over her and thinking to herself that if anyone could represent death itself, it would be this infected Ulryn.

"Okay, okay, how are we pestilence?" the doubting sister asked with her hands on her hips.

"*Touch a tree, heal yourself*," Joshua said in Rynspeak.

Dawveen scoffed, and then her face became rigid, and she suddenly felt frightened, her face a picture of fear. She glanced at a nearby tree and touched it. As her injured arm healed, the tree withered.

"That proves nothing," she said, her eyes growing wide as the rising sun was blotted out by a swirling mass of darkness heading for them. She turned to her sister in rage. "What are you doin'?"

Her sister stood calmly, her eyes closed, her arm extended, and her palm open. Large swarms of various insects heeded her call and came swirling to them!

"Bugs are disgusting, and I never thought controlling animals was all that useful in the city. But insects survive everywhere . . . *are* everywhere. When amassed throughout history, they always preceded a breakout of disease or pestilence!"

Joshua nodded and walked out among the swarm, extending his arm out into it, feeling the thousands and thousands of insects flying around and past his arm, not to mention those upon the ground that came out of the woods, blackening the ground.

"*Will you two stay and help find this murderer?*" Joshua asked simply, his arm still within the swarm.

Suddenly, the swarm attacked Joshua, and even before the insects on the ground could come close to him, the airborne swarm became a black mist, and those on the ground retreated back into the woods before they too were destroyed.

Aileen waved the thought of helping away.

"Against a human opponent, we would stand a chance. However, if the person that started this is like you, what chance would we have against him, especially if he isn't, in fact, just an infected? But is this Aluryn thing like us? No. We will continue on our way to Indiana and seek out our mom. I am not risking my sister's life in this, as eager as she is to be joining you," she said, turning to Dawveen, who was angry being thus spoken for but silenced by her elder sister's stare.

Joshua glanced at his hand still extended where the swarm had been and then returned his gaze to the two Cynryn women.

"*I understand. This is not your fight. You have a future with dreams and hopes. We can deal with this matter. Go. I hope you two find your mother.*"

Aileen looked back at her angry sister who obviously wanted to help and sighed. She turned back to Joshua and took his hand into hers, shaking it.

"I'm sorry, really."

The two ran into the woods and disappeared. Joshua turned and started to head back inside. A few of the deformed still remained alive, and then there were the bodies.

"No one can know what transpired here, lest our secret is discovered." Saying this via Rynspeak to Sara, Joshua gathered his mists around him.

*   *   *   *

Early afternoon

Theresa was changing in her room, and John was in his brother's room, in his upright, white-wolf form also donning a costume, while a very anxious Heather waited down at the foot of the stairs, eager to not only see them in their costumes but also to try hers on and see what they might think.

"Will you two hurry up?" Heather called out, tapping her foot at the bottom of the stairs.

Marcus and Tara had been waiting a while and were sitting on the couch watching a movie they were streaming until the click of a door latch told them that one of the two was ready. The proud parents stood and saw Theresa walk out in a *hanbok*, the traditional dress of South Korea. The top was white and covered the top portion of a red dress under it. Its sleeves went to the wrists, and she had traditional South Korean accessories in her hair.

"You look like a belle," Heather said, smiling.

"Well at least tonight I'll be disguised like a normal human," Theresa said unhappily in response to Heather's words.

"Theresa . . .," Heather said, now much more softly.

"Tonight, we are in costume. Tonight, I am a simple Korean-American wearing a traditional *hanbok* for Halloween."

She descended the stairs, and Tara came up to her, smiling brightly.

"You look beautiful, Theresa."

Theresa forced a smile as she glanced at Heather. "Thank you, Tara. Marcus?"

Marcus walked up beside her as Heather started up the stairs.

"Honey, I never raised you to have bad taste, so how could you look anything but beautiful?"

A door opened and closed upstairs, but Theresa chose to ignore it.

"Well, sounds like John is ready. I'm sure we'll have fun," she said, smiling.

"You going to find Steve so he can be jealous of you being with John?" Tara asked seriously.

Theresa sighed. "No chance. He told me he's in love with Elizabeth. I was told what happened at the coven. I really wanted to go there someday. I hope I still can."

Tara gave Theresa a hug. "You'll find someone. I'm quite sure, Theresa. Be patient and enjoy your youth while you have it."

They all looked up, hearing the door open again, and it seemed as if Heather was struggling to pull John out of the room.

"I feel silly," they could actually hear John say from within the room, even though it sounded somewhat muffled.

Marcus came to the base of the stairs a bit in shock. "You can talk, John?"

Suddenly, John got yanked out into the hallway, exposing him to the world in his new costume. He wore a toga across the left shoulder that draped slightly down into a thick leather belt with a large red glass gem in its center. He was waving a hand in front of Heather, and they could see that he wore matching fingerless leather gloves that came up to his elbows. His long white hair had braids on the left and right side of his face that hung across his chest. His hair was touched up so it had a chic flair that covered one of his silvery-ringed eyes. A brass circlet was attached to his left arm. He moved to the top of the stairwell and started to descend. His boots had no heel nor toe tip but otherwise covered up to his knee that ended in a slight flair, looking somewhat like a half moon. As it happened, the toga had a crescent symbol, as did the back of the boots wrapped to their sides.

His leather belt had black triangles, as did his boots and toga along the fringe.

"No, but what you hear in your mind is how I wanted you to interpret how I sound." John said still in Rynspeak. "Something like changing my fur color so I'd look more like a large Malamute before. In this case, I don't move my mouth so as to look like a fancy mask, while my voice sounds like it's coming out of said mask. Tyr found out last year, and we've been playing with this for a while now. It's very tricky to get me to sound like this," John said, smiling.

Theresa looked over his barbarian getup, and giving him a once-over, she shook her head.

"Are you about ready to go out on the town?" she asked. "We shouldn't make any stops. We can just walk for a bit. Maybe hit the park then return back for this first time, okay? Let's play it safe and see how people react," Theresa said as she extended her hand. John somewhat sheepishly took her hand into his and started to head outside as Sara's SUV pulled up.

"Joshua?" he called out, seeing Sara step out, then Kala and Amber.

Theresa was a bit of confusion even among a gathering of her friends and family.

"Sara, what's up? Has something happened?" Theresa asked as Amber glanced around after being helped out of the SUV by Kala, only to see John and starts screaming.

John raised his hands and immediately ran back inside while Theresa became upset.

"Amber? What's the matter with you? Calm down!"

She started walking up to Amber angrily, and Kala stepped between them.

"She's—we've been through a lot. We can explain inside, but you need to get that big wolf-guy out of Amber's sight." Theresa's stopped dead in her tracks and turned to Sara as she came up to her. The two watched Kala move Amber toward the house, and Marcus and Tara came out to help the terrified Amber.

"Sara? What the hell happened?" Theresa asked, watching everything unfold as Amber was trying desperately to get away from their house.

"I don't know what to do with her. She knows you are different. About the wolf-guy thing, she saw Joshua's infected form. What is worse, there are a lot more of them near the town. We got to start evacuating everyone."

"What? Who? How? Half the town is out trick-or-treating," Theresa said as she waved at several kids and their parents moving along the street, doing just that.

"Damn it, anyway," Theresa continued giving voice to her thoughts. "Why did they ever have to start trick-or-treating so early when night would work so much better, like it used to be with my foster parents?"

The group moved back inside, and Tara closed the door. Inside, they could see Amber finally fell asleep on the couch, although it seemed she is having a bit of a nightmare as she gestured and mumbled, "Werewolves," over and over.

Tara joined the group in the living room and threw her hands out toward Sara as if expecting her to start explaining. Marcus lowered his phone and shook his head, "No one is answering at the police station."

"Ma'am, with all due respect, we never saw this coming. The entire clinic outside town was filled with infected and malformed variations of an infected Ulryn type. A lot of them were nearly helpless. I saved as many as I could, shooting them with silver to keep them from starving themselves to death or invoke any powers, although that wasn't likely."

Tara grabbed Sara and shook her.

"My SON! Where is my son?"

Sara broke free of Tara's grasp and stared her down.

"Josh is just fine. He saved everyone there nearly single-handedly. But police officers may have seen what happened, and what's worse is they may have seen Joshua. I'm not all that sure myself."

Marcus sat down, completely taken aback by this new information.

"We need Lorelabs to make some calls and explain the clinic was doing illegal genetic experiments. We got to fabricate a story before this goes out over the web. If this gets out, everyone and their senator's representative will be out here, sniffing around for information and most likely turning whatever is being done here into a damn living weapon's project."

"What is being done now," Tara asked, hardly relieved her son was alone in his fight.

"He is still there with two Cynryn girls," Sara said. "I'm sure they're cleaning up the mess even as we speak."

Marcus nodded. "His Umbrage will make quick work of the remnants. But what is this about two Cynryn girls?"

Sara came up for air. "I didn't cleanly take them down, so he can just kill them."

Marcus was firm in his resolve. "If they live, this could spill over to Josh and John. You want them taken to be used for experiments? Josh knew what had to be done and sent you on so he could do that grim task in peace."

Sara, her hands balled into fists in frustration, stared at Marcus, who moved up close to her and hugged her, much to her surprise.

"I understand how you feel. They are someone's family, but they will be victims all over again if the government gets ahold of them. We spare them, and what their family gets is the grief, not the infection or additional families infected."

"Trust me. I think this might be all Lorelabs's fault," Marcus said solemnly.

Everyone was suddenly listening with undivided attention.

"It makes sense, really," he continued after a short pause to organize his thoughts. "Autumn returns with the leftovers calling themselves 'sons of Loki.' Their job . . . to awaken Fenrir. That much we already know. But what if the descendants of those meant to guard against this very thing helped Fenrir instead? They used his blood for over two decades before the breakout we caused, which allowed us to take over operations and stop the marketing of the still unknown drug to the public as a safe alternative to morphine among another remedies."

Marcus paused yet again, nodding slowly to no one in particular, and then continued relating his "epiphany" as it were.

"The drug's unlikely, and very secret, ingredient was Fenrir's blood drawn from the sap of the tree. In low doses, it provided, if not healing properties, at least a numbing effect for various pains. It replaced drugs meant for pain and arthritis, or really, anything related to easing the suffering of patients. I would conjecture the age group would be anyone over nineteen who has taken it for several years. They would likely become those deformed infected, while those who have taken it steadily over many years will most likely be those in their mid-twenties to thirties, and perhaps even older. These last may very well end up becoming the truly infected."

Sara stood, enraged. "You are telling me possibly every teen and child out there may have parents and older siblings who are living time bombs waiting to become monsters?"

"But what is the trigger?" Marcus murmured, trying to think what could have set it off.

Kala slowly raised her hand. Everyone turned their attention to where she was sitting on the couch, using her legs as a pillow for Amber's unconscious form.

"We found an old man outside the coven by the road. We took a ride from him. He fell down after touching the Kissing Tree," she said, her eyes looking vacantly up at the ceiling.

Theresa lifted her sleeve and moved her hand across the runes in her arm written by the Umbrage and invisible to all but the Eluryn.

"Marcus," Theresa began. "Josh and John gave me and Heather runes so when we changed forms, we could have clothing. They are only rudimentary runes, simple, really. What if the tree has far more powerful runes that bound Fenrir and were somehow damaged?"

Marcus and Tara stood. "We've seen something like runes on the Kissing Tree. You and John should go in case there is an outbreak here. We can't panic people, or we might lead them right to him. See if there is anything we can do. I'll continue to try to reach someone at the station."

*   *   *   *

Theresa opened her bedroom door to see Heather sitting on the bed beside John in his large white wolf form. "Tee, he's been saying sorry a lot in Rynspeak. He's freaked out. I think he was scared of something like this happening."

Heather stood up and walked up to Theresa. "He needs you, Tee, not me." Heather patted her sister on her shoulder before leaving the two alone. Her own room had changed a lot recently. Everything was picked up, and even the dish of colored gems was set nice on her vanity. She walked up to it and gently touched the gold and purple colored orbs on the small china dish.

"How long ago, Heather, did you supposedly die again?" Theresa asked herself. John glanced up at her a moment before slumping down on the bed, looking toward the door in silence. Theresa moved to sit down beside John and started petting behind his ears.

"You okay?" she murmured.

"*I never wanted to scare anyone. I never felt more like a monster than right now. It's a bit much for me. Sorry,*" he replied.

His feelings made her heart lurch for him. She touched her chest a moment to regain her composure and wiped the tears that had formed as a result of experiencing such raw emotion.

"You always knew who you were. I feel like I've been lied to all this time. I feel cheated out of anything even bordering on a normal life."

"*A normal life I've never gotten to experience.*" She could feel his pain and suppressed anger at the thought of never having what she'd had.

"John—" she started, but he interrupted.

"*What would have happened if I was born a human like I should have been instead of a wolf? How would have I turned out? Would I still love you as much as I do now?*"

"You'd probably have a lot more women chasing after you," she said, smiling.

"*While the one I love would have still ignored me and chased after some other guy.*"

"That's not fair, John," she responded quickly.

John rose and shook his wolf body before walking toward the closed door.

"One thing about life, which does, at least, seem to be constant. We should go. I've heard everything that's been said down there."

Theresa stood and moved over to open the door for him. He left in silence, and she followed him out the door and on out into town, both doing their best to cling to their own illusions.

* * * *

Elizabeth in her Wiccan gown and Steve dressed as a wizard were greeting kids at the café, handing out candy to them while Jack and a single maid almost literally fought to keep up with workload.

"Why the hell hasn't Amber or Kala called in if they're going to miss work?" Jack asked, exasperated by the pressure of the workload.

"I have barely started here, but when you guys introduce me to them, I am going to kick their butts," the young girl said as she broke her third plate only two hours into her shift.

"Oh man, that was a number 6 special!" Jack said, sighing heavily. "We should just shut down with so little help, Steve."

Elizabeth glanced at Steve and smiled, running into the back. His knowing smile was a bit too obvious as he glanced at her retreating form.

"I'm almost done with this batch of . . . there. Okay, back to the kitchen for me," Jack saw Steve returning to the back and cheered. "Thank God . . . man, seriously this is getting overwhelming."

Elizabeth came out from the back in her usual Wiccan attire, but atop her usual clothing, she wore a maid's uniform over it, grabbing the plates.

"Oh man, you are going to owe her big time," Jack said to Steve, who nodded in agreement.

"I think that was her plan all along," Steve said, smiling.

"You betcha," Elizabeth said as she started to hand out the food to the customers.

A bell hung near the door rang, and a customer came in limping. The old man limped to the seating and plopped down roughly as Elizabeth came over to see to his needs. As she drew near, his murderous glare caused her to balk, and she backed off immediately.

She turned away and started to smile at another customer, serving them instead.

Thiess sat quietly, looking out toward his ultimate goal. *So easy*, he thought. *Too easy*. Suffering, agonizing, and raging in helplessness. Once more, Elizabeth moved to wait on him.

"I'm sorry, sir. Do you need anything?" she asked quietly.

He glared at her with such venom, and then lunging forward, out of nowhere, he grabbed a handful of her hair.

"Does it look like I want anything but for you to die screaming human?"

Elizabeth tried to break free, screaming as she struggled to free herself but found the old man too strong. Steve leapt over the counter and rushed over, only to have Elizabeth pushed into him with such force that the two of them fell into a tangled heap upon the floor. The old man stood and smiled. "Yes, fight me. Die by these hands. Crippled though I am, I can still kill you all. You humans are such a plague to my master, to this world, to each other. You are traitors, every last one of you, cockroaches whose lives are mine to snuff out at my master's whim."

Steve disentangled himself, and Elizabeth and regained his feet. He turned to the simpering little man.

"Get out! NOW!"

"I have a better idea," he said, smiling brightly.

"*OBEY.*"

*   *   *   *

Suddenly, most of the parents in the area, inside and out, doubled over in pain. Even many of those in their twenties and thirties did so. Small children and teenagers balked and cried out to their parents, seeing them in so much pain. To the teenagers' horror, they saw their parents changing, their bodies contorting and stretching abnormally. The small children started crying on the spot, dropping their candy and some even offering their candies to their agonized parents, if only they would return to their former selves.

But humans were not the only ones. Jack started getting sick; the hatred he felt being too much for him much less the insanity that fueled it. Heather back at the Joneses' house balked, recognizing the voice, and started crying despite herself. In terror, she huddled into a corner of Theresa's room, covering her ears and rocking back and forth, saying over and over, "Not again, not again." Tara's head felt like it was exploding, and she became abnormally angry at her husband. John suddenly seemed to go berserk, flailing around and obviously was engaged in a terrible battle for his own mind. Watching him, Theresa started to feel sick.

"So much hatred. So much vile anger and disgust toward everything that exists," she murmured to herself. She saw John rolling over and over and then suddenly leaped to his feet and ran off into the nearest alley, away from the crowds and away from Theresa. She reached out to him, but the pain in her heart and head prevented her from actually going after him for several minutes, thus giving him ample time to put distance between them before she set out in pursuit.

*   *   *   *

DeSantos was still at Lorelabs when he felt the wave of anger and hatred wash over him. It came at him time and time again as he took his true form. He saw Tyr fall down as if in immense pain. He saw others of the staff starting to change in front of him. Their roaring mindless fury was all too apparent. They had no more control than a falling raindrop. He didn't bother to take the time to destroy them one by one. One of them leapt at him, only to slam down onto the floor, breaking his own neck. Those not close enough for him to kill easily, he took possession of, and they started to kill each other. Soon, bodies lay all over the place, with only Tyr gasping for breath, wheezing, and baring his teeth, while DeSantos stood over him ominously.

"Will you be okay, or do I have to end you too?" he asked calmly.

"How . . . how can you stand so . . . so much hate and anger?" Tyr asked.

DeSantos knelt down and ran his hand over the sweat-beaded forehead to the old wolf in an attempt to comfort him.

"I blamed myself. I've hated myself and was quite suicidal for a very long time. No one can hate me more than I hate myself. No one's more sorrowful that I couldn't end my own life. This pain is great, I feel it, and it's a bit greater than any I've felt for a very long time, for sure. However, it's like taking some poisons. Over time, you become resistant to it."

Slowly, DeSantos lifted Tyr and helped him toward the elevator.

"What can we do? How can we stop this from unfurling further?" Tyr asked, glancing around.

The door opened, and a deformed guard reached out, trying to claw, even kill, him. DeSantos's hoof came up kicking the guard, utterly smashing their assailant's spine. That one would die completely, long before he could ever regenerate such damage. Tyr flinched, hearing the bone crunching and crumbling under that awesome strike.

DeSantos helped him inside where he settled into a corner on the elevator's floor.

"Anything is better than doing nothing, Tyr," the bounty hunter said, watching the doors close.

*   *   *   *

Kala continued to watch over Amber as she split her focus between caring for Amber and wondering if she should do something about Tara. Kala seemed to be totally unaffected by what was affecting others.

"Mr. Jones," she called out, fear in her voice.

"Just stay there while I try to help Tara," came the response.

Tara fell over immediately, nearly vomiting from the bile clogging her throat. Marcus affected far less reached out for his wife, but she slapped his hand away.

"Get away from me! I can feel the beast rising even with my silver earrings and ring that are meant to keep me under control," Tara said desperately.

"I love you. No way in hell am I going to leave your side!" Marcus said, crawling to his wife's side where both of them shuddered in each other's arms. Marcus had started to recover from the initial wave. However, for Tara, it was an ongoing wave, coming again and again, seemingly without end. They could hear the screaming outside, and they could hear children crying for their mothers. Teens from next door could be heard yelling for their parents to come back to them, all to no avail, and the sounds of doors slamming as the older children started fleeing, some with their younger siblings in their arms.

"They've got to do something! This town is going to destroy itself!" Kala said loudly over the many cries and screams from outside.

*   *   *   *

A young girl holding onto her little brother ran into an alley and quickly stuffed him inside a trash bin. The young boy would not be quiet, however, and continued crying for his older sister. Crying, she kissed him and closed the bin. As she turned, she saw a great white beast round the corner. Saliva and drool came from its maw, and no sign of intelligence could be found in those dead silver-ringed eyes. The young girl grabbed a couple of plastic trash lids and started slamming them together, only to find out plastic made nowhere near the noise aluminum does, so she started screaming at the beast.

"Hey, stupid! Right here. Come get me. Bring it on, asshole!"

The girl turned to run, only to slam into the great white beast's knee, and she couldn't help but burst into tears, crying uncontrollably and knowing there is no escape. She raised her arms to defend herself, and suddenly, the beast roared in pain. She looked up to see an equally large black beast standing in front of her, blocking the white beast's access to her. The beast held two, large, shiny katanas.

"*Run, girl,*" came a command directly in her mind.

The girl turned to run, and then remembering her brother, she turned back to grab her sibling before fleeing down the alley.

Joshua turned to John. John stood wary of his older brother as if evaluating his opponent.

"Little bro, don't make me hurt you. I'm not going to plead with you. Wake up!"

John's blow came swift and deadly, but Joshua dodged gracefully, his right-hand katana cutting a deep slash into his arm. John wailed in pain and started to go berserk, wheeling and leaping around as though crazed, as he grabbed his arm savagely, injuring it even further and his claws digging in far too deep!

"Damn it, John. You'd better come to your senses, otherwise, you're going to be in a lot of real pain real quick. I can't hold back on you. If I figure this right, like when I was told to 'Obey,' I couldn't use my Umbrage. Looks like it takes a mind to summon and control it, not just instinct."

John started to calm down and growled low in his throat as he turned to hunker down, as if ready to pounce.

"Well," Joshua said as he steeled himself. *"This is either going to hurt you a lot more than me . . . or me a lot more than you."*

*   *   *   *

Theresa stopped in the middle of the street, realizing she had no idea where John had gone, except she knew that he had gone toward town. She did not want to change to hunt him and decided to continue in as far as the Kissing Tree, also known as Yggdrasil. As she moved toward the center of town, she saw people running away. Some were underclassmen running around looking for refuge. The older teens had gathered themselves together, and taking the younger kids, any kids, they quickly fled, seeking a refuge. She heard them saying things like they should break into the school and hold up there or perhaps the jail at the police station.

She continued to fight off the haze in her head as she walked ever closer to the tree's location. Soon in the near distance, she could see the tree, and she could also hear Elizabeth crying out, "Steve!" Theresa thought only a moment before diverting her steps toward the café.

She ran up to the large bay window and peered inside. She could see Elizabeth trying to comfort Steve who seemed to be writhing about in agony. Theresa sped to the couple's side, banging through the doors to the café, which were hanging open crazily and almost off their hinges. Elizabeth was shocked to see Theresa appear almost instantly, seemingly out of nowhere, at their side, accompanied by a strong gust of wind that seemed to actually blow Theresa into the café.

Elizabeth was nearly pushed over backward by the gust of wind that followed Theresa's arrival.

"Liz? What's the matter with him? Liz," she asked, seeing Elizabeth nearly in hysterics herself and fawning over Steve as he continued to cry out in pain.

"I . . . I don't know. He fell over just a few moments ago. Jack ran outside nearly in as much pain. I just recovered. The few in the café left just before you arrived except," at which point she glared at a lone elderly man sitting alone in a booth, "for that evil old man over there seemingly enjoying the spectacle."

Theresa stood, suddenly enraged, and stared at the old man. He sat at the table, smiling. "You have no idea how to stop me, or you would have girl. Even as an Eluryn, you have no power over even this body's Umbrage. So is the heritage that our first father had bestowed on all his descendants."

Suddenly, flames erupted from the kitchen stoves, and strong winds came about to lash out at him, only to see green eldritch flames devour her efforts. Compressed air formed, only to be consumed as it was being gathered by the same flames.

"Suffer, Vulryn," he said when suddenly, Elizabeth cried out. Theresa turned around and saw Steve start to grow and change, screaming in pain. Elizabeth could only watch in horror as she saw her beloved change into a fully infected Ulryn. His eyes started to turn crazed, and she could see he mustn't have eaten recently because his ribs were showing. He would be hungry from the change, if what Joshua had said about him changing in the past had any merit.

Theresa waved her hand over her arm, and the wind blew briefly around her, showing Theresa in her true, Vulryn form, covered in the black gown John gave her, complete with a tiara.

"Oh? The world sees your heritage and title, Kinguard, but I will never accept it. Come at me with elements or subdue my senses, and

I will kill everyone Vulryn, here and now. The master I share this body with will not allow you to interfere," Thiess said as he gingerly stood and started to hobble his way to the door. "You will be the last to die, child. If only you knew how to restrain my power as others before you could have. A pity."

"*How do you know so much about me?*" Theresa asked in Rynspeak as Elizabeth knelt in shock on the floor, too upset by the change in Steve to even notice what was going on around her.

"The two you captured. They heard many things while visiting the café. They were only to distract you from me. I guess using words like Vulryn or Ulryn in public would escape anyone's notice but not to those who knew the words of the formerly dead races of Ryn. The one thing the master could always rely on is the traitorous Savryns and humans."

"Steve?" Elizabeth almost whispered as terror seized her heart.

Theresa, eyeing her enemy, suddenly realized his injured physical form was his weak spot, but the power he wielded, was it as great as he had said? Theresa was torn between saving Elizabeth and chancing she could end it there and then.

"Steve? Please don't do this . . ."

Theresa continued to struggle, her entire body shaking with fury. All her powers, she thought, and still, she felt completely helpless. *Worthless would be a better word*, she completed the thought. She started to walk toward the door, and turning back, she saw the feral Steve fully consumed as his new form creeping toward Elizabeth. Still, even as he did so, she was struggling to bring him back, but then he leapt. Elizabeth screamed. Without thinking, Theresa reached out with her power to protect Elizabeth. A circling path of wind sharp as a razor ended Steve's life as his head flew past Elizabeth's screaming form. She cried out Steve's name yet one more time. His body dropped next to her feet, headless, and Elizabeth, enveloped in terror, cried out horribly as Steve's body was starving as it tried to rebuild its head. Unable to do so, it turned rapidly to ash before her very eyes.

Elizabeth couldn't scream anymore. She couldn't speak. The realization that Steve was actually dead shook her to the core of her being. Slowly, she crawled to the ashes and started trying to gather them all to her, the tears from her eyes breaking down the ash she desperately tried to pile up.

In front of her was the Vulryn who just killed him and saved her life. It was Theresa who had killed him; it was Theresa who had allowed this to happen. She could have stopped him and then gone after the monstrous old man. She could have restrained him. She could have done . . . something! But she didn't. She could have somehow cleanly wrapped it up all at once. She collapsed onto the floor rocking back and forth wailing, the pain she felt could be heard reverberate throughout the café.

Theresa gasped. No, that wasn't what she feared. Sheer horror griped her heart in realization. *I'm not innocent*, she thought to herself. *I'm not who I was. I'm not a normal girl. I'm not even human, not in the least.* She thought, in the back of her mind, that if he killed her, if that happened, Steve would be hers. She thought, *That must be why I struggled. I had time. I could have. I should have. But I didn't. Because I am as big a monster as the old man.*

The old man walked out into the deserted street. Nothing moved, and there was no sign of life as those still human had long fled the area. Now, only howls and screams of the injured and dying could be heard in the distance, and Theresa's cry joined them.

Thiess smiled as he continued to hobble toward the tree.

Chapter Ten

TYR'S STRATEGY

"Inside, everyone!" the teen said, ushering his fellow teenagers and children inside the doors that he and his friends just broke open. Some were crying, while others were talking both quietly and urgently.

"Shut up all of you—god!" the young man hurrying everyone inside said in exasperation. His raised voiced caused some of the smaller kids to start crying, and some of the older boys and girls clasped their hands over the children's mouths as they all entered the high school. Two sophomores remained at the door, keeping a lookout for more kids in need of help. They watched the large group that they had come in with disappear around a corner, further down the long hallway.

"What the hell is going on, Trish?" the young man said, peering out the doors as he brought some furniture to block the doors and keep the monsters at bay.

"I don't know. Mom and Dad were so scary, David." She started to tear up when he pulled her close and held her.

Shouts from outside grabbed their attention, and they peered out into the large yard and parking lot to see a fellow classmate running toward the school with two children in tow. The young man was being bared down upon by two infected Ulryn running toward them.

"Dad, Mom! It's us. Stop!" he was yelling while trying to run with his two siblings in tow. The monsters only howled in response. The young man cried as he pushed his little brother and sister ahead of him. "RUN!" he cried out as he turned to face his former parents.

The kids did the opposite and clung to him, desperately crying out, "Mom! Dad!" when one of the infected suddenly turned as something hit the back of their neck, and the teen saw a small bullet wound, and his former mother turned and started beating on his dad. "Mom," he cried out as she continued to beat on him. Then when he was soundly beaten nearly to death, she stood and looked at them and smiled. "Mom?" the boy asked again when he saw his former mother put her finger up to her lips as if saying, "Shh," and she was also shot. This time, he heard the gunshot from afar, and as she wavered, a huge beast draped in a cloak and long black kiltlike bottoms landed atop her, and with one blow, it knocked her out. The boy stared wide-eyed as the monster stood over his parents. The boy started pushing his siblings toward the school, and the beast remained behind with his parents.

"Two more down, Sara. Thanks for the assist," DeSantos said as he checked both of the parents he just took down. *"They're alive."*

"Until Tyr's plan is executed, we need to hold down the high school and protect them and help anyone looking for refuge," she responded linked to his Rynspeak.

"He is willing to go so far for John," the Cynryn said in Rynspeak as he started walking toward the high school. *"He must see him as if he was his own son."*

"What Joshua told me—he's been there for John through everything? I think John might see his mentor as a father figure himself," Sara agreed.

"Speaking of Joshua, I hope he can handle his end of things while Tyr tracks down Theresa," DeSantos said as he continued walking toward the school, waving at the kids peering out through the entrance while

they saw him approach, not knowing how to take the sudden change in developments.

*   *   *   *

Jack slammed into the back door of The Three Cs and started down the alley, having no idea what he was doing. Gripping his head, he was severely disoriented by the pure hate and anger that was invading his head. He struggled into the street, and he saw children and teens running for their lives. Some from the not-so-dangerous disfigured infected which, because of their partial transformation, was in either too much in pain from the change or simply so disfigured they couldn't pursue their prey.

"I've got to get my head on straight," he mumbled, staggering around aimlessly. He crossed the street near the bar and saw the old man casually stepping out of the café, and he knew one thing. That man was dangerous, and he needed to get away from him. So Jack started to run away from the crippled old man as fast as he could manage.

He was heading home close by the Jones' house when he saw some small children huddled together in a yard near him, with beasts rounding the corner looking for them. They were far too loud not to be heard, and he knew he had to do something, so with his head still pounding, he screamed as loud as he could, knowing he could do nothing else but give them time to flee while the monsters attacked him. The beasts turned toward him as they neared the children, and while their attention was diverted, the children fled, as much in fear of the young man screaming in the middle of the street as the beasts themselves.

The beasts turned toward him and started to charge. Jack couldn't manage much more than stagger into a tree near the street edge and fall through it. Jack emerged on the other side and changed into his true form to that of a Cynryn. He stood straight, his head finally calming down, and noticed he had two wooden axes in his hands. One of the two beasts rounded the corner, only to find its muzzle split in two by the rather sharp wooden ax. The beast wailed and started to scramble and flip around in agony as the other one went from the other side to sneak attack him. Jack turned to see the beast and was mauled by the creature's claws. He fell back, crying out and dropping his axes, and the beast howled as his prey was falling before him, only to have a branch of that same tree wrap around its neck and lifted it off the ground choking it.

Jack's silver-ringed eyes were wide in disbelief as he stood amazed.

"Yeah! Mess with me. Bring it on!" he cheered as the other one who's muzzle was all but healed made to tackle Jack from the side. Jack yelled in a panic and started to shove his hoof in the beast's mouth, breaking several teeth before slamming the head up against the tree, crushing its head repeatedly until it stopped moving. One corpse hung in the tree, and the other's head was crushed into small, bloody pieces. He staggered to his feet once more. His red fur hid most of the blood, his jeans ruined by the change. His T-shirt was on the verge of falling apart. He stood and picked the axes he dropped earlier off the ground. He looked over the blades and put them together to see them remold into a single long staff with bladed ends. The two infected started to turn to ash as he walked away, having survived the horror.

*   *   *   *

Within the Joneses' house, Heather Blackfeather huddled inside Theresa's room, crying. She heard again the voice that had originally drove her to commit to suicide. All she could say was, "No . . . no . . . no . . . not again . . . not again," over and over.

Downstairs, Amber woke and started to rock back and forth aimlessly, her mind trying to sort everything that occurred at the clinic. Marcus had his hands full as his wife fought with the voice that started to call all the others to change and attack everything in sight. The only thing holding her in check was the fact that her wedding band is made of sliver. The metal's contact kept her infected side in check.

"Tara? Sweetie? I'm here," Marcus said exasperated.

"Honey? Back away—I'm so, so angry! So full of rage! I feel like I am going insane," she said, clutching her head. "If only—" he started, but she interrupted. "It was stupid even thinking of that, Marcus. Infecting yourself so we can both go through this hell? You were out of your mind then, and feeling pity for me now is only pissing me off more."

Marcus didn't know what to do. He felt helpless. Outside, he could hear the screaming. Are they screaming because of dying or because they are scared of seeing an infected? He asked himself these and many other questions for which he had no answers. Suddenly, there was a banging on the door. Someone was trying to come in, and they were coherent enough to try using the door handle. Marcus took one more glance at his wife before running to the door. "Who's there?" Marcus demanded.

"Mr. Jones, you and your wife normal?" a younger voice half begged. Marcus opened the door to his neighbor's two kids who all but fell through the door. A third started screaming and pointing. Marcus looked up and saw two infected tearing the picket fence apart.

"My god. It's Marcy and Jason," he said noting the torn clothing they were wearing only a few hours before when they were still normal.

Marcus slammed the door shut and locked it, but he knew it wouldn't be long before the door would be broken through. Marcus started to back away from the doors, the kids having ran upstairs and looking through the bars of the stairwell, terrorized by the changes in their own parents. Marcus backed up to his wife to see her removing her wedding band and starting to remove her silver earrings.

"No!" he cried out, grabbing her hands. She looked up, pleading at him, "It's the only way to save those children."

"No, I said." He held her hand firm, and they turned to see the door break down, and the children's infected parents burst through the door, and they glanced briefly at the Jones before seeing the children upstairs. The two howled with their prey in sight and charged up toward their children. The children screamed, and Tara and Marcus started to yell to divert its attention as the monsters ran up. Suddenly one of them yelped, causing the other to pause and look behind it. The monster was halfway through the stairs. It was struggling with all its might, the claws ripping up the carpet and tearing through the wood under it as it was pulled into the floor. The mate looked at what had occurred, and suddenly, a ghostly hand reached up and grabbed its ankle, pulling the infected Ulryn into the stairs. It yelped and cried out, gurgling an inhuman, "Help me," before it too was swallowed by the stairs.

The children ran down the stairs, crying for their parents. Marcus ran up to them and led them to Tara where he stood, holding them both. Tara, covered in sweat, lay down on the floor, still trying to catch her breath. The five of them on the living room floor could see a dark figure coming out of the stairs covered in a long black dress. A cowl was attached to it, covering the woman's face, but they all could see the cold yellow ring about its eyes illuminating within. Marcus instantly recognized it was Heather in the rune-cast black gown of the Ryn. Her long black wings were the last to emerge from the stairwell as she floated to the entrance. The infected came to the property after hearing their own crying for help, but as much as they roared in defiance, they did not dare come closer as if they knew the danger implicit in doing so.

"Heather," Marcus said simply. "Thank you."

"You are the foster parents to my sister. I always thought of you as much the same, even when I lived with my adopted parents. I will protect you with my life," Heather said with no trace of doubt or fear.

"Are you going to tell your adopted parents the truth? They were part of Lorelabs at one time. I think they would understand what happened to you."

She turned her back to Marcus as she smiled. One of the infected leaped at her. She simply swiped her hand through the beast's chest, and it fell, flopping around as if dying.

Marcus barely caught a glimpse of its heart being casually tossed aside by Heather. With no marks on the creature's body, it was dying. She lifted the beast off the ground, and with a quick flick of her wrist, she snapped its neck and tossed it before the others. They backed off, further seeing their comrade turn to ash before them.

"Maybe," Heather replied absentmindedly.

*   *   *   *

Joshua leapt out into the street. The few people on the street fled away, screaming as a large, black wolf like creature was engaged by another huge, white creature. Joshua scrambled to get on his feet, and chomping down on the blades in his teeth, he started to run on all fours to flee from John who was slowly closing the distance between himself and Josh. Joshua led him to the small town park. Joshua did a flip and landed on his back just as John leapt at him, allowing Joshua to catch and toss him away just as he flipped back to his feet. Joshua stood, watching John slam hard into a tree, seemingly dazed. He charged his younger brother as John bolted toward him. Joshua slid toward him, slowing down enough to catch him off guard. He pulled the swords from his teeth and stabbed forward, only to have it slapped away with such force that one of the katanas was knocked form his hand. His right wrist felt broken but almost immediately healed as he spun around and stabbed through his brother's leg, with his other blade snapping it off in his thigh using John's momentum to spin him into position.

The white Ulryn roared in pain and started to claw at his own leg, damaging it even further. Joshua stood and watched as his brother tore at his own leg, losing blood fast. With silver embedded into him, he couldn't heal. Now, he had only to wait for him to pass out from loss of blood.

"Damn it, you dumb ass. Stop trying to claw the broken blade out!" Joshua exclaimed in Rynspeak, watching John continue ripping his own flesh out and trying to get the blade out. The blade was being pushed through, and though loosened, it held fast. Regardless, his brother continued to tear into his own flesh all the way to the bone.

If he keeps this up, Joshua thought as he leapt on him in an attempt to force him to stop. Even now, John was much stronger and raked Joshua's flesh. He howled and leapt back, his Umbrage kicking in on its own due to the huge amounts of blood loss his half-brother inflicted. Joshua was struggling to retain control of himself as he threw away the broken silver sword, breathing heavily. It was then when he heard other growls near him. Three additional fully transformed infected Ulryn surrounded John as he slowly started to lose himself to blood loss. Joshua saw them getting closer, and he sneered as his body healed but left him extremely hungry.

"*Takeout?*" The three infected Ulryn heard Joshua and turned to him to see him stand and roar to gather their attention away from his brother. a black mist forming at his feet like a fog all about the ground around him.

*　*　*　*

Theresa meekly threw up her arms to deflect the dishes and silverware being thrown at her, doing absolutely no harm to her Vulryn body.

"You stupid bitch! You killed him, how could you? You said you loved him. You always said you loved him more than me! How could you? How could you?" Elizabeth said, growing tired of throwing things at Theresa. The two of them, feeling exhausted from crying over Steve's death, stood there, staring at each other. Elizabeth was full of hate for Theresa, while Theresa felt only overwhelming regret.

"*I was only—*"

"Stop talking in my head! You took him away from me! He never would have harmed me! He's not a monster like you!" she said as she walked up to Theresa and started hitting her raised arms with her own tiny fists. Finally, Elizabeth collapsed at Theresa's feet.

"He was my . . . my everything. He was so loving and compassionate. He thought the world of you. Why did you have to kill him?"

The Vulryn looked up a moment then looked down again. "*I wish this had never happened, but it has. He would have lived if not for me. I'm sorry. I'm so sorry.*"

Elizabeth slowly stood. "The only good thing about this? At least, you are suffering. Seems like you should have been the one who killed herself and not poor Heather. To have you as a friend brings pain and suffering for everyone around you. You should go drop dead!"

The Vulryn looked up, shocked over the hateful words. Tears fell freely from her furred cheek. Her gold-ringed, slit eyes, moist from all her crying glanced behind her out into the street to where she could see Thiess across the road and standing before the Kissing Tree. Theresa stood and wiped her tears away with her arm before leaving The Three C's. She staggered out into the street before collapsing on the ground. Thiess's back was to her, but he suddenly turned toward her. He was intrigued and turned to see the Vulryn lift her head and cried a Vixen's cry. Most of the infected, and even those not infected, in town turned toward the sound of her cries.

*   *   *   *

The sun had just set behind the hills surrounding the town, the sky filling with the dying light of twilight. The lights in the streets flickered to life. The three infected leapt toward the injured John when suddenly, one of them was engulfed in a black mist.

"*MUCH BETTER,*" Joshua stated in Rynspeak, healing himself as the entire upper torso of an infected went missing in the black mist and the lower half slid up against John, still tearing his leg apart, almost free of the blade. The other two glanced at Joshua in fear when they all turned to hear Theresa's Vixen cry. Joshua recognized those cries as the remaining two infected started to run toward her. He was about to give them chase when suddenly, black flames, the tips which were white, engulfed them, and he stopped to see his brother standing, his leg suddenly whole, as a silver portion of a bloody blade clattered on the street.

Joshua watched his younger brother carefully. "*Are you sane?*" he queried hesitantly. John glanced back at Joshua, and he could see one of John's eyes flicker a moment from silver to gold. The silver blade, broken in his leg previously, erupted in black flames, tipped yet again in white.

Impossible, Joshua thought when suddenly, he remembered something.

"*Tyr? He's returned to us,*" Joshua said in Rynspeak.

John started to run toward the Vixen's cry.

"Johnathan, we'll get her to safety. I have a plan, but I will need your help to take out Fenrir and end this," Tyr said in Rynspeak.

John could feel remorse and sadness.

"The family okay?" Joshua asked.

"Joshua! He's too powerful. This Thiess is being possessed as he is right now. Go home and keep Heather there. She's been protecting your parents," Tyr said to Joshua. The mention of Heather and his mom being kept safe, thanks to her, made him move into action, and he took off, headed for the house.

"I've got a feeling you want Heather to stay away, Tyr. Why? I understand why I must, but she's an Eluryn," Joshua communicated with Tyr as he ran home on all fours.

"Theresa pointed out a weakness Heather has. I am sure Fenrir will know how to exploit it and kill her. Remember, he is very likely the voice that made her suicidal in the first place. I got a really good idea he was planning all this. We need to take control back, and we can't have her die before we trick him. She won't come back if his Umbrage reaches her," Tyr telepathically informed Joshua.

"Alejandro?" Tyr pressed.

"I can see into the future. It helps me choose the best path wherein I will be more likely to survive an encounter, but when I went to check on Heather's future, I found she is going to kill two, innocent Cynryn twins unless Joshua stops her."

*   *   *   *

The twins got dropped off at the town's graveyard as they started jogging into town.

"Okay, having to pass a graveyard on the way to the town is just a bit much. Ye gotta admit it be a bad omen," Dawveen said to her twin sister Aileen.

"Well, apparently, his mother's house is coming up. Why is the town so dark?" They could hear a bone-chilling cry in the distance, and it actually sent chills down their backs.

"What the nine hells was that?" Dawveen exclaimed as the two made their way to the trees and stepped through them to change into Cynryns. Emerging from the trees, Aileen and Dawveen came out gray-furred, but both of them had unique lavender- and silver-ringed eyes. The two then started running full tilt into town.

*   *   *   *

Heather stood on the porch, watching the small pack of infected walking up and down the picket fence. She sighed.

"To hell with this," she said, floating out to the beasts, slaughtering them as she went. They dropped as if having suffered a stroke, some starving immediately, while some healed themselves. Heather kept removing their organs to abort their healing efforts. However, one continued trying to heal, so she removed its brain and crushed it in her hand.

"Heal that, bastard," she murmured with a smile.

*   *   *   *

Around the corner, the twins came, and both stopped in awe to see a black-winged woman floating off the ground in matching silk evening gown draping off her shoulders. A cowl kept her face concealed, but the darkness did not hide the eerie glow from within.

"My god!" Aileen whispered, her hand over her mouth as she stared at the woman floating casually in midair. Dawveen moved instantly, inserting herself between them.

"Run, Aileen. Now!"

Aileen was frozen in terror. "I can't see her past!" she said, and Dawveen nodded.

"I can't see her future, nor ours, which means she must be involved with interrupting our powers. What kind of monster is she?"

"Monster," Heather said suddenly right next to Dawveen. "Now that's just being mean."

Dawveen pushed her sister back and swung at Heather, which would have connected had that been an actual possibility.

Heather laughed. "He sent you two . . . to stop me? What a total joke," she said, laughing.

In an instant, Dawveen recoiled in agony as she started to back off, falling to her knees in pain. Her sister ran up to her, and the two of them looked at Heather in horror. Heather opened her palm, dropping bloodied finger bones to the ground. "Are you missing something?"

The girls shuddered as Aileen spoke at Heather's approach. "No future, no past—we're doomed," she mumbled.

Heather reached out toward the girl's but paused as a black mist was suddenly manifesting between her and the girls.

"Josh!" Heather exclaimed, her persona changing the minute he showed himself. She turned and ran into his arms. The large black Ulryn embraced her and hugged her tightly.

"The girls are innocent. I met them at the clinic. They helped me there," Joshua murmured as he held Heather tightly.

The girls saw Joshua and sighed in relief. "Who the hell is this bi—" Dawveen started as the still hooded woman turned her cold golden gaze toward her once more. She settled on touching a nearby tree healing her fingers.

"This is my heart, who stands protecting my mother from harm, or worse, changing into an infected to protect her husband," Joshua stated as if to permanently end her comment.

The four started to walk toward the house. The few functional infected would not approach the house with a fellow infected so close, protecting those inside and somehow sensing that he was different and far more dangerous than any of them. They growled at them as the four of them entered the Jones' house.

"My god. Alejandro was correct? There were more Cynryn?" Marcus asked as he watched the twin Cynryns enter the house with Joshua and Heather. Tara gave them blankets to wrap themselves in. Aileen accepted them with grace as she was yet standing in torn and bedraggled garments from the change.

"We've lost all sense of modesty long ago, but thank you," she said, covering up their loose tops. The women had no bottoms either, but like others of their kind, the thick and long fur hid that portion of their bodies that might have otherwise been somewhat embarrassing.

"What is Tyr's plan, Marcus?" Joshua asked with all seriousness.

Marcus glanced at Tara, and the two of them sat down on the couch together. The sisters sat in chairs across the Jones, while Joshua and Heather stood near the two Cynryn.

Marcus continued, "I told Tyr, after what I'd heard, that it's likely due to the medication Lorelabs had been producing before Tara and I discontinued it. It was tainted by the blood of Fenrir—that, I am now sure of. That also means if he leaves this town, he could slowly infect the entire country and more. Tyr proposed a plan to stop this possessed Thiess, but the rest of us need to stay back for our safety. This all falls on Theresa, Johnathan, and sadly, Tyr."

Joshua's Rynspeak speech clearly showed his disfavor.

"*Why Tyr? He has no power. He's defenseless.*"

Marcus looked up at Joshua with sad eyes.

"That is exactly why he must go in our place," the older man softly said.

*   *   *   *

Jack couldn't believe what he saw. The formerly sleepy, quiet town he grew up in was in a shambles. He could hear screams in the distance and people crying out for help. He'd run toward the pleas, only to hear silence as he drew close. He dared not yell for them in fear of the infected hearing him and giving chase. He looked for people he could help, but even now, the streets were long abandoned except for the occasional misshapen infected crawling around and aimlessly growling, even though some did not even have teeth to bite with. He pitied them, knowing these were people at one time.

"*Jack!*"

He heard his father call out to him in Rynspeak. In a sudden burst of hope, he eagerly replied. "*Dad? Where are you? What the hell is going on?*"

"*Jack, you need to get off the streets. Head toward the Jones. Tyr has a plan to stop this madness before it gets worse. His plan is sound, and I am going with it. Head to the Jones, son, and be careful.*"

"*Dad, I . . .*"

"We will speak more after this is done. Sara and I are a bit——" his connection to his father was broken.

"Must have engaged with the infected," he said to himself as he made his way toward the Joneses' house. He continued warily on toward the end of the street, being out only a few blocks from his destination.

It was then when he saw a woman struggling as she was slashed badly by an infected feral. Jack charged the beast, his bladed staff biting deep into the monsters back. It was in the middle of biting the woman and tore a chunk out of her shoulder as its head pulled up from being struck. The woman screamed as Jack continued to swing on the beast. He kicked it off her and then swung again, beheading it. The woman lay on the ground crying, and he knelt down to her.

He tried to stop the bleeding, but it bled profusely, seeping between his fingers. He panicked and started to weep for her when suddenly, she started howling and changing. He stood in shock, seeing her change into an infected. It was at that moment that several fully-functional infected came around the corner, just as Jack leaped back away from the changing woman and espied the beasts approaching. A tree near them swatted a couple away as three more charged into him, biting and clawing.

"Off of me!" he exclaimed as he shoved one off with one hoof while he struck another with his sharp wooden staff that bit into the beast's neck. The beast bit into it and broke it in a single bite, so he put his fingers into its eyes, making the beast yelp in pain and back off. Not being able to focus on so many things, the two beasts swatted previously by the tree leapt at him. He lifted his arms to see the claws cut to the marrow. Jack cried out in pain. The woman he had tried to save now grabbed his ankles to bite him. He felt overwhelmed and staggered back to fall as the three of them came down on him.

Without thinking, he grabbed one and brutally broke its neck and ripped the jaw off another to slit the previous victim's throat. The three that had recovered, plus the victim, was slowly circling him.

He didn't wait for them to get set but selected one and charged with all his speed, throwing it up against a tree that rapped its limbs around it, crushing its body. The two remaining, and the previous victim, charged. The limbs lowered themselves as he put his back to the tree. In a focused fury, they did not see the tree limbs lower in time before impaling themselves on them as the bloodied limbs lifted them overhead.

The last one, which was originally the victim, raked him, and his blood gushed forth. He used the trees again to heal himself but was thrown from the tree by the victim, who was now in a frenzy after smelling the blood. He landed hard on the street, and she landed atop him, straddling the young man as she started shredding his arms even further. He couldn't do anything with his arms as they were about useless now, shredded as they were, so he head-butted her in an act of desperation. His small horns stabbed her through the eyes, and she started crying out in pain, and then he turned his head toward the street, pinning her as he drove his horns into her skull. Exhausted, he rolled away from her as she started flopping about in her death throws.

He just lay there for a bit after the fight, watching her slowly become deathly thin and turn to ash. He closed his eyes and mouth as it happened and turned over to let the ash fall to the side. He started coughing, and blood came from his mouth. His arms were worthless, shredded as they were, and his vision was swirling as he started to black out.

"Honey?"

"Theresa!" he said, blood seeping from his mouth. He looked up in the direction the voice came from and saw a silhouette near a tree close to the street's edge. The silhouette was that of a female, and she was beckoning him to the tree under whose branches she stood.

"Sure, we can work with that, honey. You will make it. Trust me, I know."

"Theresa," he said again. He could hear that she was in tears. She was crying for him. Why?

"Theresa . . . why you crying?"

She sniffed. "You dummy. I love you so much. Just come over here so this tree can heal you."

"You love me?" he said, dumbfounded.

"Dear god. Stop focusing on the 'I love you' part," she said, laughing nervously, "and get over here. Please?"

"Sure, Theresa, whatever you say. Anything for you, babe," he said, trying to smile with blood covering his white, fanged teeth.

He stumbled on toward her and the tree.

"Theresa? Why won't you help me?"

"Sweetie, I don't have time to explain why. You're almost there. Come on, just a little further."

Finally, Jack felt the roughness of the trees bark. He was there! He fell forward, his arms flopping into the tree, and he hungrily drained it, causing it to become a hardened thing bereft of life.

As he started to recover, he could barely make her out as she walked away. The only thing clear to him as he passed out was she was wearing red sneakers.

"I love you, Jack," was the last thing he heard as the blackness enveloped him, swirling dizzily, pulling him down, down, down. . .

*   *   *   *

To Thiess's delight, Theresa knelt sobbing in the middle of the street.

"Oh, how your pain is such a sweet delight. The would-be Kinguard, crowned among the children of the Ryn. Your race was subdued and enslaved because of your kind's arrogance, and now you sob like a child, helpless to act. You should have died alongside your friend."

Theresa could only see the end of her suffering—her hell. She was tired of being a Vulryn. She was tired of worrying about John. The end would bring her peace. She so wanted to be done with all of this to join Steve in oblivion.

"Oh, if only I could find the other daughter of Blackfeather to complete your suffering. My master made her commit suicide only to—WHAT!" Thiess could barely finish his last word under the torrent of slicing winds as his Umbrage barely came up to protect him from her barrage. He could see her standing, not crying.

"He did what to my only real friend? My sister? My only blood left? I will protect her! I will KILL YOU and your pathetic master!" she said in Rynspeak as storm clouds started to gather. The winds started to grow in strength. The buildings started to shudder under the strong winds.

"Hold, Theresa! Stop it before you tear the town apart and free his master! I need you to do something else for me. It will hurt his pride and keep him off guard until we can finally end his miserable existence. I promise you," she could hear Tyr in her mind.

Thiess was hard-pressed to stand as the winds attacked from all directions.

"Vulryn, I will put you down like the dog you are, here and now—what now?" Thiess proclaimed as he looked around, and the winds instantly died out, and he saw all the infected and partially infected fall down, completely incapable of independent action. They simply lay on the ground, drooling and expelling themselves on the ground uncontrollably.

"You dare use your power to disable my mutts! I will kill you in a single blow!" Theresa was engulfed by black flames with an eerie green glow emitting from it, only to be instantly dissipated. Thiess was beside himself, spittle came from his mouth, and he was so furious.

Thiess lifted his hands into the air, and darkness started to grow from far above him, only to be snuffed out by something that had Thiess feeling fear for the first time.

"No, NO! That is impossible! I will wipe the entire town from the map! I'll—AHHH!"

He barely dissipated the blow struck against him that came out of nowhere, black flames with tips of pure white. Thiess knelt after destroying the attack and looked around, more than a little panicked. He looked around and sneered, seeing a lone elderly man walking from around The Three Cs alley toward him. The old man was barely dressed, his lower half covered in tattered and bloody remnants of blanket that made a makeshift kilt for the man. His gray-haired body was covered in scars, but it was the old man's eyes that he truly feared once he spotted them, knowing full well he was dead.

"What? No threats? I held back my power, Thiess, surely you can overpower me knowing I'm holding back. No? What about you, Fenrir? You going all out? No? Well, that's disappointing. Now I'm the one getting bored," Tyr said, smirking. Mocking both Thiess and Fenrir, who possessed him. Suddenly, Thiess started screaming, and his cries made Theresa bend over sick from the insanity that was touching her mind. The hate, the fury, but it didn't affect Tyr at all.

"Oh, come on, Fenrir. You can do better, right? Or do you need infected humans and a half-born mutt to do your work for you?" he said, laughing this time.

Instantly, Thiess was right in front of him, smiling his nearly toothless smile as he grabbed Tyr's face, and in the next instant, Tyr dropped to his knees as if in prayer.

"You fool! My touch made Fenrir possess you! You will now forever be Fenrir's avatar on this world, and you will destroy it in his name! He will—OOF!" Thiess exclaimed as he was kicked away by Tyr, the sound of bones crunching from the blow clearly to be heard. Thiess looked on in shock as he clearly could see Tyr screaming as if having a tantrum.

"What? Master, what is happening?" Thiess called out, his eyes searching all about.

As if in reply, a loud thud of something landing behind Thiess caused him to turn as if to bat the insignificant thing away. A large white Ulryn was staring him down. His silver eyes glared with fury and unfettered hatred. His lip quivered with restrained fury, and his white fangs gleamed as his lips pulled back in savage rage. A flicker of gold in his right eye made Thiess start laughing as tears began streaming down his cheek in sheer terror. John lifted his hand over his head, and nearly the entire sky was blackened with black flames tipped with white in contrast to the last of the fading sunlight.

"It was you," he said, almost giggling.

"For this that you sought? Power? Hatred?" John said. His Rynspeak made Thiess soil himself as he started sobbing, sensing it wasn't madness that drove the white Ulryn but the loss of a loved one, which, as he knew oh so well, when focused, is far worse than any madness.

John instantly lowered his hand into the old man's abdomen. Thiess coughed up blood as he stared in shock down at himself being mutilated. John lifted him overhead and stuck his other hand within and then render Thiess's body asunder, throwing the portions away from him in opposite directions. Thiess's upper half landed, and he stared in horror, seeing his lower half wither and turn to ash and his vision starting to blur. Before he lost consciousness, he could see his upper half doing the same, his hands withering before his fading eyesight.

Tyr was unmoving on the ground. John looked at Theresa with hope, but she shook her head.

"*I have his five senses restricted. He's a vegetable like the others,*" she said softly.

John moved quickly toward Tyr and knelt slowly before the old man, his tears flowing freely. He held onto Tyr's body for several long moments that seemed an eternity.

Theresa didn't do anything further as Heather and DeSantos joined them. Jack was approaching, but seeing at the now wrecked The Three Cs and the traumatized Elizabeth within, he headed there instead. John continued to rock Tyr's body back and forth, crying between whines and howling with such remorse.

Theresa could only imagine his pain as she saw him finally lay Tyr's head gently on the ground and stand.

"*Fenrir might be in possession, but it's still his body. Give him mercy.*"

John slowly backed off, his body shaking, and turned around. He steeled himself when he felt the winds kick up. The others could see what he could not. Theresa gently lifted Tyr's body and moved him to a tree near the local bar, and DeSantos had the limbs hold the body, wrapping Tyr in leaves and limbs. Theresa then caused a lightning strike, setting the tree aflame. She then had the flames grow to engulf the body. The group watched the body burn for a long while before the entire thing was suddenly devoured by ebony flames. For some time they watched in silence until-

"*Enough,*" John said as others turned to see his back still to them, his arm outstretched before falling limp at his side. Theresa slowly came up to him and touched his shoulder. He turned his muzzle wet from tears, and he pulled her close, her head resting on his massive chest and her body leaning heavily against his. She could feel how fast his heart was beating—strong, powerful, and furious. Then he touched her mind gently with his, and she burst into tears.

"*It's the same, Heather,*" Theresa said, and Heather flew up to the two as a car pulled up with Marcus, Tara, and a reverted Joshua, the lights focused on the two hugging.

"*What do you mean?*" Heather asked as she took her sister's hand in her own.

"*When you first died, I felt like I was going to die too. I felt lost. I felt like there was no hope, no reason to live. The grief I felt—he's feeling it too, and it's exactly the same.*"

Heather stood near them and squeezed Theresa's hand reassuringly. With her free arm, she embraced John, and the three of them grieved. One for a loved mentor's demise, another for all the loved ones lost, and the last gratitude for her sister's life that was spared.

Epilogue

The luxurious car came to a stop outside the town of Fairmount's limits. Even in the early hours of the morning, after Halloween night, the police had the two main roads in and out of town blocked. The flashing lights of the police cars flickered and reflected off the nearby trees, almost hypnotically, as the chauffer exited the vehicle and approached the closest police car. After a short conversation, he returned to the car. In a span of a very few minutes, the car turned around and left, going back the way it had come.

Meanwhile, within the town, a strong contingent of survivors were pulling bodies off the streets, segregating the living and dead, with local police officers, firemen, and a great many civilians working side by side, striving to return the town to some semblance of normal. All now human in appearance, the living worked hard to load the dead and remove them from any possibility of public viewing. Those suffering injuries but alive were loaded separately.

The living unconscious ones that had been saved were headed for Lorelabs medical facilities, while the unfortunate dead were being carted off to a different area at the same location. They would remain outside, behind the main buildings, to be identified and later buried. Three other teams were doing their best to handle any visible blood stains that might be exposed to public view in the coming daylight when black flames with white tips suddenly wiped all traces away in the town.

*   *   *   *

John, Theresa, Joshua, and Heather, most looking like humans, save John, set out walking back toward the Jones' house as Marcus and Tara left in their car to supervise the activities out at Lorelabs. The night of horror having now passed into their history, the friends retired to their respective homes or hotel rooms to retire for some much needed rest. The two small gatherings waved wearily at each other as they went their separate ways, some again afoot, others in vehicles.

John walked as if in a daze. Theresa reached out a hand hesitantly then lowered it, a feeling of hopelessness seemingly settling down upon her. She looked away, tears in her eyes. Their forms made a stark contrast to the town regardless of the fact that the previous night had been Halloween. Dawn was still many hours away as they turned off the street and made their way along an alley.

"I can't do this," Theresa said, turning away from John and starting to walk back out to the street.

Heather walked up to stand beside Theresa. "Well, we all want to be loved, Theresa. He may be a bit immature, sure, but. . ." She glanced back toward John as he started coming out on the other side of the alleyway. "He loves you. You felt it. We all did back at the dance."

Theresa stared down at her feet and stared angrily at her hands. "So we 'must' be together? We have to choose each other?" Heather could feel her resentment. It was almost hatred.

Heather's wings expanded briefly and started to shake in agitation.

"Damn it, sis! You avoid Rynspeak so we can't feel it, but you love him too! We both know you do! You just won't admit it to yourself! Why? Why is it so hard?"

"Because then I have to admit I'm not some superhuman! I'm just a creature, a monster! Screw this, to hell with it all! I never asked for any of this."

Theresa used Rynspeak with such force that Joshua and Heather balked at her mental fury and denial. John still within range only sighed.

"Theresa." The three of them turned to see John at the end of the alleyway turnaround as black flames started to lick the caked blood from his claws and fur until the blood was all burned away. *"I understand. I think I won't push it anymore. I just . . . I just don't want to wait until our lives are over and the only thing we have left is regret—that's all."*

John turned quickly away; turning into a wolf and left them all, standing in the alley. The feeling of remorse the others felt from John was not only from rejection but something else, something even worse.

Joshua took hold of Heather, seeing her frustration, and held her tight as Heather whispered, "Something bad is tearing him apart. Maybe Tyr's death?"

Joshua's eyes played over his friends, seemingly as mystified as the rest of them. He said thoughtfully, "Maybe."

*   *   *   *

In a secluded area set aside to the rear of the main Lorelabs buildings, there were many weeping beside their dead loved ones, and though there were many of them, there were still others who had none to mourn them personally.

"Marcus, what are we looking at?" Sara asked as she and Marcus continued counting the dead and checking off boxes on the papers attached to their clipboards. The two of them were walking among the many corpses laid ceremoniously about the secret meadow in the woods behind the great facility.

"The town is going to need to build and support an orphanage now. We saved most of them, but still, there are thirteen families lost or torn asunder thus far, most of them being the parents. Parents therefore having left their children alone." Marcus paused, trying to choke back his frustrations.

Sara was calmer and placed a reassuring hand on his shoulder.

"You'll get through this, Marcus. We all will. Oh, and by the way, the town mayor is among the dead."

"He didn't even get to live long enough to fully change. He was trying to lose weight when it occurred. He starved his body to death before the change completed. So many elderly among us were slightly overweight, even obese. That probably allowed them to live long enough to make the change. I was relieved when I found out Joshua learned from John how to use the Umbrage to change so he wouldn't suffer like they did," Marcus mused glancing around.

"The screams were the worst part for me," Sara said, kneeling down and checking another name off the list before standing and continuing on. "It unnerved me to no end. I've been in combat and seen death many times. I thought I have gotten used to it, but those screams went from human to inhuman. They actually sent chills down my spine."

"DeSantos should have been here helping us," Marcus murmured as he checked off another block.

"He had to get Jack home, Marcus. His boy was almost killed tonight. You can't blame him for tending to his son's needs first. I'm quite confident that those who sought to bar his path will not be among the living injured."

"His son can heal. He's not human," Marcus said bitterly.

"Tara is caring for those still alive inside exactly as he's tending to his son. So why are you out here when you could be inside helping?"

Marcus plopped down on the ground, looking up into the sky and exhaling loudly, the pain he was feeling finally finding a way out via his hoarse voice.

"No matter what I try to say to myself, this was my fault. The past came back and tore our home and our town apart." Marcus turned to Sarah with moist eyes. "How are we ever going to recover?"

A sound behind them caught their attention.

"You are a hard man to find, Dr. Marcus Jones."

Marcus stood with Sara, warily eyeing the newcomer who simply was there and should never have been able to pass through Lorelabs gates.

"How did you get back here? Who are you?" Sara said, drawing her weapon.

The owner of the voice was a man well dressed in a dark purple suit with tan trimming. He was Middle Eastern looking, his dark skin and black hair slicked back. He look to be a man of considerable means, but there was something somehow cold about him as he seemed almost- not human.

"I am Azazel, and you may fire as you wish, Sara. It is of no concern to me," the man said, his hands behind his back, smiling. His voice sounded somewhat British, and there was an almost theatrical flair to it.

Sara noticed someone behind him. "Who do you have hiding behind you?"

A young woman walked out from behind the newcomer. Though it was dark, dawn not having yet broke, they were able to make her out, courtesy of some well-positioned lighting on the premises. A young woman, stepping out from behind he who had named himself Azazel, wore frayed and somewhat tattered and long unchanged clothing. Least by the looks of it and from what they could see, she was decidedly dirty but was there. With no mistaking it, they knew her, her mannerism, and the way she colored her hair and still wore makeup that gave her that unique Goth look of hers.

Marcus smiled brightly, relieved that there was finally some good news.

"What the—Karin?"

CPSIA information can be obtained
at www.ICGtesting.com
Printed in the USA
BVHW031648190819
556237BV00003B/23/P